THE

DRAGON

KEEPER

THE DRAGON KEEPER

a novel by
Mindy Mejia

www.AshlandCreekPress.com

The Dragon Keeper

A novel by Mindy Mejia

Published by Ashland Creek Press

www.ashlandcreekpress.com

ISBN 978-1-61822-013-4

Library of Congress Control Number: 2012931269

Printed in the United States of America on acid-free paper. All paper products used to create this book are Sustainable Forestry Initiative (SFI) Certified Sourcing.

Cover and book design by John Yunker.

For Andy—the composer, midnight painter,

hyperbole weaver, star chart reader,

fallen soldier

and my oldest friend.

The Dayaks of Borneo worshipped Jata, the Watersnake goddess.

Together with the Hornbill, Mahatala,

she destroyed the Tree of Life and created the world.

— from *Ngaju Religion: The Conception of God Among a South Borneo People* by Hans Scharer

Hatching Day

Meg Yancy kept a picture to remind herself where she and Jata began. The picture wasn't of either one of them; it was of the history of the relationship between Komodo dragons and humans.

Only a hundred years ago, the first white men started sailing the Indian and Pacific Oceans to Komodo Island in search of the dragons. They called themselves adventurers, without any irony, and they were on a King Kong mission to capture the biggest lizards in the world. Zoos all over Europe and America had just heard of the Komodo dragon, and everyone wanted a piece of the action, all of them trying to outbid one another for the first exhibit in the Western hemisphere. In other words, it was the typical feeding frenzy Meg always read about whenever some new, crazy species splashed onto the pages of the trade journals.

What made this story different was that the Komodo kings—those much-hyped, little-understood predators—didn't go quietly into that dark cage. They beat the men who hunted them, and no one saw it coming.

When the men landed on the island, the dragons didn't attack them. Despite what recent headlines suggest, Komodos don't regularly eat people. Humans taste bad—ask any shark. The dragons didn't run or hide either; it wouldn't even occur to a ten-foot-long, three-hundred-pound dragon to hide from some smelly, chattering mammals.

The men baited them with bleeding goats, trapped them, made the local villagers bind their jaws and legs, and measured them to make sure they were the longest, most impressive specimens to send back to the Western zoos. They loaded the dragons in wooden cages onto their ships, then kicked back in their cabins, sipping whiskey, polishing their guns—totally oblivious to what happened next.

The dragons broke free.

They smashed their cages to boards and splinters, ran past the shocked crew up the stairs to the main deck, and jumped, leaping overboard with a splash that must have sounded like "No fucking thank you," and dove through the dark waters to swim home.

They couldn't have made it. The dragons had escaped in the middle of the ocean with no land in sight. All of them died of hypothermia or sheer exhaustion, but Meg knew that wasn't the point. The point was that they died free. They died unbeaten.

Eventually the humans got smarter and found ways to contain the animals during the long trip and deliver them to all the zoos. Jata's ancestors were among the captured ones. Now, as a keeper, Meg tried to make the cage bearable for the ones who weren't lucky enough to escape and die free.

As she opened the outer door to the Komodo dragon exhibit at the Zoo of America and walked inside, Meg went straight to the picture she kept taped up on the wall. It was from around 1910, as near as she could figure, and it was a snapshot of one of the first Komodos in an American zoo. The dragon sat in a small, metal enclosure with no food, no water, and no chance for escape. After weeks at sea, that bare cage was his final destination. It was a hopeless picture, the kind that always made Meg mad, until she turned to the main exhibit door and saw what a hundred years could do.

Through the viewing window, Meg could glimpse a sliver of the ten-foot rock wall that circled the habitat. A large swimming pond took up the far side of the space, and various trees and shrubs dotted the sandy ground. Two large, flat boulders were powered with internal heaters to keep their surfaces toasty warm, perfect for afternoon basking. The area even boasted a cave for some privacy. At five hundred square feet, the exhibit was bigger than Meg's first college apartment. It was exactly the kind of environment that a Komodo dragon should live in, if it had to live in a zoo—except today Meg's job was to get that dragon out.

She unlocked and opened a window on the holding room's restraint box—which was basically a reinforced coffin with airholes—and dropped in the backside of a chicken, minus some feathers and guts. Re-locking the window, she walked to the other end of the box and lifted a steel lever attached to the wall. A low, creaking motion inside the wall signaled that the door had opened, connecting the exhibit to the restraint box. Curtain up. She paced back to the main exhibit door and lifted herself up to her toes to peer through the lead glass. The metal cooled a circle into her stomach through the uniform, and her breath fogged the window. One second, two. There was no reason to step inside to call her when the chicken would do all the work. Komodos could smell carrion two miles across the Indonesian savannah; a forty-foot distance would be like shoving a piping hot pizza in Jata's face.

The pool and basking rocks were empty, so Meg focused on the cave, which wasn't really a cave. The rock outcropping that supported the visitor's viewing platform hovered over the exhibit a couple feet above the dirt floor. It was a crevice, if anything, just a thin, black cavity tucked underneath the constant stream of visitors.

That's where Jata appeared.

At first she was just a bust, some kind of sculpture made out of copper running to green. Her square snout protruded out from the shadows, and she tasted the air with a flick of forked yellow, confirming what had woken her from her nap. Chicken. It flashed from her tongue to her eyes, which darted immediately to where the mini-door opened into the restraint box. Climbing out of the cave in two giant lunges, Jata broke into the open space in dead pursuit of a free lunch.

This was the best part, watching Jata walk. Did those European explorers feel the same awe when they caught their first glimpse of a Komodo dragon? Jata walked diagonally, one foot in time with the opposite hind leg, in a sweeping, swaggering motion. Her tail pumped out behind her like a three-foot-long, bone-encrusted rudder, stirring up dirt and leaves and even a few wadded-up napkins in her wake. Sweep, swagger, she walked. Sweep, swagger, and even though her head bobbed up and down in time, her eyes never moved; they had locked in on the restraint-box door. She passed underneath Meg's window and out of sight, and then from inside the box came the clicking of claws on wood, the rustle and brush of scales against the walls, and, finally, after a beat, the juicy rip of chicken. Meg slammed the lever down. She had to be quick. Even sleepy, Jata liked to grab the bait and wriggle back out before she was trapped.

There was a thump in the box near her ankle, a disgruntled tail.

"Sorry, sweetheart, but this won't take long." Patting the box near an airhole, Meg picked up a flashlight and a shovel and let herself into the exhibit.

The few visitors strolling down the Reptile Kingdom path cocked their heads and waited to see if Meg would do anything interesting. Behind bars, humans were just as fascinating as animals. Without breaking stride, Meg scooped up the napkins and chucked them up into the walkway. At least napkins were biodegradable. Freaking people used the turtle pond as a wishing well, and then they had to do surgery to pull $1.85 out of the turtle's stomach. The visitors, a couple of teenagers holding hands, rolled their eyes and kept walking to the exit. No one else appeared around either corner of the path, so after a quick double-check of the keeper's entrance to make sure the coast was clear, Meg clicked off the radio on her belt, turned on the flashlight, and wriggled into the cave.

As a juvenile, Jata had scampered in and out of this place freely, but as the years passed and she grew to more than six feet long and 180 pounds' worth of scale and muscle, the cave became a tight fit, and she'd started burrowing. At first, Meg hadn't even realized it— the whole place was so hidden—but then the dirt started mounding up at the sides of the rock, along with all the loose bits of gravel and sand, just like an avalanche waiting to happen. It was natural enough for a Komodo to make a burrow. They used them to conserve heat and sometimes slept in them, but tunneling wasn't exactly one of their best skills, and every once in a while on Komodo Island someone came across a dead dragon that had suffocated under the weight of its own ingenuity.

Meg crawled into the cave, military-style, and began packing the top layers of dirt back with the shovel so the walls flowed down to the floor in an easy slope, eliminating any chance of a cave-in. It was quiet work, not too bad for anyone who didn't get that buried-alive nightmare. From here, it was hard even to hear the humming of the building generators. The world shrank down to just the dull thwacks of the shovel, the smell of mossy soil, and the sweet curl of sweat trailing from her temples to the corners of her mouth. She worked her way around the cement circle and was checking the perimeter one last time when something broke the silence.

"Yancy!" The voice was distorted and distant. She switched the flashlight off.

"Yancy, I know you're in there. I can see your keys on the ground."

Shit. She must have dropped them before crawling inside. The voice was male but definitely not her boss. It had more *oomph* than anything Chuck could belt out.

There was just enough room to scoot around so she didn't have to back out ass first. After she inched back out into the exhibit on her elbows and knees, the light burned her eyes. She paused at the exact spot where Jata had stopped earlier—head out, considering and wary.

"What the hell are you doing under there? I didn't even know that was open space."

Antonio Rodríguez's voice came from directly above her, so she flipped to her back and leaned on her elbows. Ten feet of rock, concrete, and steel towered over her, a bumpy landscape that seemed to stretch all the way into the white beams of the roof, except for the round splotch breaking the horizon of the railing like a black sun. Antonio was just a silhouette, totally eclipsed by the light streaming in from the arching skylights.

"Yeah, it's open under here. Is that all?"

"You look like a prairie dog."

Dirt sifted out of her hair and landed on her nose as she shrugged, but she bit down on the sneeze. No need to hand him any more satisfaction.

"You playing tourist today, Rodríguez? What do you want?"

"Don't you have someone watching your back under there? Or a safety harness or something?"

She pulled herself the rest of the way out of the cave and stood up, arms crossed. Antonio was the head veterinarian, a tall, dark, handsome pain in the ass. When he wasn't working his Latin heart-throb angle on some hapless intern, he was using the zoo as his personal laboratory to grab as much industry attention as his endless studies could get. Now, lounging over the railing, he looked as if it were Sunday afternoon at the horse track and he had a winning ticket tucked in his front pocket. He grinned, flashing teeth that were whiter than his lab coat. He knew he'd caught her, the bastard.

"Do I look like I report to the veterinary department?" She grabbed her keys from the ground and started walking back to the keeper door. "Go piss off. I've got an irritated Komodo to release."

She fumbled with the ring, looking for the key with the sticker of a Chinese parade dragon, the tiny tumble of yellow and red that stood out from all the other keys, and hollered over her shoulder. "Aren't you supposed to be working? Injecting monkeys with microchips or analyzing bat shit or ..." Found it. As she slid the key into the lock, he stopped her with a word.

"Meg."

They weren't first-name people. She was always *Yancy*—or *Yance* in a hurry; *the dragon keeper* around newbies; *Miss Yancy* when he was being a smart-ass; and *Queen Bitch* when she was the smart-ass and he thought she was out of earshot. Any of these names, fine, but not Meg. Never Meg.

She spun around, her jaw dropping. The knowledge punched her in the gut with a breath-robbing, giddy certainty. Antonio leaned farther over the railing, practically dancing now. He looked as if he might leap the thing and fly into the exhibit.

"Really?"

He nodded. "Just now. I had to tell you in person. Come on, let's go."

Opening the door, she ran to the restraint box and knelt next to the wood that sent out the sweet stink of blood and rancid, post-feeding dragon breath. Jata rustled, rapping her tail on the box once, getting impatient. Meg leaned over the airholes, holding her cheeks to keep the smile from breaking her entire face apart.

"They're hatching."

~୨

Meg had never seen so many people jammed into the nursery before. The room was no bigger than her kitchen, and at least a dozen bodies lined the walls. Every keeper and vet intern she'd ever seen in the hallways wanted a piece of the party, all of them clamoring above heads and around shoulders for a look at the incubator and the three Komodo eggs that lay inside. Meg tried not to turn around often. Looking at all the faces was too much like being on exhibit herself—a particularly surreal, fishbowl kind of nausea.

When she and Antonio had arrived, it was already crowded, but he'd just grabbed her hand and slogged through the crowd straight to the back of the room. A couple of chairs were set up around the machine, but she couldn't sit. She stood with her arms crossed, rocking on the balls of her feet, eyes fixed on the incubator.

"Hey, down in front," someone said.

"Piss off. Where were you for the last eight months?" She didn't even bother to see who it was. They were all bandwagon freeloaders, lazy kids fresh out of college who'd rather play voyeur than take care of their own exhibits.

Antonio, who sat next to her jotting notes in his charts, poked her leg with the back of his pen. "Play nice."

"Why?" she grumbled. "None of them rotated the eggs or monitored the temperature and humidity of the environment. They didn't lie awake at night worrying about hatchling diets and exercise stimulants."

"I wouldn't admit that in public, Yancy. People might get jealous of your fascinating life."

A few people snickered behind them.

Gemma Perkins, Meg's fellow reptile keeper and the only one who apparently still had exhibits to tend, radioed in on their mobile com units. "How's it going in there?"

"The same," Meg replied, without glancing away from the incubator. When her eyeballs started to itch and water, she rubbed them with her wrist.

The egg that had started the entire circus was at the front point of the three-egg clutch. Hairline slices ran diagonally from its base up to the apex, where the leathery surface of the shell waved open into a tiny sliver of black. All eyes in the room, some with more success than others, strained to focus on that one slice of space. Meg could practically feel a dozen people's breaths pulsing around it, like some creepy fan club waiting to witness what some of them insisted on calling a miracle.

As the minutes ticked by, no more slices appeared in the shell. The tiny Komodo remained invisible underneath the crack in the egg. The initial excitement and laughter that had buzzed around the room slowly quieted, and the chatter fell to murmurs and shuffling feet. Meg tried to ignore the worry circulating in the air behind her.

"Why did he stop?" someone murmured, but no one answered.

It was the second time today that Meg had stared into a black void, but this was no cave. She couldn't crawl inside and make it safe or do anything that would ease the hatchling's way into the world. For this journey, he was on his own. Somewhere inside that blackness he'd grown a single, serrated tooth for this sole purpose—the shell tooth. Once he struggled free of the shell, the tooth would fall out, spent.

The shell tooth was at the front of the hatchling's mouth on his top palate. Meg's own tongue now pushed at the same spot, focusing the tension toward the only point in the entire world that mattered right now. The pressure in her mouth spread into her skull, seeped through her temples, and pounded against her ears, filling them with the rushing void of a seashell that silenced everything else inside the room. It brought the Komodo kings back to her mind—what the roar of the sea must have sounded like as it rose to meet them, then the cold press of water that welcomed them into the nether region between life and death. The hatchling was crossing paths with them now, trying to find his way out of his egg and into the world, fighting to be born.

At that moment, the crack in the egg ripped open.

The entire room shouted. Meg's jaw stung from the sudden release, and she grabbed someone's hand, squeezing the palm into pulp.

A long slice of shell, the size of a carrot, fell off the egg and revealed the underside of a wet jaw and part of a foreleg. The jaw moved, glistening under the incubator lights like a pearl, and thrust itself up through the hole. Suddenly his whole head was visible, a yellow and green crown no longer than two inches, and his slatted eyes blinked open.

"It's a boy!" someone said, and a giddy excitement filled the room. People laughed and hugged one another, pushing forward for a better look at the zoo's newest baby. Meg took it in, dumb with surprise. Were these the same people who grumbled alongside her every day, bitching about management, long hours, low pay, and the humiliation of being replaced by little pieces of plastic? It was as if they'd collectively shed some itchy, brittle skin and slithered out into the summer sun, as unrecognizable as the crazy pounding of her own heart.

Without warning, Antonio swooped over to wrap her into a huge bear hug and twirl her around. The antiseptic on his clothes stung her eyes and pricked tears into their corners. She protested and shoved him off, grabbing the chart out of his hand so she could look away and dry her eyes.

"April ninth," she said as she wrote down the date.

Antonio looked at his watch. "Five-fourteen."

For a split second, they both paused and stared at each other. It was there—in that flash of knowing between them, the first time in the history of the Zoo of America that Meg Yancy and Antonio Rodríguez shared a moment in which neither of them sneered or poked or flat-out tripped the other one for the hell of it—that time split open. Only a handful of people in the world had ever witnessed a birth like this. It was the beginning of a life that shouldn't be. No one inside or outside of this room was ready for Jata's babies, but here they were anyway, severing everything in her life into the distant, messy before and the impossible, triumphant now.

Meg and Antonio grinned at each other, then he grabbed his chart back, scribbling like mad. She bent down toward the hatchling, who'd shimmied out of the rest of the deflated shell and lay flanked by the two eggs that hid his sleeping brothers.

There was a hypnotic glaze over his black eyes, that cloudiness born from the inner war between determination and exhaustion. She knew that look. He was gathering his strength. He was getting ready to change everything.

5 Hours *after* Hatching

It was ten at night when the second egg started cracking. The zoo closed at six, and usually all the staff except for maintenance punched out by seven. Everyone had packed up and left the nursery while Meg watched with a fierce—but quiet—satisfaction, eager to finally be left alone. Zookeeping would be so great if it weren't for all the people.

At five foot two, Meg was a tiny blast of a woman who usually prowled the grounds with the military stalk of a disillusioned lieutenant assigned to a remote and hostile outpost. Most of the visitors shied away from her, though she could never tell if it was because of her attitude or just her face. She scraped her hair into the same severe ponytail every day and had never bothered with makeup in the twenty-eight years of her life. Appearances ranked somewhere below dental surgery and marriage on her priority list. Some of her coworkers avoided her, too, but Meg helped anyone who needed an extra hand with their exhibits—reptiles or not. If the keepers put their animals first, Meg made time for those keepers. Besides, the busier she was, the less time she had to dwell on the watching.

At the heart of it, that was all a zookeeper really did; she worked and she watched. The work ranged from feedings to cleaning the exhibits, writing logs, maintaining environments, administering medical treatments, and quarantining the animals when necessary, even when that meant wrestling an eight-foot crocodile. Working was the easy part. Watching could drive you crazy. Every zoo in the world lived by the same biological clock that ticked back and forth between birth and death, birth and death, while all the keepers crowded in the middle keeping watch. Some of them watched in patient vigils; some watched through careless, meandering logs; others poked glances through their rakes and clippers; and even when they snuck out behind the aquarium filtration tanks for a smoke, they were still watching. No matter how hard they worked, how busy their days were, they always watched their animals with the same two questions in the backs of their minds—*Can they be born healthy in this place?*—and then—*How long can they stomach it?* Sometimes the zoo had as many as five thousand visitors a day, and Meg still felt as if she were the only person who ever saw her animals. The crowds pushed through in a gawk-and-go traffic pattern, on their own little clocks that ticked from interest to boredom in a millisecond, moving in and out until they were just a blur of faces. The keeper was the constant, the only real witness to the animals' lives and deaths.

But as wrenching as it could be at times—and as many animals as she'd had on death watch in the last six years—these were the moments that made it all worthwhile. This was the birth watch.

She'd been debating whether to go home to get some sleep when the egg on the left side of the incubator started pulsing, as if to say, *Go, then, and miss everything you've been waiting eight months to see.* She leaned down against the machine, fingers splayed on the glass, and a greedy kind of joy surged through her chest because she didn't have to share it with anyone this time. The first egg had hatched with the entire freaking world watching; this one was hers alone.

This Komodo, unlike his brother, had no trouble slicing open his shell. The egg fell to pieces in soft splits and chunks, and Meg held her breath, awestruck. It was as if he was bursting to get out. The shell crumpled into garbage, and a sleek head and spine—a head created without a father, a spine that shouldn't even exist—crawled out of the waste.

She'd seen dozens of births at the zoo, and they were all special in their own ways, but calling this birth special was like saying Minnesota got a little cool in January. Komodo dragons reproduced sexually. One male plus one female equaled a heap of baby dragons, which was fine—except the Zoo of America didn't have a male Komodo. Jata had never met a mate in her life. Her eggs should have collapsed into infertile waste, but instead they grew and flourished. The technical term was *parthenogenesis*.

In other words, Jata had a virgin birth.

Completely unaware of his importance, the Komodo hatchling climbed unsteadily over the broken shell on his way to the front of the incubator, as if he wanted to say hello. Pulling on leather gloves, Meg popped the lid and lifted the little guy out.

She held him up to eye level and let her eyes dance the new-mother survey. Four legs—check. Twenty tiny claws curled into the meat of her glove. One whipcord tail wrapped around her wrist. A head, tilted, sleepy. Two almond slits for eyes staring ahead, reflecting nothing. Everything inside her beamed at him. "You can't put evolution in a cage."

He blinked and rustled weakly against her palm. Not a philosopher.

"What are you un-caging now, Yancy?"

She jumped and squeezed the hatchling too tightly, making him squirm.

"Jesus. You scared me."

Antonio pushed away from the door against which he'd been leaning for who knows how long and walked over to pet the hatchling's head with a fingertip. "Jesus saves, not scares."

"Jesus doesn't stalk either." She jerked her head toward the door.

"Are you kidding? Who do you think finds out if we're being naughty or nice?"

"Santa Claus."

He chuckled, a tired, rumbling laugh without a beginning or an end. "I didn't know anyone was still here."

"It's a good thing I was. Look what I found." She couldn't take her eyes off him. Every detail was so perfect, from the yellow streaks shot through his markings to the incubator dirt clinging to his tail.

Together they weighed and measured him and put him in the second tank, next to his brother's. He wobbled a little and took a few steps before plopping down next to a tree branch and closing his eyes. She'd set up three newborn incubators in a row that pumped heat through at a warm twenty-nine degrees Celsius, and she'd outfitted each with individual water troughs, foliage, and just enough room to recover from being born.

"I can't believe management's going to let you put them together in the exhibit. They'll tear each other apart." Antonio rested his forearms on the table, staring into the last empty incubator.

"I don't think we'll see any grudge matches."

"A little idealistic, aren't you? It's only a matter of time before they try to eat each other."

"Let them freaking socialize." She rubbed her eyes, trying to clear sleep and frustration. It was unbelievable, every time she turned around. "They'll be auctioned off in a few months and spend the rest of their lives in isolation. Then you'll all be happy."

They both shut up for a minute. There were a hundred good reasons to group the hatchlings together, but she was too tired to think of a smart way to say them. Yawning, she stretched out the cramping muscles of her back.

"Why don't you go home and get some sleep?" Antonio asked.

"Why don't you?" There was still one egg left and hell if she was going to let him get the first look at her hatchling.

Another minute passed. Finally he took a breath and pushed away from the table.

"Okay, I'm going to run home and grab a change of clothes, and then when I get back you can go."

She glanced over at him, and he smiled hopefully. Why didn't he just leave? He wasn't their keeper; he was just a hotshot vet who wanted … something. She wished she knew what. Another yawn bubbled up, but she bit down on it.

"Fine, but you're bringing back coffee, too."

∾

Ben was watching the news when she got home. His notebooks were spread out on the coffee table around a jumble of beer cans, reptile studies, *National Geographic* magazines, and empty plates crusted over with grease spots and petrified crumbs. He hunched forward in the middle of the sagging couch, legs splayed, thighs almost straddling the coffee table. At six foot two, Ben was often mistaken for an ex–college footballer going to fat, at least until he started talking. Even now, he had that puffy look of faded glory as the neon shadows from the tube flickered over his face, igniting his eyes with that for-the-win concentration.

Ben didn't watch the news the way other people watched the news. He studied it and charted it as meticulously as Meg watched her animals. Filling notebook after notebook with major world events, he measured how each network presented coverage, looking for differences. If an earthquake hit Southeast Asia, how many variations were there in the body count? Which stations concentrated on how many Americans were killed, and which ones sent a correspondent to the wreckage rather than regurgitate the twenty-second summary wired down from the AP? It used to be surprising to look over his shoulder at what he uncovered: There's something here, she'd thought, something important that lurked just under the surface of society, like a prejudice everyone had half-acknowledged but never looked at straight on. That was seven years ago, when they'd first met, and nothing had changed. Ben liked to talk about his manifesto—the paper he would someday publish to expose all the media injustices—but over the years Meg had accepted that he would never write it. This was just Ben's hobby, like the guys who collected stamps or space dolls. Each discrepancy he found was a little triumph for him, but all he ever did was reach for the next blank notebook and crack another beer.

Tonight he flipped back and forth between different recordings from the prime-time news while scratching notes with a gnawed ballpoint pen. Glancing up, he saluted her with a beer.

"The second one just hatched." She'd called earlier, high on the celebration of the first birth, but his phone had gone straight to voice mail, and he hadn't called back all day.

She was shoving clothes into her backpack in the bedroom when Ben appeared in the doorway, lounging against the door frame and scratching his belly through a black T-shirt. His floppy brown hair was uncombed, and his skin had the rumpled, waxy sheen of someone who'd sat in a dark place for a long time.

"I just got your message. Sorry I didn't call, but I figured you were all out partying like animals." He waited. He always dragged it out two beats too long, waiting for the expected laughter. She didn't oblige.

"How's it going?"

"Fine." She swiped some deodorant under her arms and chucked it into the backpack.

"Babies are healthy? Breathing fire and fighting knights?"

"What?" When she finally looked at him, he was grinning. Grins always scooped the bulk of Ben's cheeks up and stretched them wide, like pears turning into apples. Once, that grin had been contagious. It promised some kind of childhood she'd heard about in books and TV shows. She'd opened to it, warmed underneath it, forgave things because of it—but it was funny how all the years' worth of crap had piled into that grin and eventually flipped everything inside out. Now he grinned and she wanted to slap it off his face; it closed her, made her cold.

"Oh. Sure." She zipped up the bag.

The floor squeaked as Ben lumbered up behind her and laid a meaty hand on her shoulder. He squeezed her tendons and bones together, kneading the knots farther up her spine and piling them, one on top of the other, into her skull. The looser his fingers got, the tighter her neck.

"I found another story for you. This one's coming from Omaha. Hammerhead sharks."

One night right after Jata had laid her eggs and the two of them were chilling on the couch—Ben watching the news, taking his notes and mumbling, while she read up on virgin births—she'd told him about the genetics behind parthenogenesis. It was more thinking out loud than anything, trying to get the whole concept straight in her mind. She hadn't even thought he'd been listening, but something must have hooked him in. He'd started mining the news for virgin births, tracking them down on TV, on the Internet, and in newspapers, and handing them to her like gifts she didn't know how to unwrap. He'd found a succession of tree frogs from Mexico and, of course, the three preceding Komodo cases in Europe, all within the last few years.

She shrugged away from his hand. "Not now, Ben. I have to get back to the zoo."

"It's almost midnight. Babies can take care of themselves for a few hours, can't they?"

"What the hell do you know about it?" It was out before she could stop it.

He sighed. "Look, I'm sorry I didn't call you back, okay?"

Shaking her head, she slung the backpack over her shoulder and left the house, but it was a long time before she felt the weight of his hand lift off her neck. The guilt of it burned her skin all the way back to the zoo. They didn't fight. It took too much energy to fight, just as it took too much energy to return a phone call or to understand why now, two years after that night in Minneapolis, he was suddenly fascinated by birth.

~੭

Coffee and champagne had two things in common. They were both wet, and they were both drugs. It was almost impossible to mistake one for the other, unless maybe you were a blind, taste-impaired mammal with a careless keeper.

"We need to celebrate" was Antonio's only explanation when he pulled out the plastic cups and blew the cork across the nursery. They'd grabbed a couple of folding chairs and set up camp in front of the incubator, surrounded by bags of potato chips, backpacks, and … champagne.

"We need to stay awake," Meg objected. The coffee vending machine came to mind but with a shudder. No matter what button you pushed, it produced the same weak lattes, half-cold and topped with rubbery, chocolate skins.

"You can't sleep and drink champagne at the same time, can you?" Antonio poured two glasses and jiggled one of the cups in front of her face. Despite her knee-jerk temptation to dump the contents on him, the cup actually looked appealing; she wanted to toast Jata's babies into the world—not for what they represented scientifically or religiously, not for their commercial value—just for the dragons they were. She took the cup and grudgingly tapped it against his.

He grabbed her arm when she tried to take a drink. "You can't just chug-a-lug, Yancy. You have to say something. Haven't you ever celebrated anything before?"

She frowned. Everything she felt about the hatchlings would sound like a greeting card when it hit the air. She had nothing—nothing she was willing to share with him, anyway. "I don't do speeches."

"What about what you said earlier—you can't put evolution in a cage? That sounded like a speech, or at least a fortune cookie."

"I don't even know what that meant," she lied.

"Yeah, well, I do." He swirled his cup and walked over to the last intact egg. "If you could control evolution, I would have timed things a lot better. My sister had twins the week you found the eggs. I was supposed to be in Puerto Vallarta playing the good *americano* uncle, not to mention deep-sea fishing with my dad and napping on the beach. And I had a chance to go to the World Series this year, did you know that? These dragons have destroyed my social life, with all the conference calls and logs and research. Miracles are a lot of paperwork, which you might realize if you ever actually did any of it. I used to have a life outside of here, with women and hobbies and … women. Not that you understand anything about having a life."

"I don't date a lot of women, no."

"That's actually somewhat surprising. I think I just lost some money to one of the fish keepers."

"If it's Doug, he already knew I was straight because he tried to set me up with his sister three years ago."

Antonio burst out laughing, and Meg grinned at the memory. Doug hadn't known about Ben, of course, but he steered clear of her for months out of embarrassment after she'd filled him in. She wasn't surprised Antonio had taken the bet. Not many people at the zoo did know about Ben. It wasn't as if he came to see her at work or anything, and what was the point of talking about him? Ben was just Ben. Besides, bringing up a relationship always made people want to talk about marriage, mortgages, and children. She didn't need to jump on that conversation train.

"That's another thing," Antonio said after his chuckles subsided. "Who would've thought we could ever actually work together? These eggs completely destroyed my dislike for you. Remember when we hated each other?" He rubbed his chin and gazed off to some faraway, beloved place. "That was great."

"Speak for yourself. I don't recall getting past that feeling."

"You hate me about as much as you hate Gemma. Admit it."

"Maybe if you ever shut up you'd start to grow on me. Like a wart, you know?"

"All right, all right." He held out his cup again and waited. The corners of his lips quirked up as the silence drew out.

Man, he was annoying. "Fine," she said. "But if we have to toast, then at least get it right."

"What do you mean?"

She sat up straight and tried to figure out how to phrase it. "We think these animals are captive, right? They live in artificial environments, the deprived captive state and all that shit?"

He nodded.

"But it's not like that. The walls only hold so much. It's like …"

She waved her cup in a circle, pulling the thought down. "That old bat who lives on the cul-de-sac behind the Mammal Kingdom. Every month, she complains to the city about the wolf exhibit and the howling. The walls can't hold in their howls. The fences can't keep them from smelling the deer in the river valley or the bonfires in people's backyards. When I drive by that old bat's house on my way home and I blast the metal station at her, do you think she can't hear me just because she's in her little box of a house and I'm in my little box of a car?"

"You need help, you know that?" he said.

"Some things can never be contained, that's what I'm saying, no matter how hard you try or what kind of technology you have. We didn't find Jata a mate, and she went ahead and reproduced anyway. There it is." She pointed to the last egg. "You can't put evolution in a cage."

Without waiting for Antonio to say anything, she thumped her cup against his and drank. The bubbles fizzed down her throat like Alka-Seltzer with a dry pucker at the end. It was too sweet.

She slouched down in her chair in front of the incubator and stared at the last egg until its edges blurred into the surrounding dirt. One last boy curled up tight in his hot, little bed. She could hold it in her cupped palms now—an egg that shouldn't even exist, like some dark magic conjured it here from nothing—and in a few short years, the dragon inside would be two hundred pounds with a tail that could swim channels and jaws of bone-crunching, poison-coated teeth. He would be the king of all lizards, but there wouldn't be any other lizards where he was going. And what was royalty without a kingdom? Maybe evolution couldn't be caged up, but a Komodo sure could. In the last hundred years humans had gotten pretty good at that.

Antonio sat quietly next to her, rolling his cup from one hand to the other and staring at the contents as if he were having a silent

22

conversation with his drink. She took another sip of her own, and the bubbles burst sharply in her mouth. Maybe it was the stupid toast he'd made her say or the embarrassment of sharing champagne with him, but the longer she sat there, the more surreal the whole situation became. Antonio Rodríguez, corporate climber and self-proclaimed ladies' man, pulling an all-nighter like some mother hen clucking over her eggs? Not likely.

"Nobody asked you not to go to the World Series or see your father." She broke the silence. Meg's own father was halfway across the world, too, but she didn't go around whining about not being able to visit him. Then again, she and her father weren't the visiting kind, or even the talking kind.

"What?"

"What are you even doing here, anyway?"

"Same reason you're here."

"I don't think so. Is it the data? You need to gather that last bit of information to clinch your cover page?" The alcohol and lack of sleep made her words a little slushy, but she had to ask; it just wasn't possible for him to be here out of the goodness of his heart. Antonio didn't do something for nothing.

He swirled his cup again and sipped slowly, nodding. His hair curled down around his forehead, bouncing free from its slicked-back style.

"I want to make sure the hatchling is healthy, Yancy. It's the same thing I want for all the animals at this zoo."

"And microchips to match." She snorted.

He couldn't dare deny it. As the first vet in the country to chip the animals—injecting little bits of plastic and metal called Sero-Adrenal Microchips, or SAMs, into every land-dwelling vertebrate over five pounds—he'd drawn international attention. The chips radioed in to a central server every ten minutes, sending readings on serotonin and adrenaline levels, heart rates, and GPS coordinates. While the rest of the world called them everything from "artificial keepers" to "brave new microchips," management at the Zoo of America fell all over themselves congratulating one another as pioneers of the zoology field. SAMs allowed the animals to be managed with less human interaction, which meant lower overheads and reduced insurance rates. Antonio had become the overnight darling of management and had gotten his studies published in the most prestigious magazines. On paper, he was kind of hard not to hate.

"We'll only chip whichever dragon the zoo is keeping. The other two will go to less-advanced zoos." He took another sip, ignoring her second snort. "And if it weren't for the SAM data, we wouldn't be able to know the next time Jata lays eggs. The sero-adrenal behavior is completely documented now."

"God forbid we just find the eggs like I did, without any help from I.T."

He leaned in and leveled her with a black-eyed stare that rivaled Jata's for intensity. "We both know what happened when you found the eggs. Do you really want to go there?"

She sucked in a breath, looking away, and, just like that, the anger was gone. Deserted her completely. The ghost of wet sand filled her head in its place, clumping in her ears and gritting between her teeth. It was frightening how easily he could send her back there.

"The SAMs will help. That's what I've been trying to say for years, and none of you want to hear it. You're so scared for your jobs."

"I'm scared for the hatchlings." It was easier to say it from under the sand he'd buried her in, from where everything was distorted and distant—the place that had haunted her since she'd discovered the eggs eight months ago.

She stared sightlessly at the incubator. "Everyone wants a piece of them. They want their zoo space, or their marketing value, or their budget dollars. They want to bottle their fame and sell a miracle."

"Forget about that for a minute, okay? None of those people are here now. It's just you and me and a bunch of dragons in here."

He poured her another cup of champagne.

"Truce?" he asked.

He tapped his cup to hers as if everything was fine again, as if the fight wasn't just beginning. Maybe he didn't understand yet, but to her it was absolutely clear. No more fuckups. From this day on, she had three more dragons to defend from Antonio, the zoo, and anyone else in the world who tried to claw his way between her and them.

Still insulated against all that, the last egg sat motionless and intact in the incubator. Meg and Antonio settled in for the night and watched it, sipping to the bottom of the champagne around one in the morning. By two, they were both drowsing. At three, Meg felt a nasty crick in her neck and, rubbing the shooting pain out of her spine, scooted over between Antonio's sprawled limbs and dropped her head onto his shoulder, hoping he wouldn't wake up and notice. It was only a warm shoulder, after all, just a body waiting by another body, exhausted from the endless watching. A keeper could only watch for so long before something had to happen. Birth. Death. The mess in between. Something was always coming, always looming around the edges of the next day; it was only a matter of when. She rubbed her cheek into Antonio's lab coat and fell asleep.

2 Weeks *before* Hatching

D ragons attack people."

Meg paused mid-lecture and sized up the woman who'd interrupted her. The visitor stood at the front of the group with her hip cocked and her eyes narrowed in a smug, pseudo-omniscience that made Meg wish more animals attacked people. Humans were such a self-righteous species.

"They are certainly capable of it, yes, but attacks are rare and usually occur because of human encroachment into the dragons' natural territory." Meg crossed her arms, a gesture that the Member Center team kept telling her was *defensive* and *inhospitable*—whatever the hell that meant. They sent secret shoppers out sometimes to rate the quality of the tours, and that stuff always showed up on her performance reviews in the Opportunities for Improvement section.

Every zookeeper at the Zoo of America had to lead a group tour of his or her building once a week. It was a term of the employment contract, according to her boss, Chuck. Meg had tried to reason with him because, come on—it wasn't as if someone became a zookeeper because she liked people so much—but Chuck had just handed her a copy of the standard Keeper Level I job description in his usual constipated, twitchy way, and that had been the end of the discussion.

Now, standing at the front of the group that was crowded into the last exhibit of the Reptile Kingdom—Jata's exhibit—she thought for the six thousandth time that she should have fought a little harder. It was a pretty equal divide today between stroller moms and tourists, both gunning to be the biggest pain in the ass. The mothers who took the tours were like their own planets, with strollers, diaper bags, purses, and greasy-fingered children revolving like frenetic moons around them. Meg might have appreciated their efficiency a lot more if it didn't come with crying babies, children who uprooted the trail plants, and endless questions about cartoon animals she'd never heard of.

Tourists were a different breed. The Zoo of America made up one-fourth of the America compound, an interconnected group of tourist attractions packed into the tract of land between the Twin Cities airport and the Minnesota River. Visitors bounced between the Mall of America, Water Park of America, SportsPark of America, and the Zoo of America on the red, white, and blue light rail trains that stopped in front of each main gate, coming from all across the country for their prepackaged, temp-controlled, multi-pass vacations, with cameras dangling from their necks like abandoned lead ropes. The tourists' questions, while usually more grounded than demands for unicorns, were also generally more annoying. Like this woman and her thing against dragons.

The woman leaned on the railing that overlooked Jata's enclosure and didn't even glance down to look at the animal she was blindly categorizing. If she'd bothered, she'd have seen that Jata lay fewer than ten yards away, her legs spread-eagle and osteoderms bunching in lazy folds down to the thick claws that lined her feet. Her scales were a mosaic of delicate, sea-foam green and dull gray. Looking at her was like seeing the product of a gecko and an elephant. She was ancient, primordial—but some people only saw a predator.

It was obvious that the woman had no idea what Jata had done, how this single Komodo dragon blindly tried to save her entire species from extinction.

"I read about a Komodo attacking that boy in the Philippines the other day. It killed him." The woman's voice bounced off the towering skylights in the roof and around the clustered tour group, eclipsing the nearby tortoises' waterfall with the fascination that people constantly brought to this platform. The fascination Meg got, no question, but it was that undercurrent of ignorant superiority— that's what she couldn't stand. The word *it* was like an ice pick in her ears. *It* killed him, as if the *it* could have been a wheelbarrow or a book.

"You mean in Indonesia."

"What's the difference?"

"A country."

Meg knew about the attack. A young boy in the dry season. In the dry season, everything was prey.

"We're not here to talk about attacks, but there are some other headlines that I'd like to share with you." Damn, that was a nice transition, which pretty much guaranteed that no secret shoppers were here today. They never evaluated her when she said smooth stuff like that.

Meg walked to the edge of the viewing platform and swung a wiry arm over the railing.

"This is Jata, our famous Komodo. You might have heard about her recently."

At Meg's voice, Jata swiveled her head fully around and surveyed the group. Her gaze wandered the faces until she saw Meg, and then she stared coolly up at her, unblinking. Meg smiled and winked.

"She likes you," one of the kids said.

"I'm assigned to her exhibit, so she recognizes me. If you want to stick around after the tour, I'll be feeding Jata her weekly meal at one o'clock."

"Cool." The boy pushed his head against the steel bars that lined the platform, trying to see Jata better.

Meg turned back to address the group as a whole. "Eight months ago, Jata laid a clutch of eggs, which isn't uncommon for an adult, female dragon. They should have been sterile. What made the eggs so extraordinary is that they were viable."

Blank gazes surrounded her. A dark-haired man wearing a Mall of America T-shirt started chewing on his fingernails, glancing between Meg and Jata.

"Jata has never mated with a male dragon. She hasn't been exposed to a male since she was a hatchling. You are looking at one of the few known animals in the world that has reproduced via parthenogenesis."

"Oh, the virgin-birth dragon!" The boy's mother piped up, pulling her son's head away from the bars. "I read about that in the paper earlier this year. That was so cute, just like a miracle, and that reporter Nicole Roberts was talking about it, too. What did she say?" She looked around for help. "Oh, I can't remember, but it was odd, like—"

"I don't know," Meg interrupted. Heat seeped into her cheeks, flushing her skin with a mix of anger and embarrassment. She pulled her forearms tighter into her chest, imprinting her wrist with the security ID clipped to her breast pocket, and looked around the rest of the group to see if anyone else listened to second-rate news. A few of them glanced uncertainly at Jata, and the man in the Mall of America T-shirt suddenly took Meg's picture.

"You are absolutely right about the virgin birth, though." Meg tested her voice, and it came out clear and passive. Good. "Jata has reproduced asexually, although technically she hasn't quite completed the job."

She glanced down at Jata's green-and-gray scaled head. "The eggs are due to hatch any day now. Then, if everything goes well, she'll be a virgin mother to three baby boys."

"How do you know they're boys? Do they do ultrasounds?" someone asked.

"No. It's the nature of parthenogenesis, actually. It's the same way that you know if you made a human clone, it would be the same gender as the parent. This type of reproduction eliminates the possibility of females, so we know the babies will be boys."

"We're studying DNA in my science class," said a bored-looking kid.

"Oh, then let me show you." Meg lit up, her forced friendliness turning into genuine excitement at the opportunity to explain. She grabbed his visitor map and sketched it out on the back.

Male

		Z	Z	
Female	Z	ZZ	ZZ	→ ½ Male
	W	ZW	ZW	→ ½ Female

"This is how the genes would normally look if it were a typical birth with a father and a mother. You end up with half boys and half girls."

The kid's forehead wrinkled up. "I thought boys were XY and girls were XX."

"That's for humans. Komodos have the ZW genes, and they're just the opposite of us. So a male has the same pair—ZZ—and the female has the opposing pair—ZW. Now, this is what happened with our Komodo."

Female $\boxed{\begin{array}{c} Z \\ W \end{array}}$ + $\boxed{\begin{array}{c} Z \\ W \end{array}}$ *Copy* = ZZ ⟶ Male
= WW ⟶ Inviable

"See? The DNA simulates fertilization by making a copy of itself, so you get either boys or nothing."

The kid didn't seem that impressed. Meg handed back the map and smiled at the woman standing next to him. "You take that in to your science teacher. I'll bet you get some extra credit points."

Turning around, her soft smile faded, and she replaced it with something closer to bared teeth. "Now, that concludes the tour of the Reptile Kingdom. There's a tour of the Mammal Kingdom in half an hour, if you head straight out the exit and take a left at the river. Does anyone have any questions?"

Only a few people lagged behind, and Meg breezed through most of the stock questions with stock replies.

Yes, every day.

As much as we can to keep them healthy and active.

No, we don't wrestle the crocodile.

Rats and turkey parts. Yes, the bones too.

Only if a stray bird flies into the building.

The closest ones are in the cafeteria; go through the door and circle back to the round building on your right.

She smiled, spoke briefly, and took small, prodding steps toward the exit door. If she was lucky, she'd be back to shoveling shit before lunch.

～ๅ

Later, she waited in the damp concrete corridor that connected to the staff side of the reptile exhibits, with one leg propped against the wall and a bucket of raw turkey pieces at her side. The tour had gone pretty well today, though the secret shoppers never seemed happy. It was all a matter of appearances, and Meg knew how she came off to strangers. She mostly ignored the kids, didn't try to sell the animals, and refused to point out the best photo ops. Call it de-marketing, whatever. Her beige uniform was clean but wrinkled, and six years of wear had started to fray the American flag appliquéd in the center of the back. Secret shoppers liked the keepers who came in pretty and accommodating packages, like Gemma with her neat, blonde braids and easy manners. Gemma's tours brought the words *all God's creatures* to mind, all crocheted and gaggingly cute on some farmhouse wall, while Meg only inspired inquiries about the bathrooms and, now, animal stereotypes regurgitated from the media.

It was almost one o'clock. The door into Jata's holding area was directly in front of her, and through those steel barriers she knew a crowd had started to assemble. Ever since the news of the virgin birth had hit the papers, Jata's feedings were as popular as the dolphin show. People loved to watch the contrast between the giant lizard and the small woman, as thick, impenetrable scales swaggered up to vulnerable flesh with only the smell of raw meat between them. It made their bored, predatory pulses race. It made them think, *What if?*

That's why the attack stories were so popular. It didn't matter what kind of attack—a tiger jumping out of its exhibit and biting teenagers, a grizzly mauling campers in a state park, a killer whale who (go figure) killed a trainer—the public ate up every juicy, horrible morsel. The woman from today's tour group was no different. She hadn't charted the town relative to the Komodos' known habitat. She hadn't visualized the circumstances or thought about the physiology of that boy—just a young boy, weak and skinny—and what he looked like to a starving dragon.

Ben had found a picture of him from one of the news wires. He was cute, a sunbaked, grasshopper-legged kid who woke up one morning and wanted to go fishing with his uncle. No harm in that, right? Except this kid lived on Indonesia's Komodo Island.

There was only one village on the island and, because the national park reserved the rest of the land, the town was bursting at the seams. Every year, more people poured into Komodo Village for the fishing and tourism jobs. The houses were a smashed-together mass of wooden gabled roofs and stilted legs that edged out over the ocean. Every building on Komodo had stilts, which looked kind of funny until you realized that these people lived with dragons. There were no walls between the park and the people. Dragons walked through their backyards, dragons ambled onto their beaches, and dragons attacked their goats and other livestock. The fact that the dragons were there first didn't translate all that well.

Meg had read the story over and over, every version in every paper Ben could find. The kid and his uncle were walking toward the water, loaded down with their fishing nets and bait, sweating in the already roasting air, when the boy made the last decision of his life. He asked to pee.

He went to the ditch on the side of the road to do his business, but he wasn't alone in the long grasses. The dragon attacked, seizing the boy by the stomach with jaws like a shark, row upon row of serrated teeth designed for tearing flesh and bone apart, and dragged him into the underbrush. It was the dry season, and without water all the dragon's natural prey had vanished. There were no deer or pigs—none that hadn't already been poached, anyway. It had probably been weeks since the animal's last meal, and hunger made him desperate.

The boy's uncle intercepted them, pelting the dragon with his fishing gear. Drawn by the screams, the villagers rushed out of their houses and armed themselves with rocks and sticks. Together they beat the dragon back into the park land and away from the small, mangled body. They took the boy away, but there was no medical clinic on the island, and he'd bled too much. A dragon's bite was poisonous, and the lethal mix of saliva, venom, and bacteria had already seeped deep into the lacerated remains of the boy's stomach. He died within a half hour. He was eight years old.

"Ready to tame the beast?"

"Shit!" The foot Meg had propped against the wall hit the floor with a jerk, and her heart stuttered. She shook her head a little, clearing the attack vision from her brain, and took a deep breath. The concrete walls of the keeper's hallway came back into focus. Gemma stood fewer than two feet away with Desmond just behind, his uniform unbuttoned down to a sweat-stained undershirt.

"What is it?"

"A little jumpy, huh, Yancy? You on probation again?" Desmond rubbed his chest and grinned. The three of them ran the Reptile Kingdom, but each had their own niche. Meg handled the lizards, and Gemma specialized in turtles. Desmond was the snake man, and after years of the same gig, he was actually getting slithery around the eyes.

Meg ignored him, looking at her watch. "Is it time?"

"Yeah, you guys go ahead and suit up." Gemma grinned.

"What, me?" Desmond looked at Gemma, surprised. "You said you wanted to talk about something."

Meg hid her grin. Ever since Gemma started working at the zoo,

Desmond had been hitting on her. At first it was earnest—invitations to dinner or some event going on at the mall; he even bought a stuffed animal for Gemma's daughter once—but after getting the brush-off for months, he'd eventually slid back into the more familiar dirty jokes, hisses, and whistles that everyone else expected from him. He acted as though he didn't care anymore, but everyone knew he would trip all over himself to follow Gemma if she asked to speak to him in one of the dark, back hallways of the zoo.

"Meg and I—we wanted to talk to you about assisting with Jata's feeding. Today. Right now, actually." Gemma reached her arms up into the air and stretched, leaning to one side and then the other. She always looked as if she were in the middle of a yoga class.

Meg opened the supply closet and handed Desmond a fiberglass shield and a pair of industrial, elbow-length gloves. She'd just started pulling on a pair of safety boots when Desmond cleared his throat.

"Why the hell am I assisting you with the feeding?"

Meg pulled on her own gloves and stretched her fingers. The material was so damn inflexible, she might as well be wearing chain mail.

"It's not that I'm not comfortable in there. I mean"—Desmond hopped around on one leg, trying to get his boots on—"I'm not afraid of her or anything."

"Of course you're not." Gemma smiled, arching backward now.

He picked up the shield and tested it, making the veins pop on his forehead, then glared at Gemma. "But assisting is your job, sweetheart."

Meg shut the supply closet and picked up the bucket of meat. "We need to expose Jata to a variety of different keepers, so she becomes familiar with our scents. Then if I ever drop dead…" Meg shrugged. "So far, she knows me and Gemma pretty well. Rodríguez is familiar to her, but he's a vet. So you're on the rotation, champ. Think you can handle it?"

"Are you kidding?" Even with the fiberglass shield between them, Meg could tell he was rubbing his chest again. "You're talking to the keeper of the ten-foot python."

"Do you know the feeding procedure?" Meg choked up on her shield and opened the outer door to the holding area. They filed inside as Gemma waved good-bye, a finger-wagging little parade wave, and Desmond slammed the door on her, turning away from the muffled laughter. It was a cramped room for two people, jammed full of cleaning supplies, bags, and the wooden restraint box. Somewhere water was dripping. On tiptoe, Meg glanced through the window into the exhibit. Jata had moved from her basking rock to the lagoon on the opposite side of the exhibit from the door.

"I, uh, think I remember. No sudden movements, no loud noises, and ... damn, what was the last thing?"

"Stay away from her teeth."

Meg unlocked the door and stepped inside.

Jata swiveled her head and licked the air, smelling the arrival of her dinner. She pulled herself out of the pool, and the vague, swimming shapes of her body emerged into powerful forelegs, a torso that was shedding in flaky blocks along her sides, the round girth of her stomach—held regally above the ground as she ambled forward—followed by the thick, sweeping tail. Water dripped off her body as she headed toward Meg. Her tongue darted in and out, drawing closer with every second. Desmond said something, but Meg wasn't listening. The crowd of people on the viewing platform above them faded into a dull blur. She cleared her mind of everything but the bucket of food and Jata.

"Jata, Jata, chow time, Jata."

The words stretched like taffy out of her throat, long and low syllables that reached out across the mulch and sand. This was how they began. She chanted, and Jata licked the air, both of them closing the space toward the slanted rock ledge in the center of the exhibit. Jata knew the call, tasted the deep notes that never changed, and moved eagerly toward the rock. She stopped at the base of the incline, where the teeter-totter ledge touched the ground, and darted her tongue toward the keeper's door.

"What's it gonna be, turkey parts or Desmond parts? Tough choice. Hard to say." Meg's voice was easy and low as she focused in on every nuance of Jata's posture. Flat spine, relaxed tail, neutral neck. Her tongue worked in flickering swipes, processing the trace chemicals of Desmond's stink.

"Shut up, Yancy." The quiver in his voice was so satisfying, but she didn't want Jata to get too curious. Besides, a nice, long whiff was all anyone really needed of Desmond.

She took up the low call again—"Jata, chow time, Jata"—and shook the bag in her left hand. Easily diverted, Jata swung her head back around and resumed her climb up to the peak of the rock.

The rock itself was a stipulation of the public feedings and, like everything else at the Zoo of America, it had hidden purposes. The slant of it looked like a Spinal Tap mock-up of the Lion King. Even as Jata reached the edge facing Meg, the tip of her tail still swept against the dirt and mulch on the exhibit floor. The height brought Jata's head even with Meg's shoulders and, along with providing a killer view of her entire, massive profile, gave the crowd the impression that Jata was in a dominant position over Meg. Actually, it was the complete opposite. Komodos didn't hunt from above; they hid in long grasses, completely invisible in less than two feet of foliage, and struck their prey from below. That's how the boy on Komodo Island was attacked. Really, if anyone thought about it, no one ever saw a three-hundred-pound lizard dive-bombing a deer from some obscure vantage point on a cliff. And if the crowd was really paying attention, they would see that the sides of the feeding rock rose up into a small ledge that would trip Jata if she tried to lunge forward or to her right or left. Basically, the only way off the thing was back.

Jata reached the top, and her thick, dart-shaped head swiveled toward the bucket in Meg's hand.

Ignoring the crowd—*Wave?* she'd asked Chuck. *Do I look like Miss freaking America to you?*—Meg reached into the bucket with her long-handled hook to spear a chunk of raw turkey. "Guadalupe says hi."

My best customer, Guadalupe, one of the cafeteria cooks, always said as she dumped the food into Meg's bucket. *Now, you be careful in there, okay?*

Careful was so much a part of Meg's routine she barely registered it. Careful was buried in the way she held the hook out to Jata and how her biceps tensed in preparation for retracting it before Jata could bite down on the metal. Careful was designed into her boots, Desmond's position behind her, and even the rock itself. She freaking breathed caution and, like air, forgot about it as easily as exhaling. Being careful wasn't the big thing on her mind as she offered the shish-kebabbed turkey to Jata and watched the dragon's jaws fall open. It was intimacy.

Only she could see the individual rows of teeth, each like a serrated knife pointing back to her pink, gaping throat; only she could smell her wet scales and her warm, rancid breath; this was a tiny piece of space and time that only she shared with Jata, a private yet bizarrely exhibitionist dinner party that none of the voyeurs were brave enough to attend. She didn't feel careful, holding that first bite out to Jata. She felt wired and calm at the same time, as if she were swallowing little balls of thrill wrapped in soft, dark pillows. There was no other experience like it. It was how she'd always thought being a keeper was supposed to feel.

Jata tore the turkey off the feeding hook and threw her head back for a better grip on the meat before swallowing. Meg prepped the next bite, waiting for Jata to be ready. Once they began, they kept a quiet, rhythmic pace that was made up of these motions—offer, take, swallow, and repeat—again and again until the bucket was empty.

As Jata ate, a trail of bloody saliva fell from her jaws. Dimly, Meg heard the crowd murmur in response and wondered if they knew the pink liquid was the real source of the Komodos' terrible reputation. They tore their own gums apart as they ate, creating a foamy soup of spit, bacteria, and blood: a perfect, killer cocktail with a twist of venom. It wasn't fire breathing out of their mouths that gave the dragons their power. It was right here, in Jata's scary table manners. Oblivious to the crowd and her own drool, Jata shifted her weight and dug the claws of her front feet into the rock. She always seemed the happiest right here during their feedings. Meg understood.

When the bucket was empty, Meg turned it upside down and tilted it so Jata could see the bottom. Jata swallowed the last piece, cocked her head, and sneezed loudly.

"Bless you," mumbled Desmond. The crowd laughed.

Meg shrugged and tossed the empty bucket behind her toward the door, hoping she splattered Desmond with some flying turkey juice. Sometimes Jata didn't believe the bucket was empty and would walk over to investigate. And sometimes, after finding no more meat, she would start chewing the bucket itself. Unable to stop her, Meg would just retrieve the bucket—or pieces of it—when Jata was done amusing herself. Today, though, Jata seemed happy to be done with her meal. She blinked at Meg with sleepy, satisfied eyes.

"Yeah, we're done now. You can hang up your top hat." Meg cocked her head to the same angle as Jata and smiled.

Instead of retreating back to her pool or sunning rock, Jata backed down the feeding rock and walked around it toward Meg. The crowd stopped talking, and Meg could feel the hush creeping up the back of her neck.

"Meg?" Desmond sounded nervous and distant.

She waved behind her, shooing him off. Jata lumbered easily, no hints of stress or aggression in her posture, and walked around Meg's legs. As Jata circled around to the front, Meg reached out and scratched the back of Jata's head behind her ear sockets. The scales were bumpy and hard even through the thick leather gloves. Jata flicked her tongue and paused for a minute, letting Meg scratch from one side of her skull to the other, before she walked back to her pool and submerged her head for a long drink. Absorbed in watching Jata, Meg jumped, startled, when the crowd burst into applause.

Her face burned. As she tossed a quick hand toward the crowd, she spotted a white lab coat disappearing from the front rail of the viewing area. The dark goop on top of it looked like Antonio's hair, and as she frowned at the back of that head, it disappeared behind a tall, stocky man who stood as still as a pier in the center of a tide of shifting people. She blinked and focused in on the man's gruff face and smiling features. It was her father.

⟋

He hadn't really changed. The dark brown hair she'd inherited was shot with silver at the temples, but it still waved thickly over his broad forehead. His barrel chest was still broad and trim underneath an unfortunate baby-blue polo shirt. Hadn't he moved to Ireland, land of beer guts and liver cirrhosis?

He shifted uncomfortably in the seat as Meg sped out of the zoo parking lot toward home, and it came back, in one of those greedy flashes, how he'd hated to let her mother drive the few times they went anywhere as a family. He couldn't stand to be the passenger.

Meg took a corner at forty, pushing the poor Buick to its screeching limits, and bit down on a small smile as he grabbed the dashboard for balance.

He didn't say anything. Uncomfortable as he was, at least he knew damn well that she was in the driver's seat for this little family reunion. They rode in silence until she got on the entrance ramp to the freeway.

"You look good, Meg. Look like you're doing well." His voice was the same strong baritone that had reminded her of blues singers when she was little. She checked her blind spot and merged onto the highway, swerving across three lanes of traffic.

"Of course, I can only surmise that by looking at you," he continued, in a conversational voice. "You haven't returned any of my phone calls since Christmas."

"I've been busy."

"I can see that." He kicked aside some of the takeout bags on the car floor. "Feeding dragons and discovering miracle virgin births."

The surprise snapped her head around, even as she forced her way onto an exit ramp. His face was mild—always the friendly salesman—but all the blood had run out of his fingers as he gripped the door handle. She cranked the wheel around the exit loop, hugging the exact edge where the asphalt broke into rocky spinoff, then eased up on the gas as they entered residential St. Paul.

"How did you know about that?"

"I keep up." He paused. "Your mother would have been proud."

"I don't think so. She wasn't capable of that." It had been two years since her last conversation with her mother, and even though the cancer had wasted Theresa Whittaker down to eighty pounds and killed her less than a week later, on the phone she'd sounded as immutable as ever. Meg had arranged the funeral, shipped the body from Florida back to Minnesota, sold her mother's prize show dogs, and returned to work, all before her father had even booked his flight.

"Meg, there's some things I've been meaning to say to you." He started in, and she almost gagged. People said that—plenty of washed-up old men who'd alienated their families for their entire lives said that—but they were generally in twelve-step programs or banging late-life bibles, not looking healthy and even prosperous from their luxe new retirement in Ireland.

"Save it. Unless it's something that's going to change the past, I don't want to hear it."

He was quiet for the rest of the ride.

~♪

Meg pulled into the driveway of 1854 Belmont Avenue and turned off the Buick's engine, silencing the high-pitched squeak of the belt she still hadn't replaced. With its edging of rust and smatters of chips, dents, and scratches, the car looked more ancient than some of the houses in this old St. Paul neighborhood. Most of the homes in Groveland were built after World War I, and whoever built them had money. Gingerbread-looking Victorians lined up next to Spanish-style adobe places and three-story mansions with the occasional turret, if Meg looked closely enough. The neighborhood had that urban snobbery—full of mom-and-pop shops that looked more like young-and-yuppie, with tree-lined streets and private academies every mile—but it was still better than the vacuous burbs and strip malls that surrounded the America compound. Meg liked it because Groveland was its own kind of zoo, the houses just like exhibits with their meticulous landscaping and functionless ornaments, all crowded up against one another and yet still completely isolated. Driving down the street and glancing in living room windows was like making the rounds in the Reptile Kingdom.

Meg rented the downstairs apartment in an old Victorian that had been converted to a duplex in the sixties. When she and her father arrived, Ben was in the driveway, buried up to the waist under the hood of his truck. His frayed jeans bagged low under the sweaty T-shirt hem, revealing pale hips but, luckily, no ass-crack. As Meg killed the motor, her father grunted.

"Is that your landlord?"

"It's Ben."

Her landlord, a guy named Neil who lived upstairs, was probably around here somewhere. Neil was like Andy Warhol in Dockers. Meg had no idea whether he had a job. He sat on the upstairs porch most days, drinking a Bloody Mary and doing crossword puzzles, and when she came home from work, he always asked if she had set the bears free. Sure, Neil. Keep drinking.

"You're still seeing Ben?" The concerned father: It was amazing how he could pull it off with so little practice.

Instead of replying, she grabbed her lunch bucket from the back seat.

"I didn't know he was living with you now."

Everyone thought it was such a big deal. Gemma and even Paco, Ben's acid-rock-listening, pot-smoking business partner, both called it a "step," as if they were on some giant relationship staircase with a fat prize at the top. It just worked out this way. Four years ago, Ben and Paco bought a corn-dog stand from Paco's uncle and started working the fair circuits. They hit every county and state fair from Nashville to Billings, starting out in mid-May and arriving back in the Twin Cities in time for the season-ending Minnesota State Fair in the last week of August. It was a gold mine—if you could stand fourteen-hour days of sweating grease and batter—and even though Ben made more than enough cash to loaf around and watch the news the other eight months of the year, he'd defaulted on his rent last summer while he and Paco were on the road. By the time they got back in August, the building manager had sold off all his stuff. He'd started crashing at Meg's place and never got around to finding a new apartment.

And yeah, maybe the whole thing was a bad idea, but it wasn't completely uncomfortable. He made dinner sometimes, and the sex was a lot more convenient when it was across the couch instead of across town. She'd thought … well, she hadn't really thought that much about it at all, but in retrospect it could have helped them work out their issues. They'd made one terrible choice two years ago, and two years was a long time to be angry. So maybe they'd moved in to move on, or something like that—but so far, it wasn't working. They hadn't moved past anything, and seeing him every day, unchanged, untouched, was just throwing it all back in her face. Something had to change soon, but that was all between her and Ben. It wasn't anyone else's business, least of all her father's.

Ben unfolded himself from under the car hood, bringing out a torque wrench and a hasty, scared smile. Wiping the excess grease on his jeans, he stepped forward and shook her father's hand.

"Jim, hi. Long time."

His eyes were cracked-out nervous, bloodshot and darting around her father's shirt like a fly trying to find a steady place to land. Meg didn't need to see the joint stamped out in the garage-side ashtray to know he was blitzed. It was Ben's favorite way to work on cars. Or to do anything, really.

"Ben Askew. You're living with Meg now, I hear."

"Yeah—yes, sir. It's the off-season, and I was going to stay with Paco, but—funny story—his place had a fire while we were on the road. His ex torched this sweater she thought belonged to—well, I'm staying with Meg for now. I'm paying rent." He cleared his throat and played with the wrench. Her father didn't say anything but looked at him through squinting eyes.

"Are you in town for long?" Ben asked, awkwardly breaking the silence.

"No, just a week or so."

"Uh, on business?" Ten bucks said Ben had no idea what kind of business her father had ever been in.

"I'm retired. I'm just here to see Meg."

He was here for her? You'd think he would have mentioned that, maybe elaborated beyond *Hi, it's Dad, just checking in* on her answering machine.

"Well, I'll let you two catch up." Ben lifted the wrench like a clumsy salute and retreated back under the truck.

The wind licked at her face; it was still cold for late March. She walked down the path to the house with her father at her side and opened the kitchen door. He followed her in and made a big show of looking around, as if there were something to see besides a room full of empty cupboards and dusty, creaking appliances.

"This is a nice place. You've been here a few years now."

"Three."

"Meg, I know it's none of my business."

"I'm not going to marry him." She unwound the scarf from her neck, which was crocheted in uneven loops of red yarn—a Christmas gift from Gemma—and raised her eyebrows at him. "Is that what you're worried about?"

Hard to say why she even bothered reassuring him.

"You're not going to marry Ben? He seems like a catch." Her father paced casually around the kitchen, stooping to examine a teakettle, glancing out the window into the dead grass of the backyard. He picked up a saltshaker shaped like a gecko and wagged it playfully at her. "He even pays rent."

The laugh escaped before she could kill it. Once it did, the tension in the room drained a little, and the edges of his eyelids crinkled up. Smiling, he replaced the gecko next to its match.

"Ben's just … Ben." She shrugged.

"Do you love him, Magpie?" No one had called her that since she'd learned how to nuke her own microwave dinners.

"You sound like a Lifetime movie. Did Ireland turn you into a chick?"

He laughed this time and grabbed her scarf from the table, winding it back around her neck.

"What are you doing?"

"I'm going to take you out to dinner. That is, unless you had something you wanted to cook."

They both glanced at the kitchen table, where a basket of clean underwear and socks sat on top of a pile of newspapers.

Meg tightened the scarf and nodded reluctantly. "I guess I could eat."

1 Day *after* Hatching

The morning after the first two hatchlings were born, Meg was in the Mammal Kingdom discovering the existence of gnomes.

The Zoo of America segregated all the animals into six main buildings; reptiles, amphibians, insects, fish, mammals, and birds were all grouped according to their kingdoms, with the exception of the dolphins, who got their own building because their trainers refused to be part of either the fish or mammal kingdoms. Each area had designated supplies, but the Mammal Kingdom had poached one of Meg's water hoses twice in the last month, and she couldn't figure out who was doing it. Michael, the head mammal keeper, who was as giant as the bears he tended, blamed it on gnomes. The purple ones with the fuzzy butts, he said, liked using the hoses for playing jump rope. Another day she would have been mad or even logged a complaint with Chuck, just to make him fill out a stack of forms and take a wild gnome chase, but nothing could piss her off today. She laughed and slapped Michael on the shoulder, or as near to his shoulder as she could reach, coiled the hose around her head and arm, toga style, and headed back to her reptiles.

The winding path that snaked along the edge of the zoo grounds over the Minnesota River was her favorite walk, despite all the visitors and the snack and souvenir stands lining the sides. If you didn't look at the freeway bridge or the power-plant smokestacks upriver, or listen to the dull roar of morning traffic, it was really beautiful. The dark river shallows pooled into lazy lakes and bogs that lapped at the surrounding tree-covered bluffs. Sometimes, on spring mornings like this, fog danced up from the river in crazy corkscrews, and the great egrets darted through the puffs looking for an unsuspecting meal. Fog made the whole valley look different, as if the river was from another world in which subdivisions and tourist attractions didn't crowd its banks and smokestacks didn't belch into its sky. There'd been huge, dense forests here once, too, but that ecosystem was as long gone as the logging industry that destroyed it. Now the cranes and red foxes stuck to the valley, where a wildlife preserve was their last refuge, at least until the power company or the America compound needed to expand, and then maybe some zoo in Shanghai would think they were exotic enough to open an exhibit and give them a shot to bring some money through the gate. Look at all the dull American birds, white as the tundra, almost extinct.

It all boiled down to money. That was why Jata had been brought here in the first place. The world's largest lizard, king of the reptiles. That kind of bill drew crowds. Meg had a feeling the river valley species wouldn't be able to catch the same life raft; egrets weren't half as gorgeous outside the fog.

She was trying not to think about money, the zoo, or the future at all—but trust her boss to dump a four-inch binder of it in her lap. Chuck walked in front of her line of vision, ruining her view.

"Megan, it's amazing, isn't it? The entire zoo is revolving around Jata's babies." The way he said it, he might've been constipated with excitement or just plain put out that his carefully organized monthly schedule had gone to shit.

Ben talked about The Man a lot, and The Man—he was a lot of different guys. The governments, the corporations, a media empire here or there—no matter who The Man was, Meg would bet he had a Chuck. Chuck Farrelly was the kind of guy who maybe once had tried to have a sense of humor, who twenty years ago would have tagged along with coworkers to the bar, all eager and awkward, always wanting to stay for one more drink but never having anything to say. You could still see that sad sack around the edges of Chuck's eyes. Getting the position of General Zookeeping Supervisor was probably the highlight of his life so far; he could finally make use of the fact that nobody liked him. He had an office in the basement of the Visitor Center that smelled like Windex, and on his desk was a picture of him with a fat woman and three children, all wearing pseudo-safari gear; it was the only evidence Meg had that Chuck was capable of smiling. She tried to make his life as difficult as possible.

"What's up, Chuck?" She didn't bother to stop walking. The sooner she tended to her exhibits, the sooner she could go back to the nursery. Chuck fell into step with her, his tense, bulky frame easily keeping pace with her quick march.

"Marketing has taken out a quarter-page ad in Sunday's paper, a birth announcement for the Komodos. They've already sent a press release out. Channel 12 is running a spot tomorrow, and they want to come down and take some pictures of the hatchlings. We need to transfer them to the baby building as soon as possible for the news crew."

Meg felt a gut-punch of fear at the mention of Channel 12. "Nicole Roberts?"

"We don't know."

She swallowed and worked her way through to the rest of his brilliant idea. The baby building was the least private, most chaotic place at the zoo. It was classic Zoo of America: All of the baby animals born at the zoo were required to go there after birth—with their mothers, if possible—where the public could ogle them all at once without tiring their feet on the two-mile walk around the whole park. Without any permanent residents, no keepers were assigned full-time to the area, yet all of the kingdoms were thrown in there side by side. Meg knew the hatchlings had to stop through there eventually—she'd redesigned a series of terrestrial tanks with fresh shrubs and logs full of cubby holes—but the move should've been at least a few weeks out. Not freaking tomorrow.

"Chuck, no." She squeezed the hose with a death grip. "They're not even all born yet, for Christ's sake. There's one egg left to hatch."

"That one will follow soon, Antonio said."

"Oh, Antonio said, did he? Did Antonio read everything ever written about Komodos reproducing in captivity? Because I did, Chuck. It could be another month before we see the last Komodo hatchling," she lied.

"A month, hmm? He didn't mention that possibility." Chuck glanced at his clipboard—as far as Chuck was concerned, the ten-year-plan of the entire planet was on his checklist on that clipboard—and frowned.

Some people might say you shouldn't lie to your boss, and maybe they were right, but they didn't work here. Other zoos, the ones that acted as conservationist sanctuaries for threatened species, wouldn't put themselves in this situation. Those zoos put the animals first; they tried to understand and mitigate the stress of captivity, they created partnerships with organizations that protected indigenous animal populations, and they participated in breeding and reintroduction programs with local Department of Natural Resources offices.

The Zoo of America was a totally different species. It showcased big-ticket animals like Jata in high-tech, elaborate environments while cramming the "fillers" into box-like exhibits no larger than the minimum space that regulations required, knowing that the average visitor went straight for the dolphins, bears, and lions anyway. "Charismatic mega-vertebrates," the zoo called them. The moneymakers. The rest of the animals just rounded out the collection and helped justify the price of admission. Meg spent most of her time disgusted by management's bald preoccupation with the bottom line, but secretly—and she would never admit it to any living soul—she was relieved, too. Relieved that Jata was a charismatic mega-vertebrate, and a cost-effective one at that. Other than the thermoregulating heat for her exhibit and some dead animals for a weekly lunch, Jata didn't cost the zoo an extra dime. The zoo probably barely broke even on the dolphins, but Jata was a guaranteed cash cow. And that meant Meg could keep her as long as she lived.

While Chuck seemed to be mulling over what she'd said, they passed the turnoff to the bird building, a soaring triangle on a peninsula of land that jutted over the river, designed to look like a grand, golden wing. The morning light hugged its transparent walls and created the illusion that it was glowing from the inside. The Bird Kingdom was the flagship building of the zoo; marketing put the golden wing on every postcard and souvenir they sold, and people loved it. It had even been featured in *Architectural Digest* once. What most people didn't know was that the building had killed hundreds of birds. Originally, the exhibits had backed up to the windows so visitors could squint their eyes and almost imagine the birds were flying around in the river valley. Unfortunately, the birds had thought so, too. In the zoo's opening days, bird bodies had littered the exhibit floors every morning. They flew into the glass again and again, trying to escape. Maybe they would have designed the thing better if there were charismatic mega-vertebrate species inside, but birds were pretty much all fillers, so the keepers had to find their own ways to keep their exhibits alive. Tinted glass didn't matter; mesh netting didn't make a difference. The sky called to the birds, and no amount of diversionary tactics could convince them of their captivity.

Eventually, after the back of the exhibits had been completely blacked out, blocking all of the natural light, the birds finally got the idea that they were in a cage, but all the other keepers still referred to the long, narrow path out to the golden wing as death row.

Their walkway veered away from death row toward the western side of the zoo. After another minute of silence, Meg tried to drum up some more points for her case. "It can be extremely stressful to transfer the hatchlings into a public exhibit before they're ready. They'll be more likely to attack each other and possibly even go into shock."

The first part was true enough. She didn't even know if hatchlings went into shock, but then neither did Chuck. As a trump card, she threw down the m-word. "You don't want a dead miracle baby on your hands, do you?"

He was listening. Whenever he pursed his lips into little razor-blade slashes like that, Chuck was actually listening to what someone was saying. He looked a lot more pleasant when he was just blowing you off: Then he'd just nod and wait for a pause so he could give you the corporate answer he had all lined up in his head.

Meg's mind raced ahead; she was desperate to keep the Komodos out of the public eye for as long as she could. If she could keep their stress levels as low as possible in the next few weeks, they'd be much more likely to adapt well to a social environment with one another.

"Every baby at the zoo goes through that building," she said. "How can the public understand how rare the hatchlings are if they're displayed like every other specimen? Let's bring the news crew into the veterinary nursery and give them some behind-the-scenes footage. They can get clips of the broken eggshells and everything. They'll see the whole process." She jabbed him in the side of his arm. "Tell me that wouldn't be a headlining story for the local news."

Chuck pulled his arm away and rubbed it, slowing down. They

had reached the end of the bluffs, where the path curled back into the heart of the zoo. Meg could hear the bridge traffic zooming behind the two-story noise wall. When the zoo had first opened, it had hired some artist to paint a tacky mural of America across the entire thing; the Golden Gate Bridge and the Rockies bled into the Great Plains, and animals the size of West Virginia—gray wolves and buffalo, all the species that early settlers wasted no time clearing out—wandered aimlessly around the picture.

Meg glanced up at the bald eagle soaring over the top of the painting and then ahead to the Visitor Center that towered over the main gate. Was there a completely shallow and commercial angle she was missing? She wanted to rub the bald eagle's head like a genie's lamp. Tell me, favored beast of America, how to get Americans to protect you.

"We really need to distinguish the hatchlings, Chuck." She didn't know whether he was still listening. "Not only are they exotic—let's face it, the kings of all lizards—but they're a miracle. They really are."

Chuck frowned and tapped his clipboard on her toga of hose. "I understand your point, Megan, and I know how much this exhibit means to you, but, well—I tell my son that language and presentation can be just as important as action—"

"Exactly. I want to present them well."

"And," he continued, with a pointed pause, "you have to be careful with what you say about these dragons. Miracle. Virgin."

He ticked the words off on his fingers, pointing dead at her chest.

"These are words you should avoid whenever possible, especially if you're interested in the security of your job. Remember where it got you last time."

Clenching her jaw, she nodded. "Fine. Okay. I won't say it—but other people will."

She pointed to the mural of America and the roar of traffic

behind it. "People who want to pay to see these hatchlings. They believe they're miraculous. We can't jeopardize them in any way or cheapen their value. Trust me, Chuck. Please trust me on this."

He sighed and propped his hand on his hip. "You've made a good point. Antonio made similar assertions when we spoke earlier. With the veterinarian and primary keeper on the same page, so to speak, I think management will agree."

The thought of being on the same page or even in the same library as Antonio still made her uncomfortable. Her cheeks burned when she thought about that morning, waking up in the nursery with her head lolling down his chest.

She'd scrambled up out of her chair, barely registering the cricks and cramps that shot down her spine from sleeping upright on hard plastic all night. Her head pounded from the champagne, and she'd quickly grabbed the cups and empty bottle, hoping to God no one had punched in yet and seen them passed out on each other. The whole camping-out plan seemed too intimate, too inexplicable in the fake fluorescent light of day. Antonio had woken up as she was hastily checking the un-hatched egg and two newborns.

How are they doing? He'd stretched like a jungle cat, tipping backward over the folding chair.

She looked away. *Fine. No change since last night. I gave the newbies a cricket apiece. I'll check back later to see if they ate them and take some more measurements.*

Hey. He was talking, stretching, and reaching toward her, but she ducked out of the nursery and ran for the first discreet wastebasket she could find, empty champagne bottle stuffed under her arm.

It turned out that it had been six in the morning when all that business went down. She took a quick shower in the locker room, trying to scrub the night off her skin, and got to work doing anything she could find around the cafeteria until ten o'clock, when it opened and she raced inside, begging Guadalupe for a free coffee. *Those dragon babies keeping you up late?*

Kids. Meg had grinned and thrown her arms into the air. *What can you do?*

Now Chuck and Meg reached the Visitor Center, where all the supervisors and admins worked. Above them, the glass walls of the upper management offices reflected the morning sun. Meg glanced up at the sleek surface, dying to run straight up there to tell them where to shove their media relations plan. She couldn't afford it, though. The last incident had landed her a fat probation and who knew how many checkmarks on her file. She had to play it by their rules, in their language, font, and form. It was the only way to protect the hatchlings.

"Do you want me to write up an e-mail or a—memo—or something?" The word even tasted nasty. "I can point out all the studies that support this. The Species Survival Plan doesn't specifically instruct about care, but there's tons of data—"

He held up a hand in a mini Heil Hitler. "Don't do anything. I'll talk with the appropriate parties, and if we need some further information to make a decision, I'll contact you."

"You're talking about tomorrow, Chuck. Are you going to hear back on this pretty soon?"

"You'll hear as soon as the management team makes their decision and not before. And no matter what that decision is, you'll cooperate with it completely or face suspension. After your probation last fall, I'd have no choice in the matter. Are we clear, Megan?"

"You read all my paperwork, right, Chuck?" Some of the hose coils were starting to slide down her shoulder, and she bounced the load back higher against her neck.

"Most of it, yes."

"Notice how I sign everything 'Meg Yancy,' not 'Megan'?"

"Actually, no." He tucked the clipboard against his side like a football, which was his universal sign of departure. "Your signature is completely illegible."

He turned around and disappeared inside the Visitor Center.

"Fucking bosses," she muttered, making her way back to the reptiles.

She used the water hose to fill up the black tree monitor's pond, scaring him up the only branch in the exhibit when she ducked inside. It was a bare-bones space; a small pond and a piece of driftwood were the only things keeping him company between the beige walls. She fed and groomed him once a week, according to his care plan, and watched his SAMs, of course, but the only other interaction he had was through the glass. Meg scrubbed it down from the inside and watched the visitors stream by. Some stopped and waved at her. Others watched the monitor for a second and read his description on the wall. The rest just glanced in as they herded their children on to Jata's exhibit around the corner because that was the big attraction in the Reptile Kingdom. That's why they were here. Meg watched them disappear around the corner again and again and felt herself slide away with them, wondering what Jata was up to this afternoon and how much longer it would take her to finish with this exhibit. Then she kicked herself.

She stayed with the black tree monitor longer than necessary, sweeping up nonexistent dirt and watching him watch her from the security of his branch. She wiped the glass down until she could see her reflection in the drifting crowd, until the walls closed in around her and it was easy to understand how a bird could have a view like this and throw itself away.

1 Week *before* Hatching

L ike every fun moment in her childhood, just when Meg started to relax and get used to seeing him, her father left. He stayed a week this time around, which seemed about right. It would have been pitch-perfect if he'd brought her some hotel soaps and souvenir T-shirts from Ireland and promised to take her with him on one of his next sales trips. That simple gifts-and-promises strategy had served him unbelievably well for the better part of her preteen years; it was like her holy grail as a kid.

When Meg was growing up, her mother had dragged her off to some dog show almost every weekend, packing her up in their minivan along with the dogs, kennels, food, suitcases, and all the paraphernalia of competition. They drove for hours, sometimes days, for the big shows, with Meg sitting in the passenger seat staring silently out the window while her mother talked endlessly about her rivals, their inferior dogs, her hopes for the show, and tidbits about whatever part of the country they were driving through that day. Sometimes Meg saw signs for pools or theme parks, but they only ever stopped to get takeout or to let the dogs pee and play fetch to stretch their legs. She'd probably stood at the edge of hundreds of rest stops, eating chips from a vending machine and throwing a ball until her arm hurt. That part was never so bad; the part she hated was the shows themselves. A hundred people crammed into some gym or onto a field, brushing and buffing and polishing their poor dogs as if they were some kind of sculpture instead of a living, breathing animal. The dogs loved it, her mother always said: Look at how excited they were to run the ring and jump through the courses. When Meg was little, she believed it, but as she grew up she learned what dependent creatures dogs were. They were happy when their owners were happy. They looked excited when they earned ribbons because they got a treat and some affection. The ribbons weren't for the dogs at all; they were for the owners who took those little puppies and molded and trained them into winners.

It was easy to see stuff like that, to see the animals clearly, since she was always one of the only kids at the shows. For most of the owners, their dogs were their kids, and sometimes Meg wondered if her mother felt the same way—that the dogs were her real children and Meg was just some failed experiment in reproduction. Her father, at least, seemed to like her. Every weekend, she'd stand off to the side of the judging area by herself, watch her mother bask in the spotlights, and wish that her father would burst through the crowd and take her away. She daydreamed about it constantly, squeezing the life out of that hope the way only a reclusive, idiot child could, and he never once rescued her. Eventually she grew up and let go of the fantasy, and when they sat her down in high school to tell her they were getting divorced, her only question was why they'd waited so long. After that, she'd seen her father sporadically. He came for weekends in high school, dropped off care packages at her dorm rooms, and left chatty messages on her apartment answering machines.

On this visit, he'd taken her out for dinner every night and had even shown up at the zoo a few times with some random buddy in tow. He took each friend down to Meg's exhibits and pointed and waved at her like a little kid. Clapped the guy on the back and said something, all smiles, nodding toward Meg. She turned to Jata one day and rolled her eyes. "Is this what it's like all the time?"

Jata just dunked her head into the pool and guzzled some water.

One night, he'd brought some photos of Ireland to show her. There was a shot of a tiny, unmarked street that was apparently downtown, a castle that was near something famous she'd never heard of, lots of pictures of dark, low-ceilinged rooms from his cottage—before-and-after remodeling shots of walls, bathrooms, and a narrow, steep staircase—and picture after picture of laughing old men. She wasn't sure, but it seemed like the same three guys aping in the cottage, parading down a gray beach, and propped up on barstools. *Best people in the world, Meg,* he'd said. *Believe me, I've met enough to know. But they can't name a single spice apart from salt and pepper.*

Today Meg punched out for lunch and walked up to the cafeteria to meet him. The place was nearly empty at three o'clock in the afternoon; most people had already eaten their overpriced hamburgers, sipped their solar-heated coffee, and packed the kids off to see the afternoon dolphin show. Meg walked into the seating area, bright with sunlight from the bay windows that overlooked the river valley, and found her father sitting in a far booth. He'd already been to the counter and gotten two hamburger meals with fries and shakes. She grabbed the chocolate shake and started slurping, tossing the sandwiches a suspicious look.

"Don't worry, yours is a veggie burger."

It had taken him two dinners that week to remember she was a vegetarian, but after that he'd been pretty accommodating. Sales guys were good at that.

"Thanks."

"Don't thank me until you try it." He bit into his hamburger and made a face. "It's kind of like being back in Ireland already."

They ate and watched the birds fly over the river.

"I couldn't believe you today, Meg."

She mopped up some ketchup with a handful of fries and shoveled them into her mouth. "Abou wha?"

"The feeding. It was amazing." He stopped eating and just stared at her now.

Tuesday had rolled around again, so she'd done Jata's weekly feeding for the public a few hours ago. She hadn't seen her father's face in the crowd, but he must have been in there somewhere. She'd chosen turkey again today, since Jata had weighed in a little porkier than Meg wanted at her recent physical. It wasn't surprising, since most zoological specimens were fat and lazy next to their wild cousins, but Jata shouldn't get too overweight too young. She could have twenty years left in her.

Meg shrugged off her father's comment and slurped on her shake. "She trusts me, that's all."

"Don't Komodos kill people?"

"Not half as much as we kill them. They don't consider us a primary food source." She flipped off the shake's lid and started dipping her fries into the chocolate.

"And I wouldn't consider that a primary food source." He tracked the French fries from the shake to her mouth and cringed.

She laughed with her mouth full just as a white lab coat appeared next to their booth. Following it upward, she met Antonio's amused face.

"Yancy, I didn't know you could laugh."

She swallowed and wiped her mouth with the back of her hand. "I'm on my lunch break."

"I figured that out. Big brain and all." He tapped his temple.

"What do you want?"

He turned to her father. "See, this is the Yancy I know. All business. No wasted syllables."

"My girl's efficient. She's a dragon tamer, you know." Her father smiled broadly across the table.

"Dragon keeper," Meg corrected. "Jata's not tame."

"That's my point." Her father toasted her with his shake. "You can't tame something that's already tame. You tame wild creatures."

"True," Antonio said, but he was looking at her. He blinked and turned to her father, extending a hand. "I'm Antonio Rodríguez, head veterinarian."

"Jim Yancy, Meg's father."

"I didn't realize Meg"—he faltered—"had parents."

"Antonio missed the biology part of veterinary school," Meg said. "He was too busy trying to nail the prep squad."

Antonio cocked his head to one side. "It's hard to picture you as a little girl, Yancy. Did you have pigtails? Maybe a couple turtles in a bucket?"

"Whippets," her father said, spitting it out like a cuss. He shook his head and flashed Meg a long, guilty look across the table. "Her mother bred show dogs and dragged Meg across the country with grooming brushes shoved in her little hands. I was too busy with work to save her from that circus."

"Dad." She tried to shut him up, but he waved her off with a hand.

"It's true." He glanced up at Antonio. "Meg was never too fond of people after putting up with those trophy-hungry freaks her entire childhood. Hard to blame her, believe me. You ever met any of those people?"

"No." Antonio was still watching her; she could feel his stare as she sucked the last drops of her shake and stared blindly out into the river valley.

"They'll drive you bat-shit crazy. I should know; I was married to one for fifteen years."

"I'm sorry to hear that," Antonio said. "Well, I don't want to interrupt your lunch any further. It was a pleasure to meet you, Jim."

They shook hands again.

"Meg, come see me when you get back on shift."

"Why?"

"I need some clarification on your paperwork." He tapped a paper on the medical chart he was holding. She tried to see what he was pointing at, but the chart was above her line of sight. He smiled, following her gaze, and then strode out of the cafeteria without saying another word.

"I like him," her father said, watching Antonio leave.

"Yeah, he's great till he shoves a chip in your head."

"Hmm." Her father piled his empty fry carton and drink container back on the tray and set it aside. "There's something in the air between the two of you."

"Like hate?"

"Like a spark, an attraction."

Meg choked on her last fry. She coughed and shook her head dumbly. Maybe the Irish whiskey was frying his head instead of his gut. One sappy family reunion under his belt, and he was some Cupid with a psychology degree.

"Well, I should probably head off to the airport and let you get back to work." He half stood and pulled a manila envelope out of his back pocket, sliding it across the table to her.

"What's that?"

"It's for you. I know you hate flying, so I thought this would be better."

She opened the seal and unfolded the papers inside: Two tickets on a cruise line, departing from New York to Dublin.

"They're flex vouchers. You can use them anytime in the next two years." He closed a hand over hers and patted it gently. "Come visit your old man sometime, okay? You can bring anybody you like."

She flinched away and dropped the tickets on the table between them. "You always did bring gifts after being away. I guess things don't really change."

For the first time all week, he looked old. The lines on his face tightened up, and his eyes went watery, then hard. Slowly, he nodded. "I always said we'd take a trip together, too. Do you remember? I planned a dozen, you know, but it never worked out with my schedule—or if it did, your mother refused to spare you from her dog shows."

He tucked the tickets back into the envelope, pushed them toward her, and squeezed her hand.

"Come see me, Magpie, after you work out all this dragon stuff. We'll finally have a proper vacation together."

There were other days, saner days, when she'd have happily kicked the old man's ass back to Ireland for trying to pull off the father-of-the-year act this late in the game, but right now he looked weathered and defeated, like one of the animals on a slow death watch, and she just didn't have it in her.

"Think about it." He pulled his jacket on and walked slowly out of the cafeteria, leaving the tickets and all the garbage from the food on the table in front of her. This was normal again, being alone; this was how she wanted her life to be. But still she sat in the empty room and looked out at the river valley, fighting the strangest urge to get up and follow him.

~⦆

"What do you want, Rodríguez?"

She found him in one of the quarantine rooms on the safe side of the bars from a lioness lounging in a pile of hay. The animal was facing away from Antonio and flicking her tail once every few seconds, apparently pissed off at the accommodations.

"I want her to get up and walk around a bit, so I can see how the foot is healing."

Meg pressed her forehead into the bars and spied a pink incision pointing down the pad of her back paw as Antonio made a note on the animal's chart.

"Domestic dispute?" she asked. Sometimes lions got touchy about the feeding order, but the males usually started all that shit.

"Glass shard. Puncture wound went straight up, right between the toes."

"Bottle?"

"Yep. One of the interns thinks Snapple."

"Bastards."

"Sometimes." He flipped the chart closed and tossed it onto the chair. "We'll have to keep her in isolation a week or so just to make sure she's out of danger for infection. Poor girl."

He patted the bars and went back into the hallway, handing Meg a leaflet of papers on his way past. It wasn't her paperwork. It was an article titled "How SAMs Can Predict Ovulation and Birth in Animals," by Antonio Rodríguez, DVM.

"What is this crap?"

"The future of zoology, among other things." He flashed a grin at someone passing behind her in the hallway.

"Be delusional on your own time. Where's my paperwork that you can't understand?"

"That was just to get you to actually come down here." He turned the grin back to her, that same flashy smile that he used on everyone from the cashiers to the director of the zoo—the Wheaties-box smile, the I'm-going-to-nail-your-daughter-and-then-take-you-golfing smile, the white-toothed, dimpled, gleaming smile that he thought he could use to get whatever the hell he wanted. And it usually worked.

"Piss off." She tossed the papers and brushed by him, heading back to the keeper's cage.

He appeared at her side before she'd gotten two steps down the hallway. "I've got data on twelve different chipped species that had offspring here in the last few years, and there's some really interesting trends on blood-pressure patterns. During an ultrasound for the black bear, I even managed to pick up and sync the fetus's heartbeat to the SAM so that the keeper could continue to monitor the fetus's development and health between checkups."

Grabbing her elbow, he pulled her up short before she could reach the exit. His hand was warm, and it sent a jolt of energy up her arm, as if she'd hit one of the electrified fences ringing the far half of the outdoor mammal exhibits. She jerked out of his grip and crossed her arms.

"There's a section on Jata that I want you to proof for bench-marking against the general Komodo population. A lot of the other keepers have done the same for their animals' sections, and I'm giving credit at the end of the article for everyone's technical expertise."

"Not sharing your precious byline?" She raised an eyebrow.

"Bylines are for people who write, Yancy, not ones that make caveman drawings with arrows and stick figures on their forms."

"Thanks, but I'll pass. You should know by now that I don't support your brave new world."

He snorted a short breath out his nose and bunched the paper in a fist. The veins on his neck started to pop out and then, after a second, sank back into his skin as he shook his head and sighed. "SAMs are the future of animal management. You're so short-sighted. I'm not just talking about zoos here. Animal refuges, even wild fauna, can be microchipped and observed from any computer in the world without disturbing a single blade of grass in their natural habitat. We can monitor entire populations, track their migration patterns with 100 percent accuracy, which will allow us to study the vulnerability of their habitats and food supplies, even intervene and fight widespread diseases before they wipe out a species. The Zoo of America is providing the baseline measurements that all future research will build on for generations to come."

He pointed back toward the enclosures. "That lioness in there? We wouldn't have known about that puncture for at least another day without SAMs. The keeper saw a dip in her blood pressure combined with an adrenaline spike as her body reacted to the injury. The SAM helped us save her from any further blood loss and a thousand times greater risk of infection. So how can you stand there with your arms crossed and your mouth all sucked up like that and tell me that I'm not doing the right thing with this program? I'm saving animals' lives. With increased monitoring, we could save entire species from extinction."

She shook her head slowly, working her way from side to side throughout his whole little speech. An intern and a keeper wheeled a tank full of meerkats by them as he talked, but neither group stopped to acknowledge the other.

"I'm not shortsighted. I can see exactly how far your program will go. Microchipping the world, keeping every creature in it under your thumb? What gives you the right?"

"Said the zookeeper who controls every last detail of her animals' worlds."

"There's no place left for some of these animals. It's better for them to be here than in a circus or starving in the wild or being killed by poachers."

"We can change that," he broke in, really working the sale. He pulled her hand out of her crossed arms and put the papers back into her palm, closing his fingers down over hers so that she was forced to hold the article. It was the second time in as many hours that someone was trying to shove something into her hand. She tried to pull away, but he kept plowing through his pitch.

"With SAMs, we can track poachers as soon as a chipped animal dies. The GPS signal will take us straight to them."

"And how long do you think it will take them to learn to cut out the microchip? Two poachers later? Maybe three?" She finally ripped her hand away from his, and they glared at each other for a second, toe to toe. "This isn't even about poaching."

"What is it about? Besides your clear lack of willingness to evolve."

"That's just it." She drilled a finger into his chest. "You can't decide how I'm going to evolve. You can't control a species' survival, and you can't manage the planet's ecology. Stop trying to play God." She dropped the papers on the floor in front of him and walked away.

3 Days *after* Hatching

M eg paced the length of the keeper's room, trying to figure out the least humiliating way of doing what she had to do. The sign on the door read Zookeeping Administration, but everyone knew this place as "the cage." The long basement room, with its low ceilings and fluorescent lights, had a dungeon-like quality that someone once tried to lighten up by painting palm trees on one of the cement-block walls. Every zookeeper had a locker in here, and the lockers faced a row of computer kiosks where they wrote their daily logs, entered purchase reqs, and checked their SAMs. The cage and the veterinary wing were both underneath the cafeteria, and Meg could hear the last of the shuffling feet as they closed for the night upstairs. Finally, when she couldn't put it off any longer, she punched out on the time clock, pushed through the double doors at the end of the room, passed the bathrooms, and headed straight down the vet hallway to the last office on the left.

Meg knocked on the open door of Antonio's office. He swiveled his chair around and nodded her in, pointing at his earpiece.

"We'll have to make it up before next week. Maybe Sunday?"

He looked at her as he said it, which confused her. When people talked on the phone, they should look at an unassuming wall or their dirty fingernails, not at someone else who was waiting her turn in the conversation line. Irritated, Meg bided her time perusing all the crap he'd hung in his office. Diplomas and certificates—no surprise. Covers of magazines in which he'd probably published articles. Everything was framed in black and aligned with anal, T-square geometry around the room. As she glanced around, one of the framed covers caught her eye; it showcased a two-headed profile against a smudgy backdrop of garbage, like a soft-focus landfill. The profile was black, and on the left side, the face was a bird—with the stubby, hollow beak of a parakeet—and on the right side, it was a human. In the center of the two faces, right where the bird brain and the man brain would touch, was a small, glowing microchip. The headline read "Can Technology Really Save the Planet?" but the words were skinny and pale. They faded back into the pile of garbage, and the longer she looked at it, the more everything else in the picture faded, too, until the microchip pulsed alone in the middle of the page, as if there were no point in bothering with the question mark at all, as if the editors had already given their answer because the chip was the only thing in focus. The only hope for the planet.

"All right, give me a shout if you can get us set up for Sunday. I'm free all afternoon. Later. Hi."

She heard him shuffle some papers and stand up behind her. "I said hi, Yancy."

"Oh. Hi." Her heart started racing as she swung back to face his desk, and she clenched her arms tighter around her middle. There were no words for how much she didn't want to do this.

"I didn't think you'd still be here after closing time," she hedged. "I was just going to leave you a note."

He shrugged and moved around the desk, half-sitting on the front of it. The arms of his lab coat pulled tight as he crossed them and stretched his neck from side to side, cracking his spine. He looked tired but pent up at the same time, as if the exhaustion couldn't hold him back for long. She knew how that felt.

"I was hanging around until baseball practice, but apparently we just got rained out."

"Slugger, huh?"

"More of a bunter and runner, actually. They put me on the top of the rotation because I can steal bases."

Her eyebrows raised; he'd even said it with a straight face. "I bet."

He laughed and shook his head. "It's not a co-ed team, Yancy."

"Whatever." She paced back toward the wall, getting more nervous now that she had his attention. "I talked to Chuck today, and he said he got management to hold off on moving the hatchlings into the baby building."

"I know. He called me, too."

She took a deep breath, inflating the bottom of her lungs with that tight, bursting feeling, and turned around while she still had the humility left in her.

"Thank you."

He didn't say anything. It was probably the only thing in the world she could have said to leave him speechless. His eyes rounded, and his stomach even kind of sucked in, as if she'd gut-punched him. Maybe she had, in a way, but if they were trying to kill each other with kindness now, she sure hadn't thrown the first punch. She paced back his way and tried to explain.

"They wouldn't have taken my word for it. I could know everything in the world about Komodo dragons, but I'm a bitch. I know that. I haven't played on their terms in the past, and they haven't forgotten what happened last August—even though I'm trying to shut up and play along now in order to be a good keeper for these hatchlings."

He cocked his head. "This is you trying to shut up?"

The laugh huffed out; she couldn't help it. "Yeah, I guess it is.

Anyway, you're their freaking golden boy and they listen to you and I'm just saying that I know I wouldn't have been able to protect their welfare without you. That's all."

"I'm trying to protect them, too, you know. When will you get that through your head?" He wasn't letting her off the hook. Bastard.

"I guess"—she shrugged, a quick bounce of shoulders that stung the cramped muscles in her neck—"now, huh? Now I believe you. I don't trust people because they always have something to gain."

"I do have something to gain. I have three healthy parthenogenic Komodo dragons to gain. Who else but you could understand how amazing that is?"

"Yeah." He smelled like antiseptic and cinnamon, and she started to get nervous again under his eyes. They were chocolate brown, rich and obnoxiously compelling, watching her as carefully as they'd watched the hatchlings by her side for the last eight months. Her stomach flip-flopped, and she turned to leave.

"I was thinking about what you said the other day. You know, your toast about evolution."

She leaned against the doorjamb, frowning, and waited.

"I'm not trying to manage evolution, if that's what you think. I'm making a difference in these animals' lives, giving them the chance to live better, longer, and healthier with human supervision. You know how an animal evolves, how it survives? Two ways. Diversity and adaptation. Diversity—to weather the changing climates and food supplies. Adaptation—to fit themselves to the environment they're stuck with."

He ticked the points off on his fingers, and then shook his head. "And that's what I don't get about this whole thing. Parthenogenesis can't be evolution. It's devolution. Parth reduces the species' genetic diversity, making it more vulnerable to those changes in the ecosystem. So here's the fifty-million-dollar question. Why is parthenogenesis still happening when, biologically speaking, parth species should have been sucked into the black hole of extinction eons ago?"

Bumping her shoulder softly against the cold doorjamb, she inhaled, smelling the river scent that seeped into every basement room around here, and smiled at him. "I've got a better one for you. Why are seventy-five percent of wild Komodo dragons male?"

"Why?" He looked confused.

Still smiling, she watched as he made the connection, as it spread across his face. "You think they're reproducing via parth in the wild? It's not just zoos?"

"Exactly."

"Or maybe females just have shorter life spans due to disease or increased predation. You can't jump to conclusions like that."

"Are you kidding me?" Meg laughed. "You can't tell a male Komodo from a female unless you do a blood test or happen to catch them having sex. How could one gender possibly be at risk for a shorter life span?"

He nodded. "Point taken."

"So if parth is such an evolutionary black hole, why have Komodos survived this long? Maybe they got the recipe right a long time ago, and we're all just catching up."

Let him chew on that for a little while. She pushed away from the door and was going to leave—again—when he stopped her—again.

"You are a good keeper." He shifted on the desk. "You just said you were trying to do everything in order to be a good keeper for these Komodos, but don't worry about it, Meg. You already are."

She was going to say *thank you*. The second time was always easier; at least, that's what they said about murder, which couldn't be too much harder than gratitude. She could hear the words rumbling around in her chest, but before they could make their way up and out of her throat, she leaned over and kissed him.

It was quick—just four lips meeting around a fast inhale and a freeze. The flip-flopping in her stomach twisted sideways, curling up into her chest, expanding. Soft, she thought. Warm and soft. And then, straightening back up—oh God. She bolted from the office, speed-walking down the vet hallway, past the bathrooms, and back into the keeper's cage with her face burning hard through the sixth ring of hell.

Kissing Antonio? Her mind stumbled to catch up to the shocks racing through her body. What the hell was she thinking? She stood in front of her locker, staring blindly into the dark void at the back of the tiny, metal cubby.

The cage was empty. Most of the keepers packed up and headed home as soon as the zoo closed. The few late shifters were all out milling around, taking care of exhibits or cleaning up for the night. On any other day, Meg would have been watching the news on the couch with Ben by now, eating greasy takeout and ignoring whatever he said about the headlines—not here, standing stupidly in front of her locker and trying to erase the fact that she'd just kissed Antonio. No, not just erase it—suck it into the far reaches of oblivion.

"Hey."

She spun around. He was lounging against the doors that led from the cage back to the veterinary wing. She opened her mouth to say something—explain, apologize, blow him off—but nothing came out, not even air. He just watched her—not smiling, not speaking, a ready audience for her next humiliation. Forget that. She tossed her hands up, shrugged, and turned back around to her locker, pulling off her work boots and chucking them into the bottom compartment. That's all he got—a shrug. It was probably more than he tossed at some women himself. As she sat on the bench to lace up her tennis shoes, his lab coat rustled up behind her.

"What's that picture?"

"Gemma and her daughter." She refused to glance up and tried to ignore the horrible heat that pumped through her face.

"Brilliant, Yancy. Thanks. I meant the other one, the one on top."

She stood up again and tried to focus on the welcome distraction of the picture, unsure when she'd really looked at it last. She was always too damn busy, rushing through here unloading junk or packing on some more, never stopping to notice anything that wasn't out of place. Now she stopped and looked. It wasn't even a photo, just a black-and-white copy she'd made out of a book, and it was so old the paper was curling and brittle at the edges. A blonde woman smiled into the camera in the center of the frame, and an adult Komodo stood next to her. They were practically cuddling; the dragon's head tilted in toward the woman's hip, and her hand rested on its neck. The woman's hair was pinned back in waves, and her elbow jutted strongly outward, like a Rosie the Riveter of the dragons. Meg didn't know why, but she'd always loved that elbow, all sharp angles on top of the proud, cocked hand, glowing white against the dark curl of the dragon's tail sweeping behind her.

This picture was nothing like Antonio's microchip magazine cover. The woman and the animal were companions, not two mutant halves of the same head. This was old and organic, not Photoshopped and cold—but somehow the same sadness took hold of Meg as she stared at it, the same hopelessness she'd felt facing his magazine cover.

"It's just an old zoo picture." She shrugged.

Antonio hopped the bench and leaned in for a closer look. He tapped a knuckle to her scrawly handwriting on the top corner of the photograph. "Bub ... chen?"

"That was the Komodo's name, Bubchen. It's German for sweetie pie."

She could see his head nodding out of the corner of her eye. "I didn't know you spoke German, Yance."

"I don't."

"She looks pretty acclimated to humans. What happened to her?"

Meg stared at the photograph until the lines started to blur and an engine roar echoed underneath the silence of the empty building. "I don't know," she lied.

They stood there for a minute, quiet. She tried to listen for footsteps in the hallway, but no one ever interrupted at the perfect time. No one bailed her out of these situations, like when Chuck drilled her about corporate policies, or she had sixteen forms to write, or she was standing too close to the only man in the world who wanted to talk intelligently about Komodo dragons and happened to taste like cinnamon.

"This keeper"—Antonio tapped on the photo again—"is like you. She's a dragon tamer."

Meg turned around and met him head on. She could smell the antiseptic soap on his arm and the warm spice of his skin underneath it. "Piss off, Rodríguez. I'm just a keeper like anybody else around here."

"Said the dragon tamer." He smiled, and the flash of it moved like quicksilver down through her body, churning deep into her stomach and tingling through her limbs. It was as if someone had flipped a switch inside her. All he'd said was *I'm on your side.* That's it. And now she wanted—no, it was better not to think about what she wanted.

She backed up into the bench, hitting the wood with the back of her calves, and grabbed her duffel bag. Thank God for duffel bags and all those straps that kept her hands busy.

"Give it a rest, okay?" she said. "I didn't mean to kiss you. It's just been a long week."

"Fine." He looked at the floor and leaned back into the wall of lockers. The hair he usually slicked back into a Desi Arnaz knockoff was falling into curls on his forehead. It was hair little girls would stab each other to get—dark, goopy spirals that swallowed the light. As Meg tried to figure out how to save face and disappear, his mouth started working, as if he was getting ready to spit out an equally nasty-tasting thank you.

Rather than say something first and eat it later, she waited him out until finally he sighed and said, "You are kind of a bitch, you know."

Unexpected but okay. Meg zipped and unzipped a side pocket on the duffel. The zipper was broken; it never closed all the way anymore. "Yeah, you're a sweetheart, too."

"I like how you yell at people."

"I like how you sexually harass them?" It came out like a question, and he laughed. She worked the zipper faster and faster.

"You're dirty a lot of the time. And you smell like shit."

She stepped closer, pointing at his mouth. "Your teeth are practically fluorescent. That's not okay."

"I watch you sometimes." His gaze, which had been bouncing around the room, locked on hers. "Feeding Jata. Since the eggs—I—you're amazing with her."

His eyebrows buckled up, and he pushed away from the lockers with his shoulder. "I'm not trying to hit on you, and I'm not jerking you around. I just wanted to say it when we weren't tearing each other a new one, like usual. So that's all."

He threw a hand up into the air and started to turn back toward the vet wing. "Good night."

Fuck it. Meg closed the distance between them and kissed him softly, just a brush of lips and breath. They both froze. She felt his limbs tighten and wondered if his blood was racing like hers, if he felt this flush of pores opening and nerves rushing toward one another. For a moment she hovered there, pressing a kiss to his mouth—her mind emptied of everything but warmth and a thudding heart near her chest—and then she slanted her head against him, wanting to taste him, deeply, everywhere. It didn't matter why or why not.

His hand moved to the back of her neck and cupped her head. She wrapped her arms around him and tried to speed up the tempo, but he held her back, sampling her mouth in sips and lazy, get-to-know-you swirls.

Their bodies shifted and bumped into her locker door, breaking the kiss. Antonio leaned back, his fingers sifting over her ponytail.

"Damn." The word was like smoke from his throat. He rested his forehead against hers and closed his eyes. "Let's just take a second here."

Her breath came choppy and hot. She shook her head slightly, trying to think of a reason to stop, or really just trying to think at all. This was Antonio, the cocky vet who hit on every woman within a five-mile radius. He probably had sex on speed dial, but he watched over fatherless eggs and defended dragons. He wore hair gel, but he tasted hot and sweet. She felt his breath on her face, unsteady and anxious. This was Antonio. The warmth in her chest turned over and over, until she felt it catch fire and decided she might as well burn.

She rested her head back against the cold metal slats of the lockers and smiled.

"I don't think this is what you want." His eyes burned now in ambers and blacks; there was no more brown left in them.

"It is. I want you to touch me," she demanded and tightened her fingers into his back, bringing him closer. He kissed her mouth, then moved to her temple and earlobe, working his way down her neck. She'd never felt this alive, this needy, with anyone. Like a latecomer to the party, Ben's ghost finally showed up, but she shoved him aside. The betrayal was so natural, she almost wondered if it had been there the whole time, just waiting for an opportunity.

"Someone could walk in." Antonio's voice was muffled against the collar of her uniform.

"Who?"

"Security. The cleaning crew. Or … Chuck."

She nuzzled the side of his head. "Uh-oh. You'll have to take the workplace harassment training again."

"How did you know about that?" He popped up, surprised.

She laughed and pushed away from the locker, feeling freer and giddier than her body could remember. There was no memory like this, no recognition in the weightlessness that propelled her across the room.

"Where are you going?"

She didn't look back as she pushed through the doors to the veterinary wing. "Your office."

2 Years *before* Hatching

Everyone was so polite. The girl who bumped into her knees apologized twice before moving past Meg to sit on the open chair on her right. A guy with a bull ring in his nose asked Ben if he was reading *Time* magazine—the one that lay closed on the end table next to Ben's arm—before picking it up. The waiting room was full and silent, except for the corner TV that was playing a documentary on volcanoes. Every mumbled *thank you* or *excuse me* traveled the length of the long rows of chairs. It was unnatural. Even the walls were freaking polite, painted a creamy, yellowy beige that faded into nothingness, the absolute non-color, just a diplomatic middleman between the waiting room and the February Minneapolis night. An abstract painting of a sunset hung on the wall across from her. Or maybe it was a sunrise, depending on who was looking at it. Sunrise for Meg. Sunset for not-Meg. But not-Meg couldn't see it anyway and never would.

"Did you notice how quickly they processed our IDs?" Ben whispered. His dark, greasy hair flopped over one eye as he leaned toward her. "In and out, just like credit cards at the cash register." He snapped his fingers.

The girl on Meg's right startled, but she didn't look over. That was the second rule. First: Apologize a lot; apologize for everything you're about to do. Second: Don't make eye contact. She was getting it—slowly the rules of this little ecosystem were sinking in—but of course Ben was oblivious.

"They've got to be hooked in to some serious databases. Interpol, maybe. Some kind of special clearance. Believe me, they know exactly how many parking tickets you have now. The holding charge I got when we did Topeka that first year? Yeah, I could see it in her eyes. That popped right up." His right foot was tapping, bumping his knee into her leg. Little, insistent raps. It had been almost an hour since they'd arrived, scanned their IDs for the receptionist in her bulletproof cage, and gotten the green light through the steel door, and the longer they'd sat waiting the more fidgety he'd become.

"Ben." She shook her head, glaring at his knee.

"Okay." He reached out for her hand, but she moved it away. "It's just taking forever."

He let the silence last for another minute or so, just as the sunset painting started to draw her back in. "I'm going out for a cigarette. You want to come?"

It would have been nice to get some air, see the sky, but behind the steel doors and the red call button was the long, silent elevator ride and the woman with the pamphlets outside another set of doors—the woman whose reddish, pixie-cut hair looked like her mother's, except now her mother's hair had all fallen out.

"No."

He nodded encouragingly, making no move to get up.

"I don't want to be gone when they call me." She twisted the front cover of *Newsweek*, half-surprised that it was in her lap.

"Okay." He patted her hand and sat for another minute before getting up. She watched him walk out to the lobby. His sweater was wrinkled and bunched up above his pants from sitting too long. It was a relief, all of a sudden, watching him go. He'd been hovering over her for the last few weeks, barely letting her breathe, and the attention had become as claustrophobic as this room. It was her decision, after all. Hers alone. It didn't matter that he agreed. His watchfulness was as pointless as the death watch at work, as all these *please*s and *I'm sorry*s floating through the stale air.

Ben: big, loafing, greasy, boyish Ben. It was so easy for her to see a child of Ben's. Just make it smaller. Trim the too-long curly hair and remove the dusting of fur from his soft, wide chest. Inflate the gut into a half moon and shrink the penis to a peanut. There was baby Ben. Screaming, laughing, chattering baby Ben, toddling off in crazy pursuits of invisible bumblebees and, later, daddy's marijuana.

The problem was her. She couldn't project this tiny ball of nauseating cells into anything that resembled offspring, and even if she could, the logistics were overwhelming. How would she support a baby? Who would watch it while Ben was gone four months out of the year? Where would it sleep in her one-bedroom apartment? What did babies even eat? She could barely remember to keep any food in her kitchen for herself, let alone for a whole other person who would be completely dependent on her.

The day after she took the test, she caught herself daydreaming, imagining she was rocking a baby on the front porch, watching it sleep in her arms while the world drifted by, and the vision was strangely intoxicating. But the more she thought about keeping it, the scarier the idea was. Babies weren't simple. Kissing their cheeks and rocking them to sleep didn't exactly cut it. All the stroller moms at the zoo were terrifying proof of that. They carried insane amounts of stuff with them, and even though they had years of experience at motherhood they still exuded this air of harassed, vigilant exhaustion. She'd wandered into the baby aisle at the grocery store the other day and panicked at the sheer number of products for sale. What did she know about any of this? Give her a baby alligator any day—but a baby human?

Last weekend, before making her final decision, she'd even called her mother. The cancer was bad now; it had spread through her abdomen and intestines, and the last round of chemo hadn't even made a dent.

"Do you want me to come see you?" she'd asked from her usual conversation spot on the toilet lid.

"What for? You haven't visited me once since I moved to Florida. I don't see any point in starting now." Her mother's voice was as matter-of-fact as it had been ten years ago and less emotional than when she'd packed suitcase after suitcase for their endless road trips. She didn't sound as though she was dying. Meg hesitated before asking the next question, then figured, *Why not?* There was nothing to lose and no one to fight with about it later; it was almost like talking to a memory.

"Do you wish you'd had more children? Ones who would visit? Ones more like you, who would get married and have children of their own?"

"I wouldn't recommend my life, if that's what you're asking, especially not now." Her mother laughed once, then coughed weakly for several minutes. Meg breathed silently, as conscious of the air moving easily up and down her own throat as the painful gasps on the other end of the line. When her mother finally got her breath back, she was quiet for a minute before speaking again. "You've lived a lot smarter than I did, by focusing on your career and not settling for—well, it doesn't matter now. I made what I could of it. That's one thing I want you to remember, Megan, the one thing I hope I've taught you. You have to fight for what you want. No one will ever hand it to you."

"I know." Her stomach was still flat. She traced a figure eight over it.

"Although it might have been nice, I suppose, to have some

grandchildren, someone who would've liked to inherit the whippet dynasty. After all the years you were my assistant, I'd hoped you would have grown to love them as I did."

"I'm sorry, Mom." She didn't know what she was apologizing for—for not being the daughter her mother wanted, for not visiting her on her deathbed, for not having grandchildren? It was so horribly clear, when she hung up and let herself cry, that she didn't have what it took to be a mother. She couldn't even talk to her own mother without this choking resentment and regret filling the back of her throat.

In the waiting room, Meg stared blankly at a magazine page, unaware of time passing. Eventually the door at the far end of the room clicked open. A portly nurse called her in to a room, and before she was ready, they plunged needles into her arms and placed her feet into metal stirrups. She clenched her eyes shut so tight that blood vessels burst along her corneas. As the drugs coated her veins, she saw sunrises and their painfully bright streaks of color that she'd pretended to finger-paint from her mother's minivan window as a girl. The nurse hushed her and wiped the streaks from her face with a scratchy tissue. Later Ben picked up her favorite pad thai, and she ate a few bites to make him happy. She slept deeply that night and didn't speak the next day about her terrible dreams.

But part of her stayed back there. Part of her was still sitting in that Minneapolis waiting room two years later, staring through a magazine at a mass of swarming cells that changed, shape-shifting in every second from embryo into cancer, from animal to death to baby to mother.

"You don't like kids," she had whispered into the magazine as the cells multiplied and mutated in front of her eyes. "Jata is the only child you want."

8 Months *before* Hatching

And I listed off everything—the listlessness, the redness in the gums, his temperature, all after the recent laceration. I was like, it's an infection, right? And the dude's like, did you get the temperature from the SAM report?" Gemma wiped her forehead with an arm. "And I was like, no, I put a rectal thermometer in the Gila monster's butt. Come on."

Meg laughed as she dragged the biohazard bin across Jata's exhibit.

"Yeah, and he didn't even laugh."

"He's an intern." Which pretty much explained everything.

The two of them were on a serious cleaning binge. They'd already been through three exhibits that morning, and the best part about doing maintenance detail with Gemma wasn't even how focused or efficient she was—it was that she was fun. She just got it. Lately Meg had realized she even preferred working with Gemma to being alone with her animals.

Meg shoveled the piles of white dung into the biohazard bin while Gemma trimmed up the peeling bark on one of the palm trees, mainly so it didn't end up as part of the dung in a few more weeks. Jata liked to sample things.

"How come we never get keeper interns?" Gemma asked.

"Antonio gets to make his do all the worst stuff. We could have them on vomit and poop detail and get them to collect all the rat carcasses in the traps."

"I'd rather have them fill out our paperwork."

"Check our SAMs."

"Take our training classes." Meg sighed. She wrapped the shovel in a fresh garbage bag, put it back in the cart, and grabbed a rake. "But then how would we torture the newbies? There'd be nothing left to haze them with."

Gemma grinned. "How's the lagoon look to you? Do you want me to top it up?"

"No. She hasn't been swimming much lately."

Meg walked over to the beach area and looked at the clear, filtered water in the concrete pool. It should have been murky with dirt and sloshed over the nearby ground. The pool was deep enough for Jata to fully submerge and long enough to swim a mini lap, but unless Meg dumped a bag of minnows in the water, she usually just lay in the shallow end. Recently, though, she hadn't even been doing that. She was depressed, lethargic, and Meg couldn't figure out why. Jata wasn't even making a fuss about being in the restraint box while they cleaned the exhibit. Antonio had been a jerk about her behavior the other day, big surprise, and his words circled her mind—*death watch*—but she shook them loose. What did a microchip-happy vet know about the behavioral patterns of Komodos, let alone her Komodo? Not a goddamn thing, as far as she was concerned. There was no death watch here.

Meg backtracked to the mounds and furrows on the beach. She pushed the rake into one and started redistributing the sand.

"Hey, speaking of swimming," Gemma said, "I promised Ally we'd go to the beach this weekend. Wanna be our date?" Gemma flipped her braid over her shoulder and winked at Meg.

"Sure."

Gemma attached a hose to the hidden wall hookup and started watering the trees, bobbing her head to some imaginary music only she could hear. That was Gemma, doing whatever had to be done, but with Zen. She'd grown up on some farm in the middle of the state and gotten pregnant by her high school boyfriend, who'd freaked out, joined the army, and blown himself up on a land mine outside Fallujah. Her parents hadn't kicked her out, but they opened the door plenty wide when she got enough grants and scholarships to go to college in the cities. Gemma didn't tell stories like that, though. Meg hadn't heard any of that until they had a few too many at the Christmas party one year. Gemma's real stories were all stuff like the time Allison turned three while they lived in a student-family co-op, and Gemma bought her a turtle for $2.00 from a kid down the hall. They watched it swim around the bathtub all night and had peanut butter sandwiches on the bathroom floor. That was a Gemma story. She stayed cool and even-keeled in a place full of Nazi dolphin trainers and administration drones so she could go home and have peanut butter picnics. It was as if some lotus blossom had unfurled from the land of easygoing mothers to reveal Gemma, their bohemian child, sitting cross-legged and shaking sparkling corn seed from her hair.

A day at the beach. Meg raked and remembered: Earlier that summer, she and Gemma had stretched out on beach towels while Ally decorated sand castles with lake weeds and rocks. *Pretty groovy, sweetie*, Gemma said from underneath her hat. *Tell us about who lives in your castle.*

Before they met, Meg hadn't known people like Gemma existed, and it was years before she accepted that Gemma's personality wasn't an act. She had genuine skills when it came to mothering, and Allison was living proof. The kid scored off the charts on all her tests, was interested in absolutely everything, and showed this awesome quiet concentration whenever you gave her a problem to solve. It would be amazing to have a kid like that, to watch her grow and learn and take on the world. Meg hadn't known Gemma that well when she and Ben decided to get the abortion. If she had—

No. There was no point in thinking about it. Meg worked the sand into smooth lines, raking forward and back, forward and back, as intently as if her own brain were sprawled out in front of her and if she just raked hard enough, she could obliterate all these *what if*s that had started to haunt her lately.

The rake scraped over something solid. A dull crunch sounded under the metal teeth, and Meg yanked the rake away from a small sand pile next to one of the palm trees. The noise echoed in her ears, clear and untouched by thought for two endless heartbeats. Then she gasped as the realization hit her.

"Oh my God."

Falling to her knees, Meg smoothed the darkening mound of sand away from the indentation of her rake. The granules slid through her fingers in clumps, revealing oblong patches of bumpy tan and brown mottled curves. Eggs. Her throat caught somewhere between shouting and choking. There were two, then four. Gemma's hands slid in among Meg's, and together they cleared the top of the nest with butterfly fingertips. The more they revealed, the lighter their touch.

On the side closest to Meg was a shattered eggshell, its gelatinous, milky contents seeping into the sand and onto the eggs below. The destroyed shell was darker on the inside and filled the air with a faint musk. A second, nearby egg was also cracked. She could barely hear Gemma's voice over the roar of the building's ventilation system in her head.

"We should radio this in. Chuck will want Antonio to take over.

We shouldn't disturb the area." Gemma backed off and nudged Meg's arm.

Meg drew back but didn't reach for the walkie-talkie hanging from her belt. Frozen, she stared at the second, cracked egg. The hairline fracture looked like a tiny flash of lightning, and a dark fist seemed to take hold of her lungs. A cracked egg was as good as smashed. Her fault. She should have recognized the depressed behavior and unusual appetite, both egg-laying hallmarks of a healthy, breeding-age female Komodo. God.

"Meg? Hon, can you believe this? I mean, wow. Hey, are you okay?" Gemma touched Meg's shoulder.

"Yeah." With a flat-eyed smile, she patted Gemma's hand and stood up. "I'll call it in."

∽

"Hey, Meg. Did you free the animals today?"

"Maybe tomorrow." She didn't bother raising her head to Neil. He was in his usual spot on the screened-in porch above her back door.

"One got loose, anyway."

Inside, she threw her keys on the crap heap of a kitchen table and understood what he was talking about.

Ben's spare key was on the top of a pile of mail, with its square, plastic keychain that read IN DOG YEARS, I'M DEAD over a cartoon dog skeleton. She'd gotten it for him when he turned thirty, and even though he'd bitched about it like an old man, he'd carried it ever since.

Ben was back. Paco must have dropped him off after the fair closed. They always wrapped up fair season in Minnesota, but usually Ben called before coming over. It was ten-thirty, and except for the stove light—which she left on every morning for nights like this, when she needed that comforting ball of light in the window—the house was dark.

Meg went straight to the bedroom to change, grabbing whatever clothing her fingers stumbled over on the floor. She pulled on some shorts, but instead of the smooth elastic waistband, she felt wet, grainy clumps of sand hug her stomach. Her skin crawled. Sitting on the edge of the bed, she covered her face. The eggs shone against the back of her eyelids, pulsing in their leathery shells. They rolled, oblong and wobbly along the ground, each one smacking into her rake and cracking, oozing amniotic fluid into the sand. God. She shook her head, rubbing her eyes until they were filled with purple sunbursts of pressure, crowding everything else out.

When her vision cleared, she saw the flickering light in the hallway. In the living room, she found Ben half-sitting, half-lying asleep on the couch with his mouth gaping open. CNN shadows ran like ticker tape across his face, and even from across the room Meg could smell the deep-fryer grease. And something else. Mustard?

He woke up with a snort when she turned off the TV. Twisting up on the couch, he yawned and stretched.

"Hey, stranger." The words were distorted into the end of his yawn. "Have a nice summer?"

He'd called once or twice. The last time she'd heard from him was Independence Day weekend, when he and Paco had pulled into Tulsa. Or Tennessee. Somewhere in the middle, anyway.

"It was normal. Until today."

Ben grabbed her hand, lacing his fingers through hers, and pulled her down to the couch. His palm was sweaty.

"They finally fire Chuck today?"

"No." Her other hand pressed over her pitching stomach. "I

broke some of Jata's eggs."

Ben scratched his neck and yawned again. "That's your Komodo, right?"

"Yeah." Her voice sounded tiny in the dark room.

"Won't she lay more?"

"Yeah." It might have been true. She could've been laying a second clutch right now, for all anyone knew. Every captive Komodo female was different. Some laid once, others laid multiple clutches over several weeks. She read that one time Bubchen, the German Komodo, laid only a single egg and then ate it. And they were all unfertilized, for God's sake. They would just shrivel up and rot anyway, unless by some miracle they were parth, which was a huge dice roll—if the dice had three billion faces and only one winning side. The two eggs Meg had destroyed would never have hatched anyway.

"So no worries, then. You're still the best thing since raw meat to that dragon."

She smiled, and suddenly she ached with the relief of seeing Ben, of being able to lean into the warm bulk of his body and rest her chin on the shelf of his collarbone. She'd been so cold this summer.

"You wouldn't believe the shit I've had to put up with from Paco this year," Ben said. "Angelica dumped his ass mid-July, and he's been drunk ever since. Smoking over the deep fryer, bitching at other vendors, blasting the RV stereo. We almost got kicked out of Iowa, and Cincinnati told us not to come back next year." As he talked, he petted her back in lazy, sleepy strokes. "I was so busy babysitting I forgot to mail rent in for a few months."

"What?"

"I'm homeless. Funny, huh? I can stay in the RV, but it might be kind of a bitch in the winter."

She drew her finger over his stomach. She'd forgotten how his belly punched out over his jeans, not soft like baby fat but solid and thick like an animal hide. It was skin that could withstand anything. "You can stay here until you find a place."

"Thanks." He paused, kissing her temple and letting his lips linger. "It's been a while, hasn't it? You smell like zoo."

"You smell saucy."

"Creamy horseradish. I invented it this season. It's a huge seller."

"Yuck." She leaned into his neck, letting his hand drift up her back and work out the knots in her shoulders.

"Well, since we're both already dirty ... " He let the sentence trail off.

Meg didn't reply. His skin was warm, and she leaned into the heat the way Jata hugged her sunning boulders, for comfort and the instinct to survive. They stripped off their clothing, and Ben ran his hands over her body. When they came together, the abortion was there—it was always there in that moment—but she ignored it and reached for him anyway. It didn't matter anymore. There was nothing she could do about it. Remembering was as pointless as trying to fit the pieces of a broken eggshell back together.

7 ½ Months *before* Hatching

I don't know if I should be doing this." The girl glanced nervously behind Meg as they approached the nursery door.

"That's why you're here, isn't it? What kind of an intern doesn't assist the staff?"

It was humiliating enough that Meg's badge wouldn't clear the security on the nursery door, but then she had to go dig up one of Antonio's girls and actually ask for help. The girl's hair covered half her face and exploded over her back in waves like a blonde kelp forest. Meg remembered this intern, mainly because she'd pinned two weeks on her in the pool. Michael from the Mammal Kingdom had gone for the long haul, and he'd cleaned up when the girl made the six-month mark. The cut-and-run theory had seemed like a winner, especially considering the huge hair. It was hard to believe there was intelligent life inside that, but then Michael had pointed out the kelp forests and how if his sea otters could take cover in them, maybe so could a damn good intern.

It was a standing rule that the keepers always made bets on how long the interns would last. Gambling wasn't allowed on the property, but they just called it a football pool, and nobody seemed to wonder why the score sheet tacked on the announcements board in the cage had teams named "Cincinnati Sally's" and "Texas Curry

Breath." The girl in question, who was stubbing her toe into the floor and blinking through a break in the forest, had gone to the Super Bowl as the "Milwaukee Mermaids."

"Maybe I should check this with Dr. Rodríguez first. He assigns all the security clearances."

"There are animals in there under my care. Do you want to answer for them if they're neglected?"

"I don't want to get in trouble."

Meg leaned in closer and found the girl's other eye hiding behind a glossy kelp leaf. "And I don't want to have to make trouble for you, so open the damn door and we can both get back to our days. Okay?"

"One of you can, anyway," someone said behind her. Relief flushed the girl's face, and Meg stepped back, gritting her teeth.

"Winifred, go see Michael from the Mammal Kingdom about increasing the cheetah's antidepressants. I'll handle the wayward keeper."

Meg waited until the girl rushed off and silence settled back in the corridor before swinging around. Antonio was in full bouncer pose—arms crossed and feet spread as if he owned the hallway and everyone in it. "You lost, Yancy? This isn't your side of the zoo."

"Maybe it should be, since your people can't even manage to open a door."

"You're just bitter because you lost on her in the intern pool." He grinned.

Rolling her eyes, she changed the subject. "The cheetah's on antidepressants already? We just got him a year ago."

"Go figure. An animal that can run seventy miles an hour gets depressed about living in a fifty-yard box."

"Maybe he sensed that they named him Chester."

Antonio chuckled and casually swiped his badge against the nursery lock. The door immediately unbolted. Swinging it open with an arm, he ushered her inside.

Tanks and incubators lined the walls, all the baby machines that housed little cubbyholes of life. Eggs, larvae, and cast-off newborns from all over the zoo came through here. Sometimes the animals just didn't take to their young as they would have in the wild or—in Jata's case—the mother would have cannibalized the eggs if she'd stumbled upon them again. Antonio walked to the far wall and pulled a chart from the pocket of a large, metal enclosure fitted with a bay window. Flipping a switch, the interior of the tank lit up to reveal three leathery eggs. Jata's eggs.

"There's only three?" She was at the incubator window before realizing she'd even crossed the room.

"One collapsed right after the transfer, and you made omelets out of the other two so, yeah, we're down to three." His pen scratched the paper in shrill little shreds. "Nice work, by the way. They teach you that in keeper school?"

He must have been waiting to throw that in her face for two weeks because he was practically dancing with the satisfaction of it. She vaguely registered the silence over the scratching pen, the anticipation in the air as she was supposed to lob back an insult of her own. It was her turn, but there were only empty places in her vision, the dead air among the three remaining eggs where two more should have been sitting. Her fault. She was getting so good at killing things.

"So in the interest of actually keeping the eggs viable, I had to tighten up security around here. You understand, right, Yancy?"

"Piss off." She grabbed the clipboard out of his hand and turned away. He was noting temperatures and moisture levels for the tank but only weekly, and it looked as if he was weighing each of the eggs periodically. Why did he need weights? She flipped through a few pages underneath—all blank. No other instructions, no person assigned at the top of the chart. He hadn't even created electronic logs. The paper could just be crushed into a ball and chucked in the garbage as easily as the next egg collapsed.

He shuffled around behind her, moving instruments and checking on other animals. She finished reading and handed back the chart.

"Chuck said you knew they were parth. They even invited a news crew out."

Antonio smiled, closemouthed. It was the first time she'd ever given Antonio the opportunity to brag, but he kept his smug mouth shut, and she knew exactly why. The bastard was waiting for her to ask.

"It doesn't say anything about parth on the chart. Aren't you the champion note taker around here?"

"It took a little more than observation and note taking." He broke his silence out of self-defense, and they circled around each other in the center of the room, neither backing down.

"But it's not true if it's not written down, right? If it's not on a log or a SAM or in a trade journal? We just have to assume you're a showboating vet hopped up on gator tranqs." That did it. She could always beat him with vanity.

"It is true," he admitted, making her heart race. "Winifred collected a sample of the amniotic fluid from Jata's exhibit when we picked up the eggs. The cracked ones came in pretty handy. I ran some experimental tests last week—protein and enzyme analysis, some elemental DNA sequencing." He leaned against a counter by the door, too full of his own brilliance to stand up straight. "And I guess we have you to thank for providing the specimen because now we know the eggs are parth."

Everything dropped away when she heard it confirmed, but she kept her face expressionless. "You're sure?"

"As positive as I can be about tests I completely made up in the lab. Of course, if it turns out I'm right, I'll patent the procedure. No royalties for you."

She walked back to the incubator window. "So the eggs I destroyed were viable. They could have become dragons."

Her voice was a small, dead weight amid the heaters and humidifiers humming around the edges of the room.

"Hard to say. Odds are that they had the wrong DNA match anyway."

"Are you going to put them through more tests? More home-grown experiments?"

"I have to personally oversee the health of every animal in this zoo. When do you think I'm going to have time for three unplanned eggs? In fact … "

Suddenly, she was yanked backward by her hip. Antonio had grabbed the chain for her ID badge and was walking across the room as though her pants weren't attached to the thing.

"Hey! What the hell?"

He keyed in a combination on the number pad next to the door and swiped her ID across the scanner, pausing to snicker at the picture on the front. It was a crack-house mug shot, no question, but she grabbed it back and shoved it into her pocket before he commented.

"Now, you'll need to come at the same time every week to check the environment, and I promised the AZA we'd chart weight throughout the incubation for some study they're doing. Think you can handle that without getting in my way or terrorizing my interns?"

She crossed her arms and sneered. "Don't do me any favors, Rodríguez."

"I'm not. Believe me, you'd actually be doing—" He cut himself off, screwing his mouth shut, and walked back to the incubator to put away the chart.

"What was that?"

"Nothing."

"Are you asking me for a favor? You need my help with these eggs?" The smile ate up her face, seeping up her cheeks and warming her whole body. He paced around to some of the other incubators, peered inside, fiddled with knobs—anything to avoid looking at her.

"I've only got the two interns right now, and the dolphin trainers are up my ass about some cyst they found on a flipper. Purchasing wants me to fly out to some veterinary supply vendor in Korea who could save us a whole forty bucks a year on syringes." Antonio worked his way around the room to where she was standing, finally looking up when she didn't move out of his way. "And ... fine. You know what? Forget it." Digging into her pants pocket, he grabbed the ID badge and pulled her back to the security scanner.

"No, wait." She yanked on the chain, but Antonio was a lot stronger, so she only succeeded in stumbling into him as he leaned over to punch in the code. Darting in to grab his wrist, she clamped down on the ID card in his other hand.

"I want to take care of the eggs, Antonio. You know I do."

He stopped, considering. "You want to help me?"

"I want to help Jata. I'm her keeper, and that means keeping every part of her safe and happy, including those parts." She gestured over her shoulder, and he glanced at the eggs before grinning.

"Say you want to help me."

"I want to help you choke." A laugh bubbled up, but she turned it into a huff and looked down to see she was still holding onto him. Dropping her hands, she stepped back. "And there's this other thing."

"How monotonous your life is when I'm not around?"

"Channel 12 news, smart-ass." She glared. "They're going to be here later today for a puff piece on the dragons. They'll probably want to see the eggs."

"Chuck's letting you handle the interview?" Antonio opened the nursery door and gestured for her to go ahead. "He doesn't look much like a masochist."

"Pure sadist."

They walked to the double doors where her zoo started and his zoo ended. As she swiped her ID on the reader, he gave her a condescending pat on the shoulder. "Try to remember to think before you speak, Yancy. I know it's foreign for you, but it's a good rule of thumb with reporters."

She paused, tilted her head, and looked deliberately thoughtful for a second.

"Piss off."

He was laughing as she pushed through the doors and back to the rest of her shift.

~୨

Nicole Roberts looked hungry. It wasn't just the hollowed-out skeleton holding up her boxy skirt suit, or the flashing whites of her eyes, which ate up entire rooms in seconds. When Meg and Chuck greeted the news crew outside the main gate, Nicole Roberts had been pacing up and down the side of the news van like the big cats just before feedings. She masked the hunger underneath the shiny poof of red hair and the thick skin of makeup that glowed under the camera lights, but Meg could tell it was there. Nicole did the entertainment beat for Channel 12, and, according to Ben, she was positioning herself for bigger and better things. On TV, the hunger looked like fitness-craze energy, like an infomercial but without the clarity of the special offer for the next one hundred customers. In person, it was just awkward. She either needed a giant candy bar or a good push into the howler monkey exhibit.

Meg and Chuck took the group straight to the nursery and

showed them the eggs. The camera guys did some close-ups, but Nicole refused to shoot the interview in the room.

"Trust me. This particular shade of beige just doesn't translate to TV." Fanning her hand at the walls, she turned back to Meg. "This is the Zoo of America, right? Let's find some true greens, maybe bamboo or some jungle foliage. We should showcase your gardeners as long as we're here."

"Of course, of course." Chuck bent slightly at the waist, as if he'd thrown his back out in a curtsy. "We have some lovely vistas of the river valley or a one-of-a-kind mural of American animals."

"How about Jata's exhibit? You could see the mother Komodo and there are, you know"— Meg waved a hand for help—"plants."

They agreed, so she led Nicole Roberts and her entourage up through the cafeteria—"Snack, anybody? Nicole? You're sure?"— and through the exhibits to the Reptile Kingdom. They set up on the observation deck while Jata watched the camera and microphone pole with unblinking interest from her pool. Chuck stood off on the edge of the main trail, apparently supervising, while visitors jostled up behind him and whispered to one another, pointing at Nicole and craning their heads down into Jata's exhibit to see what was so newsworthy. Meg turned away from them and waited for Nicole to get ready.

"You want a little touch-up before we start shooting?" Nicole tipped a round jar with a piece of fur on top of it in Meg's direction. "You've got a bit of a sheen, as we say in the industry."

"Uh, no."

"You like the sheen?" Nicole smiled and checked her teeth in a mirror.

"Yeah, it's a trademark."

"Okay, then. Let's talk baby dragons." Grabbing a microphone, Nicole angled herself in front of the camera. A light came on, blinding Meg to the crowd behind the camera.

"We're here at the Zoo of America, where an extraordinary event has taken place in the last few weeks. The Komodo dragon right behind me has laid eggs in a process called parthenogenesis. Meg Yancy, the zookeeper in charge of the Komodo, is here with me today. Meg?" She turned and injected some confusion into her smile. "What exactly is parthenogenesis?"

Looking somewhere between Nicole and the mini-sun seemed like the best possible middle ground. Breathing deeply, Meg launched into the explanation, making sure to dumb down the scientific terms as Chuck had instructed. *Layspeak*, he'd said. As if that was a word.

"It sounds like you're talking about a virgin birth." Nicole's head bobbed up and down, and her heel tapped out a drum solo on the cement floor. Maybe it wasn't just her ambitious energy; the camera lights were enough to make a rattlesnake squirm. Meg squinted up at Nicole.

"Technically, yes. Jata has never mated before, so if the eggs prove viable—if they, um, turn into dragons—then it will be a virgin birth."

"So if they're born around Christmastime, will you name one after Jesus?" Nicole's smile turned sugary, coating Meg's throat with something like bile.

The smile said *isn't this cute?* and sent that cuteness out into the world, telling everyone who watched the news that *cute* was the end product of Jata's stunning genetic effort to aid the survival of her species. There were fewer than four thousand dragons in the wild, fighting to live in a precarious habitat where humans took over their land and poached their prey. It was only a matter of time before zoos became their last refuge. Five years ago, the species had been hissing at the door to extinction, then quietly, in a handful of zoos around the world, female Komodos started having babies. Some secret genetic knowledge began taking over and changing everything anyone knew about Komodo dragons. Meg's knuckles curled into fists against her sides. She felt Nicole's smile cracking something deep inside of her. Jata had just become the fourth dragon in the entire known world that was reproducing without a mate, and it was *cute?*

"This is a lot different than a Christmas story." Meg's voice sounded tight and foreign in the bright lights that eclipsed their bodies.

"Of course, I was only joking. After all, you don't exactly have the Virgin Mary here, do you?"

"I wouldn't say so, no. After all, we have no documentation on Mary's sexual status, and Jata has done a lot more work to reproduce."

"Excuse me?" The microphone bobbled, and Nicole glanced toward the camera, her expression changing into something bright and sharp.

"We don't know anything—scientifically—about the Christmas story. There's no proof that Mary was a virgin." Vaguely, she heard Chuck scrambling around behind the camera and whispering, so she switched gears. "Anyway, Jata's status is completely documented. She's produced a genetic miracle all on her own, without the help of angels or prophets or—whatever. We're witnessing a step up the evolutionary ladder here, and it's not just a story in a book; it's happening right here in front of us."

Suddenly Chuck darted in front of the camera to cut her off, but it was too late. Elation bubbled underneath the makeup layer on Nicole's face, as if someone had finally slipped her a giant, gooey candy bar.

"Well, you heard it here." Nicole turned back to the camera. "The Zoo of America's Komodo dragon is having a virgin birth, and they're not taking kindly to comparisons."

Chuck tried to interrupt, but Nicole was already signaling the camera to cut.

"This was fascinating. Really, really great stuff. Really. Thanks so much for having us, and make sure to watch for the segment." Nicole shook hands with both of them, oblivious to Meg's clammy palms and Chuck's sputtering objections. "We've got to go if we want to make the deadline for the evening news."

4 Days *after* Hatching

The reporters were late. Meg stood outside the zoo's main entrance with Pam, one of the PR women, and Chuck flanking either side of her, both of them wound so tight you could bounce quarters off their puckered mouths. The elephant in the room—the huge, unavoidable thing no one had the balls to mention but couldn't stop replaying in their heads—was the virgin birth interview. Meg's job was on the line here—she couldn't have been more aware of that fact—but Chuck and Pam acted as if their necks were sticking out just as far. Today was a test; Chuck had made that obscenely clear that morning in his office. Management wanted to see if she could handle the media, or they would reconsider her animal assignments—which was a backhanded way of saying they would pull Jata from Meg's care. She'd been preparing for this for the last two days—or maybe eight months, if preparing for it meant trying to ignore the possibility that she'd ever have to talk to a reporter again.

Meg stared at the edge of the parking lot. Channel 12 hadn't confirmed who they were sending out for the story, whether it was Nicole Roberts or someone else. Anyone, Meg hoped, but Nicole Roberts.

Chuck cleared his throat nervously. "Maybe we should call Antonio to assist with the tour. He's very good with the media."

"No." Blood surged into Meg's face, and she shrugged out of Chuck's line of sight. "I think he's tied up."

She hadn't seen him yet today, but every time someone even mentioned his name, her gut twisted up, hot and guilty. They'd destroyed each other last night. She didn't even recognize herself in the memory—that laughing, gasping, demanding woman—and even though she planned to pretend the whole night never happened, it kept replaying over and over in her head, and she hated herself for wanting more.

The Channel 12 news van pulled around the corner and into the parking lot. Meg held her breath as the three of them silently watched it approach. God, not Nicole Roberts. Please.

As the van pulled up to the curb, a shaggy-looking guy hopped out of the passenger seat and walked over to shake their hands. He was stoop-shouldered, wore khakis, smelled like onions and rye— and he wasn't Nicole Roberts. Meg exhaled.

Pam still seemed nervous about the whole thing but overcompensated by shaking the reporter's and the camera guy's hands a dozen times and making a big show of handing them their visiting press badges and a couple of gold envelopes.

"It's going to be a wonderful event," she gushed. "We're so excited about it."

As Meg and Chuck led them inside to the exhibits, Pam half-followed them, her hands clasped as if in prayer, eyebrows crunched together. Chuck nodded at her and raised his clipboard in reassurance, but she kept trailing behind the group until Meg shot her a sarcastic thumbs-up. Scowling, she reluctantly doubled back to the Visitor Center.

The reporter acted all touristy, commenting on every animal they passed. He even crouched down when they came to the gecko exhibit and made the whole group stop and wait. If Meg didn't know better, she'd think he was decent. The thing to remember was that even though the guy looked all wrinkled and harmless, he was the media, and the media were bees.

It had all clicked one evening during Ben's nightly news hounding. She'd been talking to one of the insect guys earlier that day and had learned that honeybee colonies could have thousands of members, but the colony itself was essentially a single organism. Each bee played out its role in the interest of the whole. When part of the colony was wounded, the rest banded together to heal the wound. If an intruder came into their sphere, the colony reared up as one to react. Just look at the Nicole Roberts incident. They claimed to be unbiased, individual reporters, but how far did they all ride on the Virgin Mary bit together? It took days to float from the front pages and morning shows to the editorials and the Internet, where the general public finally got its turn with the whips and gags. There were hundreds of TV reporters, newspaper journalists, radio talk show hosts, and web writers working in the Twin Cities, and maybe each had little distinctions they thought of as individual personalities—a Clark Kent demeanor here or a Jackie O. outfit there—but underneath they were just a huge colony of honeybees looking for the next hit of nectar to bring back to the hive.

"Are you coming?" Meg called from several yards ahead of him. Chuck and the camera guy both stalled next to her. The camera guy shook his head, as if this kind of thing happened a lot. Chuck cleared his throat loudly and wrote something on his clipboard.

The reporter caught up with them, grinning. "Sorry. I used to have geckos in college. A whole family of them, actually."

She forced the edges of her mouth up. "No problem. I was just saying that the new tank is almost ready for the hatchlings. We're hoping to get them moved in by the end of the month."

She led the way on to Jata's viewing platform. "The tank is

actually in the baby building, which we can check out later. This is the Reptile Kingdom, where we're building a new outdoor, multi-dragon habitat."

"Is this where the mother is?" The camera guy craned his head around the empty exhibit.

"Yep. Jata's probably napping in her cave, right underneath this platform." Meg walked ahead to the outside of the building and unlocked the temporary plywood door to the new exhibit, leading the group inside. A construction light inside the exhibit illuminated the almost completed space. Three walls of steel-enforced glass revealed a four-hundred-square-foot enclosure filled with grasses and boulders. Meg stepped into the center of the stone slab viewing area and felt as if she were peeking into a wild and humid savannah. Maybe Jata would feel the same way.

The reporter stood next to her, jotting notes while Meg pointed out the highlights of the exhibit: the heated waterfall that fed into the lagoon and constantly cleansed the water; the multi-tiered terrain with several basking spots; the radiant heat skylights, which would keep the space toasty even during a blizzard.

"This is nice," the reporter interrupted, "but is it big enough for four Komodo dragons? They get pretty huge, don't they?"

"Over two hundred pounds and ten feet long." The smell of drying paint fought with the reporter's onion stink, and Meg stepped deliberately backward. "We aren't going to exhibit all four. The three hatchlings will be housed together temporarily in the baby building. By the time they're three to four months old, all but one will be moving to other zoos around the world. The one we keep here will share this exhibit space with Jata, the mother, and we'll rotate the two of them in between the indoor and outdoor area."

"Can we see the hatchlings, to get some video for the news?"

"Of course." Meg deliberately smiled at Chuck, who gave a tight, approving nod toward the door. He'd finally started to relax a little, maybe realizing that she wasn't going to fuck it up this time. There was too much to lose.

The nursery was vacant when they got there, thank God, but Meg—so trained by the click of that door handle and the antiseptic air—hurried automatically to the incubator to check on the last un-hatched egg, letting the door swing shut in the news team's faces. Chuck caught it and shot her a glare before ushering the guys inside the room.

As Chuck showed them the setup for the nursery, Meg hunched over the last egg that lay all alone in the middle of the incubator dirt. A tiny slit ran up the side of the shell, and she blinked, squinted, and grinned.

"You guys are living right today. Are you ready with that camera?" She waved them over and pointed out the fracture in the shell. Chuck made some constipated noises that she took for plea-sure. He knew as well as she did that with the rare exception of an escape or attack story, the media used the zoo strictly for puff pieces, and here they were, serving one up on a silver platter.

Meg leaned in over the incubator, and Chuck and the reporters followed her lead. There was a strange silence for a while, the kind that came from the proximity of relative strangers. And even though it was quiet, Meg could hear a sort of hum in the air from the tension generated between their bodies. She held her breath, partly out of anticipation and partly because, well, onion and rye just never got better over time.

It only took a few minutes. The tiny hatchling fought his way free from the eggshell and dragged his body out onto the dirt. He walked a few hesitant steps and lay exhausted on the incubator floor, oblivious to his audience.

"Wow." It was all the reporter could say at first, but then he rolled into a million questions. What will the hatchling eat? How big will he get? Where will he live for now?

She answered everything as patiently as she could, considering she'd already told him half this stuff, and showed the crew the two other hatchlings in their individual tanks, explaining her process of moving them gradually to the new exhibit in the baby building.

"When will that be?"

"In roughly two weeks," Chuck interrupted. "As you'll see in the invitations Pam gave you earlier, we will be hosting an exclusive VIP reception for the Komodos' debut, and I sincerely hope you can both join us."

"We're hosting a what?" Meg couldn't quite close her mouth.

"Cool," the reporter said, waving the gold envelope. "Do you want us to send a copy of this footage?"

"Yes, we'd be very grateful for that. Perhaps we could incorporate it into the reception somehow."

"We're hosting a what?" Meg repeated, louder, because they were all moving away from her toward the door. Chuck's eye twitched at her as he ushered the guys out the nursery door, but that was all. No explanation, nothing.

She couldn't follow them out; she felt as if her legs had filled with concrete. Screw the reporter and management and anyone else who wanted to test her public relations abilities. She'd failed, all right? What did it matter when they couldn't even bother to tell her about an invitation-only party starring her Komodos? Hers.

She turned back to the incubator and prepared the last hatchling for his new tank. Carefully, she took his measurements while the word *reception* pounded in her temples, and her hands kept shaking between 11.5 and 11.7 on the tape measure. Hell with it. She wrote down 11.6 and released his tail, letting it gently curve into a dark question mark over the new log form. Watching his eyes droop closed, she weighed him and placed him in the last individual tank. After a few minutes he was sound asleep, recovering. Meg closed her eyes, too, and pushed the palms of her hands into her eye sockets, waiting for the wave to pass so she would be steady enough to take the other hatchlings' stats.

The door clicked open, and Chuck cleared his throat. "Why didn't you accompany the news crew back to the main gate, Megan?"

She opened her eyes and glared at him. "I asked you a question first."

He sighed and flipped through the papers on his clipboard, pulled out a memo, and handed it over. The title was AN EVENING AMONG DRAGONS. Oh God. The guest list looked as if it had been copied straight out of the black-tie fundraisers they hosted at the aquarium every fall: corporate sponsors, local government, private donors, and media groups. The date of the reception was a Friday night at the end of April, less than three weeks away. In less than three weeks, they expected her to transport three Komodo hatchlings to a completely foreign environment and acclimate them to each other, not to mention to hundreds of pairs of inquisitive, circling eyes. Meg skimmed the schedule for words like *jumping through hoops* or *breathing fire for your amusement*. Nothing yet, but there was still time.

"Why am I hearing about this now?"

"Because apparently you haven't been checking your e-mail or your in-box. The initial correspondence was sent out yesterday morning, and PR hosted an open meeting yesterday afternoon to seek our input on the reception. You chose not to attend."

Chuck nipped the memo back out of her hand and slid it neatly back into the same place on his clipboard.

"I didn't know about it." She threw her hands in the air, fingers itchy with the need to wrap around something and choke it. "Someone should have talked to me first. I'm their keeper."

"They tried. You didn't respond. The reception will be held as planned, and you and your Komodos will be there. Now, I suggest you take the rest of the afternoon to read and respond to your company correspondence as expected."

Chuck walked back to the door of the nursery, then turned. A small smile played around the corners of his mouth. "And congratulations. With the exception of the last few minutes, you handled the media very well today. I'll make a note of it."

His neatly combed head disappeared a split second before the pen she'd been holding cracked against the doorframe.

6 Days *after* Hatching

So you've got eleven hours of daylight with lows down to—what? Nineteen? No, come on. Nineteen?"

Ben said something like "Shelshus" through a mouthful of ramen and flipped the channel.

"Gus, you don't even get snow." Meg shifted the phone from one ear to the other, trying to juggle the papers littered over her lap while listening to Gus's broken English.

Nothing made sense. Ben was home again after spending the last few days with Paco, watching his news lineup as if it were any other weeknight. Play along. She'd had no other choice but to roll out her diagrams of the new exhibit on the coffee table next to his notes, jot Xs on random spots, make busy noises, and breathe carefully, not too shallow or too deep. This was their routine. Ben would hunker down off the lip of the couch, making notes and eating dinner, while she curled into the far corner and read a magazine or a trade journal. It was either this or tell him the truth—and this play-it-normal option was oddly surreal, as if she'd broken into two selves. One Meg followed the routine in which everything was fine, and that Meg knew when certain things would happen: 1. The channel changed; 2. Ben spilled broth on his shirt and wiped at it with a sleeve; 3. Paco called, and Ben's phone vibrated around the coffee table, ignored; 4. Ben called Paco back during the next commercial break as he flipped the channel; 5. "No, I hate that place. The fuck do I wanna go there for?"

She made notes, murmurs, whatever came next. It was a game, a show that the other Meg, the one who'd been sucked inside some deep recess of her mind, watched like a keeper who was taking bets on just how long this stupid animal could last.

After twenty minutes of mindless scribbling, Gus had popped into her head. Thank you, Gus. He worked at the Wildlife Refuge in Jakarta, Jata's first home, and had been her contact for the last five years about all things Komodo. Gus was the one who had first told her about the boy who died in Indonesia. Gus had been on Komodo Island at the time, doing some research when news of the attack came over from the village. If there was one person in the world who knew Komodos, for better or for worse, it was Gus. Meg had gotten used to running her ideas by him, and the new outdoor exhibit was a little risky, considering that Minnesota wasn't exactly a tropical savannah, so she'd been meaning to check with him on minimum daylight lengths and temperatures. Now, though, the surrealism of her evening seeped into the phone, skewing Gus's words, making her head pound in panicky jumps.

"Are you sure, Gus? Nineteen degrees?"

"Yes." He spoke slowly into the static, the chirpy, bodiless voice that would have made her smile any other day. "Never below nineteen or twenty in the winter and up to thirty-three or so in summertime."

"Thirty—oh, Celsius. Duh."

"Shelshus," Ben slurped again, nodding at her. She rolled her eyes and mimed a pistol at her own head.

"You can make the heat and light to work for the space. No problem, Meg."

She sighed. "*Terima kasih*, Gus."

"Sure, sure. Everything else okay?"

"The hatchlings are all doing great. Strong vitals. Fat appetites."
He laughed. "Jata's children. They hunger for the world."

It was Gus who had named Jata, for some tribal goddess in Indonesia. According to the legend, Jata was an underworld serpent who teamed up with another goddess to create everything on the earth. When Meg first told Gus about the virgin birth, Gus had gotten really serious for a while and asked if there had been any birds in Jata's exhibit lately. She tried to imagine giving that explanation to the news. *No, Jata hasn't mated with another Komodo, but there was this bird ...*

After saying good-bye to Gus, she gave up trying to look busy and tossed the exhibit diagrams under the table. Shivering, she pulled her hands up into the sleeves of her sweatshirt and curled tighter into the cushions. The old house was drafty, full of windows that didn't quite shut and doors that let cracks of streetlight slice across the hardwood floors. The radiators in each room belched out heat in short, unpredictable blasts, and every time Meg complained, her landlord reminded her about the single house thermostat and claimed he was roasting upstairs, wearing Speedos and chowing down popsicles in the winter so she wouldn't freeze. On any other day, she would have just snuggled up next to Ben, who pumped out so much heat he practically had steam coming off him, but that was impossible now.

She could sit here and watch the news and make conversation and eat dinner, but that was all. She couldn't touch him as if she'd done nothing wrong. She couldn't take comfort in his body after she'd betrayed it so carelessly. Some animals could sense when their mates had been with different partners; they could smell it, as if the mate's pheromone signature was chemically altered by the encounter. Could Ben smell Antonio on her, three days later?

"What the hell?" Ben set his empty bowl down, wiping broth

off his chin, and rewound the newscast he'd been scanning in fast forward. Meg saw a picture of a Komodo flash on the screen and then a poof of sleek red hair—Nicole Roberts. Her stomach dropped even as she jumped to grab the remote from Ben.

"Wait, I got it." He found where the story began and hit play. Both of them sat on the edge of the couch, frozen, waiting.

"—have shown some footage a few days ago of the new Komodo dragons at the Zoo of America, but these seemingly harmless babies have a much darker reputation than most of us realize."

The screen cut to the hatchlings and then to Nicole Roberts interviewing a pale, bearded man Meg didn't recognize.

"Mr. Anderson, you're a skilled amateur diver, and I understand you recently traveled to Komodo Island to swim the reefs there?"

"That's right, Nicole. We were there for a week and decided to take a hike in the park one day to see the Komodos."

Nicole held up a camcorder and twisted her face into horrified concern. "And this is what you saw?"

"Yes."

"We're unable to show the tape on the air due to the graphic nature of the material, but it will be posted on our website. Parents are strongly cautioned to review this shocking footage before determining whether their children should be allowed to see it."

Ben was already pulling his laptop onto the coffee table and booting up the site. They watched both screens as the interview continued.

"Tell us in your own words what you experienced that day."

"We hiked for an hour or so until we came upon a water buffalo that had fallen down the hill and was tangled up in a patch of mud. The poor thing couldn't get up, but we didn't realize why until our guide pointed out the chunk that was missing from the buffalo's rear flank. It was hard to see the blood at first, against the black fur and dark mud, but the animal had clearly been attacked.

"Then three huge Komodo dragons crept down the embankment and circled the water buffalo. The biggest one lunged first, diving into the water buffalo's belly, followed by the other two at the back and hindquarters. We couldn't do anything to help. The buffalo was still alive and bleating while the three dragons tore him apart. One of my friends threw up; the smell was so putrid. The guide tried to hurry us along. Later we learned that more Komodos would be drawn by the smell, and he didn't want to run into any dragons in the midst of a feeding frenzy. As we left, nearly ten minutes later, the water buffalo was still twitching. I hoped to God the poor thing was dead."

The guy narrated exactly what the choppy video had captured. Meg and Ben watched it in silence until the footage ended.

"Was there any point when you were afraid for your life?" Nicole asked.

"I don't know how you could be human and not be afraid."

Meg snorted, lunged up from the couch, and jabbed the TV off.

"They're alpha predators!" She paced in front of the coffee table. "What did she think they ate for breakfast, tea and scones?"

Ben let her fume for a minute without saying anything. She made another couple rounds and gave the TV stand a passing kick.

"Afraid for his life," she muttered. "They should post some footage of a slaughterhouse and see who the scariest predator is then."

"It was the five o'clock news," Ben said.

"So?"

"So they're gearing this toward the baby boomers and what's left of the greatest generation."

"What does that matter?" Her voice kept rising, as if she had no control over it.

Ben drew her back over to the couch and sat her down, as patient as a kindergarten teacher.

"It matters because that's not your core visitor, is it? Your stroller moms are still running after their kids at five o'clock, right?"

She shrugged.

"And this is regional news, babe. It won't even touch the markets where the tourists are coming from."

He got up and went to the kitchen while she stared at the blank TV, feeling the story seep into houses all over the city and brand Jata with its ugliness. Even if what Ben said was true, it was still on the Internet. It could be halfway around the world already.

A beer can popped open in the hallway, and Ben reappeared, sipping a Leinies. "So? What do you think? Is this guy just some pansy-ass liberal who couldn't kill a chicken for his own dinner?"

He sat back down and threw an arm over the back of the couch, resting his hand on her shoulder. She tried to will her muscles to relax and force a smile. They always went round and round about the merits of vegetarianism, but she didn't take the bait this time.

"Probably."

Ben motioned toward the TV with his beer can. "And that shit about the buffalo? Come on. There's no way it would have still been alive."

"No." The words were smaller and smaller on her tongue, shrinking underneath the weight of the story. "No, the buffalo shouldn't have survived that long. There was no hope for him from the beginning."

"It's unbelievable what some networks will air. Making your Komodos look like monsters, just to get a few market share points."

"My Komodos? They're all mine now?"

"I think anyone who has an evolutionary tree of a species drawn on their bathroom wall gets to become the unofficial guardian for that species."

He laughed, and she felt her mouth changing, melting into a tiny warm place in her cold body. The Meg who was watching the whole conversation shuddered and drew further into her shame. No right, she thought. No decency. The other Meg, the one covering Ben's hand with her own and smiling back at his laughing, boyish face, moved closer to the warmth he radiated. It would be strange if she didn't touch him. He might know; he might smell something if she pulled too far away and left too much air between them.

Later, after he finished jotting his notes about the day's news and drank his beer, he pulled her into his arms and rocked her back and forth, down into the belly of the couch. He pulled her earlobes lazily between his teeth, and they peeled off clothing, rolling over each other in groans and sighs, but no matter how much she tried to focus on Ben, all she saw was a mud pit beneath them. She couldn't remember why it mattered that Ben was lazy and childish or that he'd acted so relieved when she'd gotten the abortion. Would he even care that she'd cheated on him? Did it even occur to him that she'd never really let him into her life? The mud pit sucked them down, swallowing their bodies into a black place where it was impossible to know where the water buffalo ended and the Komodo began.

10 Days *after* Hatching

Bob the Gila monster was having a bad day. Stretched out flat on his back and spread-eagle—or as spread-eagle as a Gila could be—he wore a choke collar chaining his lolling head to the operating table. Sure, Bob was poisonous, but he'd been knocked out cold fewer than thirty minutes ago, and the thickness of the chain seemed a little excessive, especially when combined with the intern that hovered around Antonio's shoulder as if Godzilla were in the room, his eyes rolling over his surgical mask toward Bob's head about once every ten seconds. From nose to tail, Bob measured one foot and ten inches. Scary stuff. True, his claws and teeth were both wickedly curved, razor-sharp miniature scythes, but the shy lizard only used them when he was forced into a corner or—probably—when he woke up in an operating room surrounded by three blue humans with knives.

"He's out cold. Vitals are low and completely stable." Meg glanced at the computer where Bob's SAMs were displayed, the graphs and charts blipping out new data points in a steady line with no significant variation. She pumped the oxygen mask at an even pace, making sure air was getting in. A lot of reptiles stopped breathing when they were under anesthesia. On the other side of the operating table, Antonio positioned Bob's foreleg open and revealed the inch-wide bubble that Meg had noticed growing in his armpit.

"Solid." Antonio tested it with a gloved finger. "Feel that?"

The intern patted a finger against the scaly bubble, depressing it down into Bob's body.

"A liquid deposit would feel spongy," Antonio said. "Even underneath the thickest osteoderms you can generally tell the difference. This is either fatty tissue or a mass, so we can do an incisional biopsy."

He reached for a scalpel and explained how to choose a spot for minimal bleeding, the type of scalpel to use for scales, and on and on, while the intern nodded, taking notes with his round, bloodshot eyes. Meg watched the SAM screen, hoping the lecture didn't outlast the anesthesia.

When Antonio finally cut into Bob's bubble, slicing the tissue with minute, confident jabs, it was over almost immediately. He placed the sample on a petri dish and sealed it, handed it to the intern, and looked up at Meg.

"So, Miss Yancy, have you been thinking about it?"

"I don't know. It's a growth of some kind. Gila monsters don't get a lot of cancer that we know of."

"So it's just a cyst?" the intern asked, as he and Meg both watched Antonio disinfect the incision area. The SAM computer beeped softly.

She'd been thinking about this constantly over the last eight months, and no matter how it formed in front of them, no matter how many different labels and categories appeared, it still came down to one single principle, and here it was staring right at them, as a cyst this time. Deformity, mutation, adaptation. Whatever the hell anybody called it, it still boiled down to just one thing: change. Bodies evolving.

Meg answered the intern's question. "Who knows? You know, if

Jata had some physical precursor to parth, something that looked like an abnormality, we'd have cut it off. I bet you anything."

"Mmm." The intern looked at Antonio, whose eyes crinkled up as he opened the Gila monster's transport tank, removed the tape from his claws, and unlatched the collar. Meg supported Bob's neck, gloves clamped tight against his skull in case he woke up and got nippy, and they slid him back inside the tank. He opened his eyes just as Meg slid off the oxygen mask.

"Bob's poisonous, right?" she said. "Bad for us, right? But now the pharmaceutical companies are synthesizing Bob's spit to help treat diabetes. So wait, Bob's good for us now."

"Unless he bites you," Antonio threw in.

"You just can't call something a deformity. Bob's bubble? Rodríguez just took a snapshot of it, just a single point in its growth. The bubble's not the end product."

The intern stared at her. "It's a cyst."

"What is a cyst? Describe it to me."

"An abnormal clot of cells."

"What do the cells do?"

"Nothing."

"Nothing yet."

The intern rolled his eyes and asked if they were done. As soon as Antonio said yes, he took off as fast as the surgical gown could be balled up and dunked into the biohazard bin. Meg pulled her own gown off and was heading toward the door when Antonio cupped her shoulder and turned her around.

"That was really interesting, Yancy, but not what I meant." He peeled the mask from his face, revealing a mischievous grin to match the gleam in his eyes. "Have you been thinking about it?"

They were alone, and his fingers were like flash paper, transporting her back to the last room where they had been alone. Papers flying off his desk. Clothing unzipped and unbuttoned, skin meeting greedy skin.

She met his smile and basked in it a second, just a second, before shifting back to the door. "No."

2 Weeks *after* Hatching

I don't think those chairs were made for that."

Wearing one sleeve of her uniform shirt, with her purple Hanes underwear as an anklet, Meg lifted her knee to trace the cherry bloom rubbed over its outside. She was half-leaning, half-lying against the wall next to the nursery door, and the wheeled office chair in question was propped against the door handle and missing an arm.

Antonio crawled over to inspect her knee and gave a nice show of shoulders flexing and stretching across the floor. He still wore his socks and shoes, and his pants were caught around one foot in an inside-out wad of beige and lime green with frogs.

"You want me to bandage you up?" He gave her knee a light kiss and rolled over to his side, propping his head on one hand. "I've got some monkey Band-Aids around here somewhere."

"That's sweet, Rodríguez, but I think I'll live."

She stretched her leg up into the air and twisted it back and forth, flexing the banged-up muscles. It wasn't the only bruise he'd given her, and apparently, glancing down his torso where a rosy patch was developing on top of his hip, she gave as good as she got. Sex hadn't stopped their fighting; it just moved the fight into a new habitat. She'd convinced herself she was staying late to get extra work done—typing logs and checking her e-mail while all the other keepers punched out and went home—until Antonio showed up in the doorway of the cage, leaning against the doorjamb and smiling wordlessly, daring her. They'd ransacked the security guard's station last night while trying to figure out where the cameras weren't pointed (*Hey, there's no cameras here ...*) and now tonight the nursery floor. He'd tried to push her into the chair, and she'd flipped him, throwing him down onto the seat instead, snapping the chair arm and sending them rolling across the floor into the walls. When she tried to speed up, he wanted to slow down, and neither of them seemed to mind the fevered chaos that ensued.

Animals fought during sex all the time. Lions nipped each other in the flank, raccoons screeched and tumbled all over each other, and banana slugs, the poor schmucks, got their penises chewed off if they couldn't maneuver properly. It was a natural part of the courtship process. Most species, though, except for the doomed slugs, reached some point during mating when the dominant animal subdued the other, when one body moved while the other body fell still, accepting and in sync with each other. Meg and Antonio hadn't come close to that point. They fought, again and again, driving each other to the brink of submission but never reaching it. Hell if she was going to be the first one there.

She spied the chair arm underneath the exam table.

Antonio ran a finger up and down the outside of her thigh, a warm callus on a highway of nerves.

"Why'd we come in here again?" he asked.

"Hatchlings." The word sounded a lot more confident and less breathy in her head. His finger was almost scratchy, a delicate scrape back and forth along her leg. He started down by her knee and traveled all the way up to her hipbone, which stuck out in an awkward and pronounced hill, and her body picked it up from there, shivering all the way up her spine and into the top of her head and ears. The shiver refused to go away, tingling her scalp and teasing the line where her neck met her hair.

The electricity of his touch was fascinating, and the zookeeper in her recognized it for what it was—the biology of new chromosomes meeting, the subconscious excitement when a new combination of alleles becomes possible. It had been years since she had felt that pull, and never like this. Ben was everything old and comfortable: all submission, no fight. She could have sex with Ben in her sleep, pulling him over her like a worn, heavy duvet. That wasn't possible with Antonio. He was something out of a textbook: human, male, at prime. The picture would rotate his body under glass, arrows signaling various points of his physiology. Here were the muscular deposits. Note the bone density and normal, hyper-functioning genitalia. The textbook, though, like all other textbooks, would cover the basics, the generic facts, always oblivious to her favorite parts of the subject matter. On Rodríguez, her favorite part ran along the inside of his right thigh, a splotchy birthmark that colored his skin a deep, baboon-butt red. It was like some undiscovered continent, full of peninsulas and tiny dots of islands that she wanted to chart, mapping all the hidden species that lived there.

"Right. The hatchlings." He watched his finger trailing along her skin, as if he were equally aware of this strange magnetism.

"I need to transfer them to the community tank, and you need to … do whatever it is you do."

She lifted and shook her leg half-heartedly, jiggling the underwear back in the direction of her torso.

"Blood samples. I need to take some samples for a first round of testing, little bit of training for the interns, genetic mapping."

"Yeah, yeah." She jiggled the underwear close enough to reach and drew them back over her hips. "Where're my pants?"

"A question for the ages." He grinned and continued to stroke her thigh. "Let's not try to answer it. Leave a little mystery in life."

She batted off his hand and spotted them behind the substandard chair. Rolling up, she heard him shifting behind her.

"You in the monkey Band-Aids already, Yancy?"

Glancing back, she followed his finger toward her triceps and reflexively scratched the area around the small square. "Birth control patch."

"Hmm. That's why you didn't freak out about not using a condom."

"I'm still thinking it over. Do you have rabies or syphilis?"

"Syphilis—definitely not. I haven't gotten checked for rabies in a while, so who knows? And that one redhead a few months ago was foaming at the mouth, now that I think about it."

She pulled on her clothes, which—thanks to the fact that she didn't own an iron—didn't look any worse than they did a half hour ago. What was the point of ironing when you never knew if you'd be containing an alligator or cleaning up random fluids? Or jumping the head vet, apparently.

"What about you? Are you rabid?" Antonio asked. She threw his lab coat at his head and watched his body jump, muscles tensing like lions the second before they leapt between outcrops. The reaction ran down him in one long ripple.

"Doubt it."

He stood up and dressed, a grin hanging off the side of his face. "I don't know. Have you even been tested, Yancy? I should probably grab some shots as a precautionary measure."

She lifted from the floor a small animal carrier that was slightly dusty but not bad overall. It would work just fine to taxi the hatchlings to their new exhibit in the baby building. She was so focused on the carrier that she barely heard herself reply. "Not worth it. I've been sleeping with the same guy for the last seven years."

It wasn't until she wiped out the carrier with a rag that she realized ... and turned around.

Antonio was buttoning his shirt, and his chest disappeared almost as fast as the joking. Neither of them had mentioned other lovers in any real sense—no spouses, partners, nothing specific that could incriminate them—and the silence had created a delicious bubble where the outside world didn't exist, not in any important or consequential way, at least not until now, when she'd popped the bubble with a big, fat *fwop*. Now all that reality rushed in with a suffocating weight, filling the room, pushing them back into opposite corners of the ring.

He finished the last button and finally looked up. "Not married. There's no ring. Boyfriend?"

"No. Ben's just—" Another mistake. His name was huge and oppressive. How the hell did people have conversations like this? It was like walking through viper pits. "He's just there, like the kitchen or the TV, you know? Except he's leaving soon. He leaves every summer and he—you don't need to know this. I'm sorry."

Antonio hooked his fingers in his belt loops and leaned on the opposite side of the carrier, ducking his face to hers. She could feel him trying to make eye contact.

"It's okay. We all make do."

"Okay." She nodded, pretending she knew whatever that meant, and glanced over. He looked expectant, as if he wanted her to say something or maybe as if he were going to say something, and whatever it was—whatever was humming at the edge of his eyes—looked like the kind of thing that would be impossible to ignore in the light of day when they pretended none of this was happening. Whatever it was, she wasn't ready to hear it.

She flipped the sink on full blast and scrubbed her hands raw.

"Are you just going to sit around and watch while I transport these guys to the baby building? That's a little creepy."

Gloved up, she lifted the first dragon out of the tank and waited, torn between the terrifying silence behind her and the comforting dig of claws into her hand and wrist. The hatchling met her eyes, steady and fearless, as if even at twelve inches long he was ready to swagger into his place as an apex predator. She concentrated only on him, on how he didn't seem bothered by the crazy sex noises or loud faucets, on how he was untouched by the mess brewing behind her. It was classic Komodo behavior. The earliest explorers thought the dragons were deaf because they didn't react to shotguns fired right next to them. Turned out, Komodos just didn't give a rat's ass about what the humans were doing. Smart dragons. She needed to learn how to do that.

"I'll give you a hand with the transport," Antonio finally said and opened a cabinet behind her, clanking some glass together. "But you have to help me first. Hold them still while I collect the blood."

They worked together. She lifted each dragon out one by one and contained them while Antonio pricked their tails with a small needle. He only took a few cc's per draw, lining the marked vials up on the exam table and making little comments, like "Easy there" and "Steady," his voice just a murmur over the scales, needles, and blood. Each word sent the hair on the back of her neck up and cramped her muscles tighter, drawing away. She'd brought Ben into the room, and Antonio was back to acting as if this were cuddle time, as though nothing had happened.

After each draw was complete, she tagged their legs with ID markers. He watched her strap the second ID onto a hatchling and reached over to give it a tug, then let his hand drop onto hers.

"They're going to get out of those."

"We'll see." She pulled away. It was the exact same thing she'd said to Gus when he told her that's how they ID'd the community hatchlings at the Wildlife Refuge, but then he went and suggested microchips. So ID tags all around.

"We wouldn't have an identification issue if they were segregated."

"We'd have other problems. Aggressive behaviors, inability to acclimate to new environments, difficulty mating."

"You don't think the AZA is really going to allow these guys to breed, do you?"

Leave it to him to bring up the Komodo Dragon Species Survival plan, which was basically a lot of charts and endless hoops to jump through. The AZA, the Association of Zoos and Aquariums, were the guys who sat up in the proverbial clouds and looked down on the desert island scenario. If you had three women and four men, all with unrelated DNA sequences, could you successfully propagate the species without turning their descendants into a race of idiot flipper children? This was one of the pressing questions of the AZA.

"Why not?"

"You know why not." He was getting irritated again. Good. "There's a limited gene pool of Komodos in the U.S., and these guys unbalance the whole population."

No one had said anything yet, not officially, but everyone knew Jata's place on the breeding list was crossed out because of the tiny dragons wriggling one by one beneath Meg's hands. Underneath their delicate yellow, black, and green scales pulsed the same genetic code as Jata's. Four dragons with the exact same genetic signature were three too many, according to the AZA. If they bred them at all, it might be only Jata, or maybe one of the hatchlings after they reached maturity.

Meg understood that. Empirically, scientifically, she could read those charts and draw her finger along the line of hope for survival.

If she were in those clouds looking down, she'd make those same decisions. But she wasn't there; she was here, surrounded by hatchlings that shouldn't exist. Deprived and cut off from any possible mate, Jata had reproduced anyway. When there was no life to be found, Jata created it—and now the AZA was going to punish her genetic code for taking an unauthorized step up the evolutionary ladder.

"It figures."

"What figures?"

"You, jumping into the clouds with the AZA. It must be pretty easy up there, away from all these messy, real lives."

"What the hell are you talking about?" Antonio sealed the last sample and turned to face her. Gently, she lifted the last hatchling from the table and set him into the makeshift taxi, locking the door. He skittered back to the far corner and adopted a threat pose: head cocked and neck puffed out.

"It doesn't matter. I should get these guys over to their new home."

"I told you I'd help you."

She shrugged. "Whatever. I don't want to keep you. You probably have a date lined up."

He opened the nursery door and waited for her to walk through, with the carrier in tow, before asking, "Is it men in general or just me?"

"What?"

He didn't answer.

It took half an hour of going back and forth with the taxi from the nursery to the baby building next door. When the last hatchling was safely deposited inside the new tank, she and Antonio sat on opposite sides of the long stone bench that paralleled the glass and watched them.

She'd chosen a completely terrestrial exhibit, filling it with organic dirt and sand and setting just a few large sunken water pots in the corners. Pruning trees and palm shrubs, she'd planted them at various points in the tank and scattered a few rocks around the bottom, too, but those were mostly for show. Juvenile Komodos lived in trees in the wild, and her hatchlings turned out to be no different. Meg watched them scramble from limb to limb of their pseudo-trees until they found a comfortable vantage point, and then they sat, poised and warily alert. If they acknowledged one another at all, it was too subtle to detect. At least there was no aggression. Not yet. She'd designed the enclosure to be three-sided, like a square U, so each could have his own mini-territory without even having to see the other two. The added benefit, of course, was that there was more glass for the visitors to belly up to. After a few minutes, Meg dumped a bagful of live crickets into the middle of the enclosure before returning to the bench next to Antonio.

One by one, the dragons descended to the ground, moving hesitantly around one another, training their awkward limbs to crouch and hunt. They had amazing concentration. Only two weeks old, and their sleek trunks and tails pointed straight at their prey with the purpose of a poisoned dart. It was the rushing attack that still needed some working out. Meg laughed as one of the hatchlings lunged for a cricket and came up with a mouthful of sand.

"I thought we agreed to give them dead crickets to start."

"I did. But they need to start working on their coordination, not to mention their hunting skills." She chuckled again.

"I don't understand you, Yancy." He stood up and walked over to the glass, crouching to see one of the hatchlings beneath the foliage. It would be a perfect height for kids to peer underneath the canopy. "You put these hatchlings together when every other zoo in the U.S. segregates because they're afraid they'll rip each other apart rather than learn to live together."

He glanced back, and his gaze was dark. "And yet you think

everyone at this zoo, including me and probably everyone else in the world, is a self-centered asshole just trying to get ahead and use whoever's handy, right?"

The exhibit lights bounced a sharp glare off his head and threw his face into shadows.

She tried to shrug it off. "I don't know everyone in the world."

"You don't know the people standing right in front of you. What did you really want from this, Meg, just a warm body?" He hooked his finger between the two of them. "Did your boyfriend cheat on you and you're playing catch-up? Whatever it is, I've heard it before."

Behind him, the remaining crickets panicked and fled across the dirt. "I'm sure you have."

"You know what your problem is?"

"Oh, you're going to tell me?" She raised her voice, spoiling for a fight.

"Your problem is that you have more faith in dragons than people." He picked up the empty taxi and walked away, leaving her alone in the darkened building.

~⁀

The late-night maintenance crew mopped its way down the public trail toward the reptile building exit. Meg watched them through the leaded glass window of Jata's exhibit and waited until they finished up and left. It wasn't that she was forbidden to be in the exhibit after hours; she just wasn't supposed to be alone.

Quietly she opened the door and slipped inside. Jata was inside her cave but popped her head out the minute the door squeaked.

"Hey, there."

Meg carried the bucket of minnows (also known as her

"accompanying staff," if it ever came up) across the floor and dumped them into the pool. Jata lumbered up beside Meg, her dart-shaped head appearing next to Meg's hip, and licked the air with her tongue. Her eyes were intent, a midnight swirl of attention and calculation as they followed the bouncing streaks of minnows through the shadowy water. After a few minutes, she waded into the pool and submerged underwater.

Meg watched her, reminded as she always was of the other Komodos, the ones who didn't care about shotguns and got captured by the explorers a hundred years ago, the ones who tore apart their cages and leaped from the cargo ships. They disappeared from the sailors' sight just as Jata's body now faded away from Meg, slipping into the far shadows of her pool. Had they known, when they jumped, that there was no going home, that they'd gone too far to survive the journey back? A dragon wouldn't understand, of course, but say it was a human. Say she was standing on the edge of a ship, and her life as she'd known it was over. She could let the powers-that-be throw her into a box for the rest of her life, or she could jump, desperate and alone and free in the middle of the ocean. How was she supposed to have faith in people when her entire life was distilled into those choices?

As Jata nosed her way around the bottom of the pool, Meg propped herself against the same palm tree where she'd discovered the eggs. This irony was that this *was* her escape. The ocean and the cage were the same thing for her; she had no home that called her anywhere but back here, just here, in this glorified box with Jata. Everything was simpler in here, away from the crazy lovers, the deadlines, and the media. She didn't want to think about any of that, didn't want to deal with this stupid reception Chuck was planning or the hurt she'd seen in Antonio's eyes. They were just distractions from what was actually important. Rubbing her temples, she spoke to the massive shadow that snaked along the pool floor.

"The boys are doing fine in the new space. One has a big yellow splotch on the center of his forehead, and he's the only one I can tell apart from the others. Today I fed them live crickets, and one smashed his head into the sand trying to attack. You should have been there—that is, if you could promise not to eat them … "

15 Days *after* Hatching

B en, the hatchlings are in their new tank, and we need to break up. I can't see you anymore. They said it was impossible, did you know, for the dragons to live together, but Gus keeps them in communities in Jakarta. This isn't working. I cheated on you. No, I don't love you. They're so beautiful. I want to cry when I think about it. You have to go. I can't keep lying."

The house was dark and Ben's pickup was gone when Meg pulled into the driveway. Shit. It was barely six o'clock—the earliest she'd arrived home since the birth—and the sun was still high above the houses across the alley. She dropped her head onto the wheel and pushed the bridge of her nose into the warm vinyl. Maybe tomorrow.

She'd been practicing the speech during her drive home for the past week, and it changed as quickly as she changed radio stations. Yesterday's song was a sappy number about reconciliation and possibilities. Tomorrow might be an angry metal anthem, kicking him out of the house. It was hard to predict the playlist these days. She rolled her head to the side of the steering wheel and raised a hand to Neil, who was lounging in his usual spot on the porch with a Bloody Mary and a newspaper. He toasted her back.

Staring at the dark windows of her apartment, Meg pulled the phone out of her pocket and—before she could talk herself out of it—dialed the number. There was a long silence, then an odd ring: two short, even bursts and then a pause before it repeated.

"Yes?" The voice was gruff and sleepy, and Meg rubbed her temple on the steering wheel and smiled. He never said hello like other people did; growing up, she always thought he was too important to say things like hello or good-bye. It never struck her, until after the divorce, that not saying them made it easier for him to show up or leave whenever he wanted.

"Did I wake you?"

"No." He was surprised, she could tell. "No, I barely sleep anymore. All that crap they tell you about getting old? It's all true. That's the big joke."

"I'll remember that." Meg drew an outline of a dragon on the window with her finger, trying to figure out why she had called. What did she want to say? "What time is it there?"

"Eleven or so."

He waited. That was one thing he was good at, waiting until she was ready to say what she wanted, or answer the trivia question, or order from a restaurant menu. He didn't distract her with small talk or rush her into a conversation. Suddenly, she missed him with the intensity of that idiot girl who'd stared out a minivan window over nameless roads twenty years ago, while her mother's voice ran shrill over the radio and the smell of wet dog feet and feed bags saturated the seats. The sensations shuddered over her like ghost fingers. She thought she'd forgotten all that, that she'd buried the memories with her mother and never looked back, but here they were, popping into her life again just the way he'd done, without any warning or reason.

She'd longed for him on those never-ending trips, had spent hours imagining how he might appear during the next competition— ripping through all the bunting and trophy tables, scattering combs and hair dryers and leashes behind him like a finger of God—and claim her, declaring that Meg belonged with him and promising her that she would never have to go back.

Now a lifetime had passed, and yet here she sat, in another car, feeling just as powerless, as if Jata and her hatchlings were the stars of a brand-new dog show. Did she honestly still want her father to save her somehow? She sat up straighter and traced and retraced the dragon on the window. The phone grew sweaty against her cheek.

"I'm cheating on Ben. With the veterinarian you met. Antonio."

The line was quiet, and she thought maybe they had been disconnected.

"Hmm. Have you told Ben?"

The dark kitchen window was framed in the belly of her dragon. "He's not home."

"You have to decide what you want."

"I know."

"The sooner you decide, the better it will be for everyone, especially you. Believe me, there's nothing worse than living in indecision."

She dropped her hand into her lap.

"I'm glad you called, Magpie." The old endearment sounded easy on his tongue, and a strange flood in her chest had the whole freaking story pouring out. She started at the very beginning, when she'd discovered the eggs with Gemma so many months ago. He let her talk for almost an hour, interrupting only to get a clarification or ask a question, and Meg began to feel as if for all these years he'd only been waiting for her to be ready. Maybe he was never supposed to rescue her at all; maybe she was supposed to find her own way home.

Afterward, just before they hung up, he said, "I think you just need to take a trip to Ireland. Come see the old man for a while. Use those tickets I gave you and bring whoever you want. Even Ben, if that's what you decide."

She shook her head, even though she realized he couldn't see it. "I can't leave the hatchlings right now. They're too vulnerable."

There was silence for a minute, and then he sighed. "You sound like your mother. She was always chained to those dogs, always putting them before anything and anyone else. Even when there wasn't a show coming up for months, she couldn't spend a day away from them. She'd sit out in their kennels talking to them, for Christ's sake."

A few months ago, Meg would have snapped or just hung up the phone, horrified by any resemblance to her rigid, trophy-hungry mother. Anyone who'd spent eight years of her childhood trapped in the crazy competition circuit would have felt the same way. But now, after everything that had happened in the last few weeks, tiny dragon claws clutched her chest and warmed her to the indisputable biology of the matter. Theresa Whittaker had been her own sort of keeper, as devoted to her dogs as Meg was to her Komodos. If she hadn't been in that minivan, hadn't watched her mother coddle and love and race and sweat and win, would she be a zookeeper today? If her father had taken her away from the dog shows into the world of normal kids, signed her up for a baseball team or a drama club or whatever those strange, happy kids had been doing, would she ever have known Jata?

"Maybe I do sound like her," she said softly into the phone. "Maybe I am."

18 Days *after* Hatching

The map was the first thing she saw; it was one of those Rand McNally U.S. travel maps that tented and creased like a deformed turtle shell, hiding all but the legs of her living room coffee table. Paco leaned over it, dragging a Sharpie between an erratic pattern of stars scattered across the Great Lakes and Plains. Ben sat on the floor on the far side of Paco's legs, smoking a joint and talking through a haze of smoke that made his face look like an ash moon, gray and tranquil. As Meg walked into the room, he looked up.

"You're home early." He glanced at the clock, which was edging toward six. "Or early for you."

"I'm going ... shopping with Gemma and Allison."

He coughed, scissoring his knees into his chest. "It's not even Christmas."

Paco laughed. Tall and bone-thin, he was the Olive Oyl to Ben's Wimpy. She ignored him.

"It's for that stupid reception. I can't wear my uniform, and Gemma, well—she's making me."

Meg walked up to the nearest side of the couch, turning Paco into a human barrier between herself and Ben, and made a show of looking at the map. Ben continued his one-sided conversation—something about the new menu he wanted to try at the fairs. Paco grunted occasionally, but he didn't seem to be paying much more attention to Ben's chatter than Meg was.

She would have just hopped the light rail to the mall side of the America compound after work, except today was the day. It had been two weeks since she'd slept with Antonio—the first time—and she had to tell Ben before the guilt ate her alive. It was like acid in her stomach now, digesting little bits of her insides every time she saw him and acted as if everything were normal. Or normal for them. The whole thing was insane; she didn't even know what she was cheating on. She choked on the word *boyfriend.* Lover, roommate, friend? None of it was really Ben. Didn't everyone have some sort of Ben, a person who was just circling in the same habitat, putting up with you while you put up with him? Someone who met you in the middle to pay bills, call for pizza, and trade orgasms?

He wasn't even in this habitat for part of the year. She stared at the map and counted the days. Soon he would migrate south, leaving a bunch of half-filled notebooks, a scattering of roaches, and the ghost of an empty waiting room with pale, skin-colored walls.

Ben passed the joint to Paco, still talking, and she thought she caught something with her name in it.

"What?"

"I want to go with you to that reception thing. See the miracle babies."

Paco shook his head and mumbled something in Spanish as he exhaled a cloud of smoke and drew a curvy line between St. Louis and Cedar Rapids.

"Give it up, man," Ben said, swiping the joint back. "They are miracles, better than nature intended. Right, babe?"

"Why do you want to come with me?" The acid turned into a vacuum, sucking her heart and lungs down into the pit of her stomach. Antonio would be at the reception. Ben and Antonio in the same room, breathing the same air, swigging the same beer.

"See the kids, babe, like I said."

She met Ben's eyes for the first time since walking into the room, trying to keep herself steady, but her gaze slithered down somewhere closer to his chest. "It'll be a circus. Sponsors and bigwig donors all milling around, while management tries to milk everyone for money. You'd hate it."

"Exactly," he said as he puffed. "I know you'll hate it, too, so I'll come with you and keep you company."

"I'm talking about the mayor of St. Paul and the media. Chuck even told me today that they invited Nicole Roberts."

Bet lit up at the name, which was the exact opposite of her reaction when she'd gotten the news. "Perfect! That's perfect. I'm coming with you for sure. I'm not going to let you face her alone this time."

"Just make sure the heretic leaves the Virgin out of it this time, okay?" Paco didn't even look up as he said it. He was connecting Joliet to Wichita and writing dates next to each city.

"Why am I the only heretic in the room? Do you see a rosary around Ben's neck?"

Paco said something in Spanish that sounded like spitting.

"What was that?" She took a step closer.

"Rosaries aren't necklaces."

"Doesn't matter. Doesn't matter." Ben flexed his arms into the air like an overly excitable bear waking up after a long hibernation. He waved vaguely toward both of them. "Don't worry, either of you. We'll get her where it hurts. You leave her and the media machine to me."

"No."

She fled from the living room, choking on the word. Even the thought of seeing Nicole Roberts again made her nervous and sick. She'd been panicking since Chuck had told her about it a few days ago, and having someone there to support her, to keep her from making any more mistakes, was exactly what she needed. But why was Ben all of a sudden—now that she'd completely destroyed any hope for their relationship—being exactly what she needed?

Pulling her uniform off, she hugged her elbows into her ribcage. Maybe she was making too big a deal out of this. She'd just seen Antonio this afternoon, and he'd barely said hi to her.

She'd been catching up on some paperwork with a few other keepers in the cage when Antonio had passed through on his way to the vet wing.

"Hey, Rodríguez." She'd jogged over. "You seen the hatchlings today?"

She'd felt pretty smug about it. It had been four days since they'd transported them to the community tank in the baby building, and there wasn't a scratch on any of them, not even a chipped claw to be found.

"I've seen them, yeah ... but it can't be right." If his pupils hadn't been normal, she'd have thought he was stroking out. His eyelids were red-rimmed, as if he'd been staring at a computer screen too long, and he'd jumped when she'd called his name, then looked confused.

"It is right. There's no law that says dragons can't get along."

"I have to go. I have to check something." It wasn't their usual nonchalant nothing's-happening-between-us behavior. He wouldn't even look at her, and before she could say anything else, he disappeared behind the double doors. She stood there, watching the door swing shut and feeling inexplicably rejected until she remembered their last conversation. He still thought she was hopeless. No faith in humans, he'd said.

"Meg, what's the deal?"

Ben had followed her into the bedroom and lounged on the mountain of balled-up blankets in the middle of the bed.

"Why do you want to come with me? You never came to the zoo when the dolphin had her baby or when we imported the python. Why now? Why are you suddenly so interested?"

"This is stuff for the history books, Meg; this is the animal revolution. Virgin births? Come on, people start religions around this stuff, and it's happening right now. Here! At your zoo. All that stuff that I document from the news is old. Wars, famine, terrorist attacks. It's the same old human story. This is finally something new."

She shook her head, hugging her arms in tighter as the draft chilled her skin. "It's not new. You've already seen the articles from the other zoos. It's parthenogenesis. It's just"—she shrugged—"science."

He sat up farther, leaning over the mound of covers. "Yeah, but the other zoos have only started reporting these virgin births in the last few years."

"Just because humans finally start to notice things doesn't make them new."

She grabbed a shirt from her dresser and pulled it on. Getting up from the bed, he pulled her toward his chest, rubbing the goose bumps back down into her arms. He'd seen that she was cold.

"So, along with the rest of the world who's not as smart as you, now I'm noticing the zoo and Jata and the babies. I want to come with you, okay?" He smiled. "We'll party."

She dropped her forehead to his chest and let his arms wrap around her. His heart thumped lightly, a dancing joint-laced beat she knew as well as the soft hills and valleys of his body. She was comforted, warmed, and completely defeated.

"Just don't make a scene with Roberts, okay? It's a really important event for the zoo. I could lose my job if anything goes wrong."

"Don't worry, babe. You'll thank me afterwards. Trust me. And when did you become Miss Corporate America anyway, huh? Remember the Meg that used to challenge her professors and lead PETA demonstrations on the capital?"

She didn't answer. That Meg wouldn't have cheated on him either.

~ᶎ

"Now turn the other way."

Meg sighed, considered mutiny, then obediently shuffled in a circle in front of the dressing-room mirrors. Allison sat on a puffy footstool with her knees drawn up to her chin, her entire concentration focused on the electric-blue dress that had taken Meg's body hostage. They'd been in the department store for half an hour, trying on anything Allison shoved underneath the dressing-room doors. This blue number was actually a step up from the last one, a baby-doll rainbow dress that had physically gagged her.

"This one isn't right," Allison finally decided. "It makes you look sick."

Gemma joined them in a tie-dyed halter dress, pirouetting gracefully in front of her daughter. "How about this?"

"Hmm. Maybe." Allison's forehead scrunched up as she thought. It would be pretty adorable how seriously the kid took this whole business, if Meg weren't one of the lab rats. She elbowed Gemma in the side.

"You know this is your fault for not buying her Barbies."

Allison shook her head. "Barbies are creepy. Girls in plastic boxes. Maybe you should try the rainbow dress again."

Meg crossed her arms and tried to look intimidating. "Your

stock is plummeting, sweetheart."

"What does that mean?" Allison's eyes brightened at the prospect of learning something new.

Gemma checked the price tag of her dress and cringed a little. "We'll teach you, and then you can make Mommy lots of money on the stock market."

"I'll go get some more." She bounced off the chair, but Meg caught her in a bear hug before she squeaked by them. Allison giggled and pretended to fight her way free. It was kind of addictive, hearing that laughter and knowing she was the one who had caused it. It almost made this horrendous shopping trip bearable.

"Get black ones this time," she growled into Allison's ear. "If I see pink, there'll be consequences."

She turned Allison loose and watched her scamper away, unable to completely stifle the smile on her face. If she and Ben had kept their baby, it would be toddling around by now. Meg could almost see Allison holding its hand, leading it around, teaching it how to choose really ugly dresses.

"Check the clearance rack, honey," Gemma called as they walked back to their dressing rooms. The salesgirl, a friend of Gemma's, was keeping an eye on Allison up front. Maybe she'd start showing some mercy toward them and send something back that didn't look like a parrot at the prom.

Meg sighed. The reception almost felt like prom except, unlike her high school prom, she couldn't skip it. It was the day after tomorrow, and every time she let herself think about it, her insides twisted into nervous kinks. Antonio and Ben were going to be in the same room, her hatchlings were being put on display like trophies, she had to wear formal wear, and, to top it all off, she had to stand up in front of hundreds of people and actually talk.

"Chuck asked me today if I'd written a speech," she said from somewhere inside the torso of the next dress, before finding her way clear of the thing. "A speech! He wanted to review it and make some comments."

"Yeah?"

"I don't do public speaking. I might vomit up there, and then, hey—I could invite him up to review that. Give me some pointers, maybe. God."

"You give the reptile tours every week. What do you call that?" Gemma's voice sounded muffled from her dressing room.

"I call the tours babysitting. An unfortunate hour of my week."

"Then just call this an unfortunate evening and think about better things. Your body is perfectly capable of working while you groove your mind elsewhere."

"Isn't that a prostitute trick?"

Gemma laughed. "Yeah, I picked it up at that whorehouse over on Seventh."

"What's a whorehouse?" Allison asked from outside Gemma's door. Meg stifled a laugh while Gemma backpedaled and made something up before shooing her back out into the front of the store. Meg waited until she was sure Allison was gone, then poked her head out the door.

"I have to tell you something."

"What? Damn, I need to step up my Pilates."

"I slept with Antonio." It was barely a whisper.

"I can't hear you."

"Antonio Rodríguez."

"Yeah? What about him?"

"Me. On top of him."

There was no reply for a minute. Meg stepped back into her dressing room and leaned against the wall. Gemma'd heard her this time; Meg could tell by the deliberate, absorbing silence between their rooms. She screwed her eyes shut and waited, ready for the worst.

"How was it?"

Meg laughed once and caught herself. "Really? That's all?"

"Well, I could say lots of things."

"Go for it. Please, I need someone to say them out loud."

"You hate each other."

"Not really, not anymore."

"He's a complete womanizer."

"True."

"He's probably got a dick full of STDs."

"No rabies, though."

"You're in a relationship. At least what you call a relationship."

She dropped her head. That one got her every time. "I know."

"When did it happen?"

"Just after the eggs started hatching."

"And you didn't tell me. Until now, when—oh, I see, when both of them are going to be at the reception together. Now you tell me."

"I didn't know how to tell you. I'm no good at this stuff."

"At this human stuff, you mean? Relating to people? Not shutting everyone down or biting their heads off?" There was an edge to Gemma's voice, but there was warmth, too. Meg spoke to the warm side and tried to ignore the rest.

"Yeah, all that. I'm sorry I didn't tell you. The next time I cheat on my boyfriend, you'll be the first to know."

Allison came back again with an armload of new selections. A pile of animal print appeared underneath the door, and Meg sighed, bracing herself to try the thing on. From Gemma's giggle next door, Meg guessed Gemma must have gotten something equally ridiculous.

"Hey," Gemma whispered in the hallway when Allison went down to the dressing room mirrors to wait for them. Meg poked her head out.

"You never answered my question." Her eyebrows shot up in expectation.

"What?"

"How was it?"

A smile spread over her face; she couldn't help it. "Raw and dirty. Like the world is ending, you know?"

"Apocalypse sex," Gemma breathed. "Fantastic."

They grinned at each other, then Gemma nodded, ending the discussion. "Now go try on your pretty animal skins."

20 Days *after* Hatching

Sometimes, standing on the south walkway that overlooked the river, Meg could sense a bad storm rolling in. There was no hint of it on the horizon or in the thin, white clouds overhead. If anything, the air was too still, the sun too warm. The whole day was playing perfect, Simpsons-opening-credits kind of stuff, but somehow she knew it was coming. The great white egrets spiraled up into the sky like bird tornadoes, calling to one another, gathering close. The raptors stopped circling, and the roar of traffic from the bridge seemed hollow, eclipsed by the absence of some quality she couldn't name, a normalcy that governed the day-to-day interactions of the refuge and the wide, lazy river. She looked to the northwest and could almost see something stirring, an echo of thunder rippling upstream, a psychic rumbling that spread the eerie knowledge that this nice day in the river valley was coming to an end.

That's how the air felt as she walked into the zoo grounds for the Komodo reception. "Damn." It was the only word in her vocabulary when she and Ben stepped through the double doors of the baby building.

Someone—marketing or PR, whoever handled this crap—must have seen one too many awards shows because the entire place looked as if the Oscars had thrown up in there. They stood on an honest-to-God red carpet flanked by red ropes and two bronze statues of S-shaped lizards propped on their hind legs, apparently PR's idea of a Komodo.

The baby building was a circular space, with exhibits lining the curved outer walls and a big multipurpose area in the middle of the room where the animals could be brought out for display and educational talks. Tonight the benches had disappeared, and in their place was a stage with a podium and a giant screen elevated above the crowd. Dozens of people had already packed into the room, their combed and sprayed heads bobbing around a portable bar in front of the baby sea horse tank. Music played, an instrumental version of "In the Jungle" that floated over the crowd while waiters in white suits carted trays of food.

They walked in a little farther and stood off to the side of the growing crowd. Meg didn't recognize anyone and felt increasingly conspicuous, as if she'd grown way too many hands and had nothing to occupy them. It wasn't fair that men got pockets on their dress clothes and women didn't. The short, black dress she'd finally chosen was simple, wide-necked, and sleeveless because she couldn't move her arms in any of the ones with sleeves. Apparently women at cocktail parties had nothing to reach for more than a foot away from their hips. She'd pulled her hair back into her usual ponytail and applied a tinted ChapStick, which was all she could find for makeup in the bathroom vanity. Even though it was still April, a permanent tan line circled her biceps, and her legs looked awkward and pale. She'd shaved, but no power on earth could make her wear nylons. They could throw her into the bear exhibit soaked in barbecue sauce first. She eyed Ben's dark brown suit, which was short in the sleeves and begging to be stained before the night was over. They didn't match, she guessed, with his brown suit and her black dress, but she'd never understood the color thing. Brown and black always looked fine together on the python.

It was only seven o'clock, and the presentations didn't start for another half hour. Chuck had taken her through the whole lineup earlier. Gerald Dawson, the director of the zoo, would speak first and welcome everyone, then they would play the video of the last egg hatching, then Meg was supposed to talk about Jata, and finally Antonio would talk about parthenogenesis. Then she could escape.

"No sign of Channel 12 yet," Ben said, scanning the room.

"Maybe they won't show up." Please, please, if there was a God who didn't already hate her.

"It's only a matter of time. People like that can't stay away from spotlights." He pointed at the stage. "Let's go check out your babies."

She led the way to the side of the building, where a small group had already gathered in front of the exhibit. Most of them were lining the glass and leaning down to look through the tree branches for the hatchlings, but Meg stopped short when she saw Antonio sitting on the exhibit bench. Hunched over, he faced the nearest section of the exhibit with a look of dazed concentration. A blonde stood in front of him wearing a dress that looked as if it were made out of red wads of Kleenex, tapping her foot impatiently and staring at the top of his head, but he didn't even seem to notice her. He stared straight through her, and his lips were moving slowly, talking to no one.

"What is it?" Ben asked.

"It seems a little crowded there right now. Let's get a drink instead."

Thankfully, Ben was never one to turn down a drink. They snaked over to the bar and met Gemma on the way there. She glided in a leopard-print sundress and had a white flower in her hair.

"Hey, you crazy kids," Gemma said as Ben punched her lightly on the arm.

Someone bumped into Meg's back, and the music switched over

to a medley from *The Lion King*. If they played "Puff, the Magic Dragon," she was out of here.

"You look fantastic, Meg. Stop fidgeting."

"I look like an asshole." Her throat started to close off as she eyed the stage. "I really need a drink."

Ben squeezed her arm. "I'm on it."

He dove through the crowd. For a big man, he could really shimmy through tight spaces—one of the many random skills he'd picked up from working fairs and festivals for the last four years. She watched his head until it disappeared, then turned back to Gemma, whose eyebrows were practically hiked up to her hairline.

"Well, Bachelor Number One is in good form tonight. Where's Bachelor Number Two?"

"Over by the hatchlings. He seems … distracted." She glanced that way but could only see straight into the cleavage of a tall woman who was gesturing to several people with an olive from her martini. The group laughed at something, and Meg looked away, in case the funny thing was her.

"Distracted by that blonde I saw him with earlier?"

"No. I mean, maybe. I saw her, but he just looked preoccupied. He must have stage fright, too."

Gemma laughed. "Yeah, and maybe his teeth are naturally that white."

"You don't think so?"

"And maybe he's gay."

Meg rolled her eyes. "Fine. Sue me for not wanting to be the only one scared to death of the fundraiser brigade."

"Just remember you're here to work. This is a job, and you'll get it done and then go home."

Ben returned with three glasses of champagne and handed one each to Gemma and Meg.

"Thanks, Ben." Gemma toasted him. "What got into you?"

"Can't a man support his lady during her shining hour?"

"God." Meg started to drink, but he held her arm.

"Wait, wait." He raised his glass and waited until Gemma and Meg followed suit. Clearing his throat loudly, he said, "To Meg, the best zookeeper and dragon mother that any little dragons could want."

He continued on like that, his voice too loud even amid the thunder of conversation around them. Meg lost track of what he was saying as the memory of the last time she drank champagne bubbled to the surface of her mind—Antonio's champagne the night the first hatchlings were born. Had it really been only three weeks ago? So much had changed between them since. If he didn't have stage fright, what was his problem? Even though he'd blown her off the last few days, she still wanted to talk to him, to see if she could get him to forget about that stupid fight. There had to be a way to lose Ben for a few minutes, and the blonde—she didn't give a shit about the blonde.

Gemma and Ben clinked their glasses into hers and she jolted, coming back to the present, then flushing with shame as Ben smiled at her and she realized she hadn't heard anything he'd said. Maybe he proposed. Maybe he broke up with her. Maybe he was moving to Guatemala to make hats for the tourists. She smiled back, and it felt weak on her face, a nauseous smile.

Shifting away, she caught sight of the Channel 12 news team from a few weeks ago. The scruffy guy looked completely different now—he wore a nice suit with flashes of cuff links, and his hair was slicked back. Completely comfortable surveying the crowd, he chatted to the cameraman amid the flux of jewelry, dinner jackets, and money-crusted greetings called back and forth around them. He barely resembled the wrinkled-khaki onion lover. Bees did that, too, she reminded herself. Most people knew that bees had specific roles in the colony, but they didn't realize that bees shifted into different roles during their lifetimes—house bees became guards, and guards became scouts. They evolved into whatever was needed in order to best serve the hive. Scruffy Guy here must have been upgraded to the entertainment beat.

Just then he looked over and caught her staring. He started to lift a hand in greeting, then paused and nudged his partner. Freezing, the two traded some words and then darted toward Meg's group, squeezing blindly past everyone in their way. The cameraman walked with his head down, adjusting dials on his equipment, but the reporter had a dead lock on Meg. She downed another gulp of champagne and wondered how obvious it would look if she bolted for the bathroom. As he got closer, though, she saw his eyes darting back and forth between her and something else behind her.

"Gemma, do you see this guy? It's weird, like he's—"

Gemma's face had gone cold, and Ben looked as if he'd drunk at least five more glasses of bubbly at the bar, with that sloppy grin eating up his face. Both of them were staring at the same spot behind her shoulder.

"Hello, Ms. Yancy."

Meg turned around to face Nicole Roberts. She looked exactly the same as she had eight months ago—eager and fake, wearing a black-skirted suit thing with little diamonds lining the lapels. Her hair burned orange in the reflected spotlights as she tapped a microphone against her thigh and nodded to her coworkers when they arrived from the other side of the room.

Some of the party guests hushed and stood back, which, oddly, made Meg feel even more surrounded. Ben, on the other hand, raised his glass to both of the reporters as if they were long-lost friends and rolled his shoulders in the tight suit jacket, loosening up.

"Congratulations on the dragon babies. You must be so proud." Nicole's eyes dropped down to Meg's dress, as if she were checking for postpartum damage.

"Thank you."

"Can we do a quick interview before the program? My viewers would love to hear what you have to say about them, for the record."

"No." Meg gulped the last of the champagne and crossed her arms.

Gemma chimed in. "Interviews should be handled through PR. They'll be happy to help you."

"But Ms. Yancy is the dragon's keeper. She's really been the one most affected by the birth." Nicole spoke to Gemma but kept her eyes on Meg.

"We should all be affected by this birth, Ms. Roberts. Ben Askew." Ben grabbed her hand, pumping it hard. Nicole flashed him a passing smile and turned back to Meg, but Ben shouldered into her line of view. "Do you realize that these virgin births are popping up in zoos all over the world right now? They're rare, but they're starting to happen. Where was it, Meg?"

"A hammerhead shark in Kentucky, a Mexican tree frog in Amsterdam, not to mention the three previous Komodo cases." As she listed them off, she warmed up to the idea of talking to Nicole. This was exactly what Channel 12 viewers should be hearing about, not some stupid feeding frenzy over a water buffalo.

"That's right." Ben squeezed her shoulders. "Unfertilized eggs that turned into little sharks and frogs with no males in sight."

"So it's not just a story about Jata. This is happening with multiple species in multiple different locations," Meg said.

"That's very interesting, Mr.—"

"It's not just interesting." Ben interrupted Nicole. "Why do you think this is happening? Why now, in a sweeping global movement like this in these zoos?"

He leaned across Meg, tucking her into his side as he ramped up, his voice growing louder and more demanding.

Nicole shifted away. "I really don't know. It's not my job to speculate. I just bring the stories to the public."

Meg glanced over at the guys on the Channel 12 team who were watching the whole thing like a tennis match. "Is eavesdropping part of your job description?" she asked.

"I consider it more of a perk." The scruffy-turned-slick reporter smirked.

The other guy was adjusting the camera mounted on his shoulder, but Meg waved him off. "No, you don't. This is none of your business."

"Actually, it is," the reporter said. "We're invited guests here."

"I didn't invite you."

She turned back to Ben, but he was still talking to Nicole, unaware of the camera pointing at the back of his head. "These births are the outliers that are going to start shifting the evolutionary paradigm, Ms. Roberts, and you can quote me on that. You can't ignore the pattern. Why are they happening in zoos? Because the animals are cut off from their mates and the natural order, so they're starting a revolution. An evolution revolution."

Nicole and the other reporters started laughing.

"Ben." Meg elbowed him in the side, but he ignored it.

"I'm no scientist, but it seems to me like the stories are coming from zoos because those are the animals that people have the opportunity to observe." Nicole shifted the microphone from hand to hand, losing patience. "How would we know if this was happening in the wild?" she continued. "We aren't exactly following—hammerhead sharks, was it?—around the ocean to monitor their sex lives, are we?"

Ben bounced on the balls of his feet, shifting his weight boxer-style. He nodded through Nicole's speech, the flush of alcohol creeping above his collar. "That's just like a reporter."

"Excuse me?" Nicole said.

The laughter died instantly, and even though the room was

louder than ever, the rest of the party seemed to fade off into the distance. Ben's eyes reflected a manic glow. Oh God—Meg knew that look. There was no stopping him now.

"You concentrate on one little detail and blow it up like it's the only possible truth, while completely ignoring everything else that doesn't fit in to your little schema of the world. Think about it. Why would virgin births be happening in nature? There are mates out there, animals that aren't under the human thumb of breeding schedules and survival plans."

"Ben, we don't know that." Meg tried to interrupt, but he didn't even hear her.

"Animals in zoos are trapped—that's why—sucked out of their natural environment, taken from their homes, and plugged into little plastic boxes full of fake trees and synthetic suns. They're forced up against a wall. It's either die, or evolve. And they're freaking evolving."

Meg focused on breathing and threw a glance around the room, hoping to land on anything that would give her a reasonable excuse to leave this airless nightmare. The clock above the entrance read 7:32 p.m.

"You people—"

"You people?" Nicole's mouth dropped open, but Ben kept plowing ahead.

"—have influence over the public, and you goddamn know it. You're presenting these insignificant slivers of stories that are totally irrelevant to what's actually happening. A Komodo attack? Yeah, that's a headliner. The Virgin Mary dragon? Who gives a shit about the Virgin Mary when something this mind-blowing is taking place right here—"

Suddenly the lights went up on the stage, and the crowd broke into applause, drowning Ben out. Gemma took advantage of the interruption and jumped in between Ben and Nicole, loudly trying to usher the reporters toward the stage. In the confusion of shifting bodies, Meg ducked out from under Ben's arm and did the only thing she could think of—she ran as far away from them all as she could get.

"Welcome, ladies and gentlemen." A boisterous voice carried throughout the packed room. "My name is Gerald Dawson, and as the director of the Zoo of America it is my privilege to welcome you all to this truly extraordinary celebration."

As Meg stumbled to the edge of the crowd, a gap opened up to reveal Antonio, still sitting in the same position in front of the hatchling exhibit. Automatically she darted toward him. Gerald's speech had cleared everyone else from the exhibit, so when she arrived only the glass-fronted trees and rocks surrounded the three of them—Meg, Antonio, and Antonio's date. One of the hatchlings wrapped himself around a tree branch and licked the air as Meg fell on the bench, shaking.

Antonio startled when she sat down, breaking out of his bizarre thinker pose. She barely had time to breathe before he grabbed her hands and pulled her across the bench. What the hell? A few days ago he'd avoided her as if she were rabid, and now he was squeezing her palms down to the bone and practically dragging her onto his lap.

"Meg! It's impossible. It's absolutely impossible, but I double-checked everything. We ran the tests twice—and they were expensive tests. I'm way over budget now."

His eyes were huge, their irises surrounded by stark, glowing white. As he babbled on, his gaze roamed her face, the exhibit, the floor, seeming to ride the general wave of Gerald's speech without landing on any stationary object. His hands were clammy.

"What the hell are you talking about?" She was only half paying attention to him, still trying to calm down from the confrontation with Nicole Roberts.

"A splice. Some kind of mutation. Frogs!" His hair fell into his face.

"He's been like this all evening." The blonde sighed. She sat on the other side of him, texting on her phone.

"Booze?" Meg asked, even though he didn't smell like alcohol—more like cedar and cinnamon. The scent steadied her, focusing her overloaded senses in on him.

"Nope. Not with me, anyway."

"Drugs?" Meg leaned in and tried to check his pupils. Odd, how she wanted to brush his hair back and get him some water. Help him concentrate and spit out whatever was eating him. As she hovered, Antonio's head snapped up. Normal pupils.

"Drugs! Yes! Maybe there was some chemical reaction, something that caused her to … " His hopefulness trailed off, but he seemed to register that she was sitting with him, that it was her thigh pressed against his and her gaze searching his face. He lifted a hand and brushed it against her cheek, watching the trail of fingers on her skin. When he spoke again, his voice was grounded. He was talking to her now, not some mysterious figment in his own mind.

"No, it couldn't have been drugs."

"Who's got some drugs?"

Ben strode into the exhibit with two fresh glasses of champagne. The acid that had been digesting her guts for the last three weeks surged through her stomach.

"I got you another glass of champagne." Ben stopped short of the bench, his offering arm freezing as he stared at the two of them. She looked down. Antonio dropped his hand from her face, but his other hand was curled in her lap, and somehow she'd laced her fingers through his without even knowing, just absorbing that clammy skin into her own flesh automatically, like osmosis.

"I'm not thirsty."

She disengaged her fingers and scooted away from Antonio, crossing her arms to hide the tremors that suddenly shot through them. Every movement felt huge and guilt-soaked. Even with Ben and Antonio both here in the same room, breathing the same air, she'd never really believed that they'd come face to face. She never thought she'd be forced into this moment, stomach free-falling through her body, sweat breaking out on her forehead, heart racing, knowing absolutely, inarguably, that she'd finally been caught.

Nobody touched her like that, and Ben knew it.

"Who is this?" he demanded, pointing at Antonio. Another burst of applause drowned the room for a second, but Meg barely noticed. Ben's stare trapped her completely; she couldn't look away. She opened her mouth, but nothing came out.

Ben took a step closer, forcing her to look up. "Meg, I asked you a question. Why was he touching your face?"

"She had something on it," Antonio offered quietly before burying his face in his hands.

Ben swung toward him, towering over both of them. "I didn't ask you a goddamn thing."

Meg jumped up, going toe to toe with Ben. Heads were starting to turn away from Gerald's presentation on stage, a mixture of irritation and interest mingling on their faces. "Keep your voice down."

"I'll do whatever I want. What's going on here?" he asked, anger starting to churn up to the surface.

She felt the welcome rush of retaliation and latched onto it. "Yeah, obviously you're doing whatever you want, including trying to get me fired. What the hell was that back there with Nicole Roberts?"

"I was supporting you. And you—" Ben pointed at Antonio with the extra glass of champagne, sloshing it over the rim, but she cut him off.

"If that was your idea of support, take it somewhere else." She tried to keep her voice as low as possible, but people near the back of the crowd were still shooting them sideways glares. "This is why I didn't want you here in the first place."

"Bullshit." Ben looked through her to where Antonio sat. He shook his head in tight, heavy drags back and forth, and a spasm of hurt crossed his face as if the full weight of the knowledge were sinking into him. He knew what she was now.

The pain on his face hit her unexpectedly. She thought he'd be surprised and probably put out, but this was so much worse. It was enough to drain all the fight out of her, and she took a step toward him, desperate to make it better even as she knew there was nothing she could do or say to fix this.

"Ben." She opened her mouth and closed it. Antonio started mumbling again, but she wasn't listening. Ben shoved one of the glasses of champagne into her stomach, and she had no choice but to take it before it dropped to the ground. The liquid splashed onto her dress. He turned around and lunged into the crowd toward the exit. She stood there clutching the half-empty glass and watching until there was nothing left of him but a sour curl clogging her throat.

"I'm sorry, Meg." Antonio's voice sounded closer; he'd stood up behind her.

She swallowed, staring at the place where Ben had disappeared.

"I know I'm acting crazy, but it's the hatchlings. I tested them earlier this week. Standard stuff, basic hematology with the DNA workup to confirm the parth, and that's when we found it. I thought it had to be a mistake, somehow."

That single word did it. It was the only word in the universe that could find her in this haze of pain and guilt and snap her back into the present. She forced Ben to the back of her mind and turned away from the crowd, toward the tiny black eyes that were peering out at her from under a palm leaf. Her stomach, already clenched, seemed to reach up into her throat and choke her. "What's wrong with my hatchlings?"

"Nothing. Everything." He blinked off into that vortex again, and she shook him by the shoulders, all patience for this act long gone.

"Quit stroking out on me and spit it out."

"They're female. The hatchlings' chromosomes. I checked all three of them. All of them have the 500 bp DNA band; they have opposing alleles."

She laughed once, a hard, scoffing sound. "Are you going to tell me the real problem or not?"

"They're female," he repeated.

"That's not funny."

"It's true."

He mirrored her move, grabbing her by the shoulders and staring her down, repeating the words until they burned into her eyes and ears. It's true. They're female. It's true.

Denial paralyzed her for a moment, and then she shook her head. "Jata has never mated. She couldn't have produced female offspring. It's not genetically possible."

His five o'clock shadow cracked open into a crazed, insomniac smile, and finally she understood. His distraction. The blood tests. Babbling incoherence from the veterinarian with a plan for every warm body under the sun.

"It's impossible." It was only a whisper now, losing conviction.

"It happened anyway." His smile grew bigger and saner as the news numbed her body. Shock was strange like that; it got handed over, passed off to the next unsuspecting idiot. She could feel it now, moving out of Antonio's body and into hers. He got taller, or maybe she shrank. As her hands fell off his shoulders, his moved to support her elbows, holding her on her feet as another wave of applause rolled through the room. The lights dimmed, and she leaned into

161

his side for balance as the screen on stage flickered. The video was going to roll.

"It's a miracle," Antonio said, his voice quiet but filling up with excitement as the projector beam reflected off his profile. She was completely dumb, unable to do anything but watch the light play over his face in splotchy blues and yellows.

"Can you imagine?" he was saying. "At our zoo? Do you know what this means? Every scientist and reporter in the world will be knocking on our door. It'll make this reception look like nothing." He waved his free hand at the room, and she followed it up to the stage where the final hatching was being projected onto the giant screen. It replayed larger than life, bigger than anything she could remember. The giant egg cracked open, and it looked as if the walls themselves were breaking apart as the mottled shell shuddered and splintered under the force of the thing inside.

Everything else in the room stopped. Glasses stopped clinking. The music, which must have trailed off before the speeches, was replaced by the video's recorded cracks and muffled scratching. The conversations peppering the crowd died little deaths, and everyone turned to watch something that they couldn't possibly understand. A ten-foot dragon snout broke through the end of the shell, and some people clapped as a single black eye gazed blankly over their heads. Maybe they clapped out of respect for the birth, or the fact that the birth was magnified to Godzilla proportions, or because they were drunk and it demanded applause on the invitation, but no one clapped for the most stunning reason of all because they couldn't. They were watching a miracle blindfolded.

The dragon shuddered out of the rest of the shell and flipped over to its stomach, poised as if to crawl right out of the screen, snake through the crowd, and ascend to its rightful place in the food chain. At that moment the video paused, and Gerald turned back to the microphone.

"And now, for a brief discussion of our brilliant Komodo mother, I would like to present one of our reptile keepers—Megan Yancy."

She didn't remember leaving Antonio or walking through the crowd, only the hatchling—that frozen dragon hatchling that grew and grew, consuming everything in her field of vision until there was only a giant black gaze in a nest of glossy scales. She climbed up to the stage and stood where Gerald had stood, looked at the empty podium and wondered how it could be there, how something so mundane could still exist after her entire world had just turned upside down.

Later, she didn't know what had happened first—if the reporters had rushed to the stage or if Antonio had jogged to the podium and grabbed the microphone. The questions tumbled over one another, hesitant at first, all variations of "How is that a problem?" and "What are you saying?" rising above the stage lights, into the air, circulating through the baby tanks in growing rumbles and sending the animals into hiding, the swelling of the crowd pumped up by the beat of waiters and staff as the impossibility of the thing started to sink in, heads swinging wildly from expert to supposed expert, cross-examining, demanding explanations that didn't exist, grasping for any conclusion, any reasonable excuse why Meg had stood in front of them, shaking, and blurted out: "They're girls. The dragons are female."

21 Days *after* Hatching

Garbled faces moved in and out of spotlights, attacking her with gaping mouths. The hatchlings, projected up onto the giant video screen, broke free of the picture and one by one climbed down onto the stage, towering over the room. They ran for the doors, but as they tried to escape, their bodies shrank in a panic of whip-cracking tails. The crowd dove for them, ripped their bodies apart, and ate them in a whirl of flashing canines until nothing was left except a stain of blood and saliva. In the back shadows, the water buffalo stared at her with shuddering glass eyes, and as the dream twisted and faded, the crowd inched toward the buffalo in hungry, determined steps.

～

The city slept as Meg roared past the cozy, dark houses lining the St. Paul streets and onto the empty freeway, where the sun kissed the other side of the horizon, warming the sky from a pale gray to blushing pink. Her shift didn't start for another two hours, but the nightmare chased her all the way to the zoo.

Only security beams lit the baby building, and the wood floor, littered with garbage, felt sticky and wet under her sneakers. The red carpet was bunched and curled after a night of being trampled, and the empty stage and bar still haunted the far side of the room. The mess looked huge and irreversible; it seemed impossible to go back to how things had been before last night.

She flipped on the exhibit light and found the hatchlings in the trees, wrapped around branches and staring steadily back at her, gauging how much of a threat she might pose to them. After a long silence, the one closest to the door shut her eyes, dismissing Meg and the intrusion of the light. Meg pulled on a glove and carefully unlatched the exhibit door. The hinge was soundless, but Meg's scent sent the closest hatchling skittering down the tree trunk into her waiting hand. Re-locking the exhibit door, Meg sat down on the floor and cradled the dragon in her palm.

The dragon opened her thumb-sized jaw and tasted the air with a shot of her tongue. For eight months, Meg had been thinking of them as males, but the dragon she held was female. The delicate pointed head—female. The miniature folds lining the skin of her neck that rippled in and out from a balloon of nervous oxygen—female. From the pinpoint claws to her bright black, green, and yellow splashes of infant scales—every detail was perfectly, impossibly drawn in front of her eyes.

"How can you be?"

The question breathed out into the room and surrounded them. They were alone—she and the dragon and the question—and Meg felt the uneasy certainty they would remain alone. Questions about creation could only be answered at the source, by the creator, which meant that all the media, management, and every scientist in the world who demanded explanations would march past these doors without a sideways glance and go straight to the reptile building. They would go to Jata.

Jata held the answer.

22 Days *after* Hatching

Ben came home on Sunday afternoon. Meg was in the living room, poring over books and journals of dog-eared field studies, looking for clues, a whiff, anything that could possibly explain how Jata had produced female offspring, when she heard him unlock the kitchen door. She hadn't seen or heard from him since he'd disappeared from the reception on Friday night—no phone calls, no texts, nothing. Not that she'd expected him to call.

The washer lid banged open, and she heard him start a load of laundry before going back to the kitchen and opening the fridge. She'd been holding her breath and let it out carefully, unsure whether she should go talk to him or not. But what could she say? She'd never really understood her relationship with Ben; it never fit into any of those easy labels other people used for their partners and friends. So if she couldn't even identify the animal in the first place, had gone out of her way to stab it and try to hide the wound, how could she possibly hope to treat its injuries now? After a few minutes of queasy indecision, she buried herself back in the books, where at least she knew what she wanted, if not how to get it.

She had to find out how Jata had daughters.

The principles of parthenogenesis were fairly simple, just as she had drawn out on that kid's visitor map so many weeks ago.

The DNA replicated; it created a mirror image of itself. It was impossible for something else to stare back in a reflection. She rubbed her eyes and concentrated. It was all in the chromosomes. ZW. Z and W. Copy it, fold it onto itself, and you have ZZ and WW. One male and one worthless eggshell. How could you get females out of that equation?

Compound replication, DNA recombining, gender switching, and all the other far-fetched, science-fiction possibilities swarmed through her head. She turned the pages of her case studies, searching for an answer that didn't exist.

"What's going on here?" Ben appeared in the doorway, along with the smell of resin and booze—not the nice yeasty waft of beer but a sharper stink, something with the pouncing meanness of gin. It filled the room, rolling off him in waves as he collapsed on a rocking chair, which shrieked under his weight.

"The hatchlings are female." She picked up another book, flipping to the index.

"Yeah, I mean what's going on with us, Meg?"

The glare heated up the corners of her mouth, and she dropped the pretense of research. "Well, let's see. You stay here at my apartment during the winter and smoke and drink and sit on your ass. I go to work every day and pay the rent and the bills, and now one of my animals is ripping apart everything the scientific world knows about reproduction and maybe even biology itself. Oh, and sometimes you try to get me fired. For fun, I guess. To keep things interesting."

He launched himself up, grabbing the gauntlet with both hands. "I spent hours researching those animals for you, collecting the articles, documenting the births."

"For me?" She almost laughed. "The only thing I asked was that you wouldn't make a scene with Nicole Roberts. That's all. That's what I wanted, Ben. You picked a fight because you wanted to, because you've been dying to go head to head with one of these reporters for years, so don't try and pass it off as some favor to me."

"I was trying to make her see outside the system. See what the dragons really are."

She jumped up and stood on top of the couch to get closer to his eye level, waving the book she held in the air between them. "No one knows what they are. I don't know what they are. They're impossible! And you want to piss away your time making some nobody reporter 'see outside the system'? What the hell does that mean, anyway?"

"I live outside the system. I don't slave my life away in the big sparkly cage that this society lures everyone else into—even you. You're stuck in there just like the rest of them, and you don't even know it."

"What are you talking about?"

He closed the gap, inches from her face and still towering over her. The ceiling light eclipsed the back of his head. "You're going to these goddamn receptions and cozying up to management and pandering to the money and media machine. You say it's for the animals, but you're lying. You're so fucking blind. You're like one of those prisoners who starts to need the prison. That's how they get you. They make you depend on them, and then they break you, like—what's the word you guys use? Death watch. You're on a long, slow death watch, babe, except nobody's watching you but me."

"Don't compare me to them." The words boiled out of her. "I am nothing like them."

"Then why are you fucking him?" He kicked the front of the couch, and she fell, her whole body flinching back, then slamming down into the cushions. The reverberations from his steel-toed boots jolted through her. The anger, pumping so pure and bright just a second ago, exploded in a heart attack of adrenaline, and she was suddenly afraid in the way you only can be when an animal that seemed harmless and vaguely lovable transforms into a deadly hunter.

She shrank into the couch and fought the urge to hide her face in her hands. The rage seemed to freeze on his face, contorting it into an ugly, ripping mask that looked nothing like Ben.

I made this person, was all she could think. This is what I've turned him into.

"Answer me," Ben shouted.

She dropped her head and forced the words out. "I don't know why."

A moment passed in which neither of them moved. The air in the room changed—it twisted from the echoes of their shouting into something raw—the combined relief and terror of exposure.

He cursed and kicked the couch again, making her jump. Without another word, he left the house, banging doors and screeching tires in the driveway. She sat on the couch for what felt like hours, in the exact place she'd been when he arrived, except now with her eyes clenched shut, heart breaking, and dragons all chased back into the books that were stacked like silent witnesses around her.

～୨

The news didn't report anything that night about Jata's daughters. So far their identities remained hidden, unrevealed to the world. Meg turned the TV off quickly, ashamed to be watching it without Ben, and paced the edges of the empty house. The tickets for the cruise line remained on her bedroom dresser. She stared at them and, for the first time since becoming Jata's keeper, wished she was on the other side of the planet. Maybe when all this blew over, when she could be sure that the hatchlings were safe and out of the spotlight, she would take that trip to Ireland to see her father. Alone, of course. She swallowed the knot that swelled in the back of her throat and nodded at the swift realization. She would always be alone.

23 Days *after* Hatching

Whenever something changed at the zoo that wasn't part of the three-year plan they handed out to everyone in January, management called an emergency meeting. It was like some kind of elixir for them; why work the problem when they could sit around and discuss what they didn't know? Maybe even get lunch brought in. Meg had never been to one, but like everyone else who actually worked around here, she felt the trickle-down effect of policies that came from sedentary, overfed managers.

Normally it was all in a day's work, no bigger a deal than the time it took to wad a memo and dunk it into the trash, but today the emergency happened to trump everything known to science.

The meeting was supposed to start at 8:00 a.m. on Monday, and, still shaky from the confrontation with Ben the night before, Meg shouldered her way into the overflowing room at 7:45. A sign on the boardroom wall said the room's maximum capacity was thirty, but it didn't say thirty what. The fourteen chairs lining the mahogany table were filled, and people circulated at least two rows deep behind them on all sides. Working her way into the herd, Meg sandwiched herself between Gemma and the bay window that overlooked the zoo grounds. The two of them comprised the grand total of zookeepers in attendance; the rest of the room was full of administration, management, and the entire PR department, who must have arrived early because they had grabbed almost half of the chairs. It didn't even smell like animals in here; there was only the scent of coffee, with the sick lemon undertone of commercial cleaners. If you didn't turn around to see the zoo outside the window, you could have been in any corporate boardroom in America.

Antonio showed some files to a couple of men near the head of the table. She'd left him two messages over the weekend, but he hadn't returned her calls or stopped by her exhibits. And now, after seeing the pain that had ripped apart Ben's face last night, she couldn't bring herself even to speak to him.

"It's weird that there aren't more keepers here. Do you think we're supposed to be here?" Gemma whispered.

"We're the reptile keepers. Jata's a reptile. Who's gonna kick us out?"

"Right now my money's on the fire marshal."

More people crammed their way into the space between the table and the walls, but no one was talking above a murmur or making eye contact with anyone else.

"It's creepy up here." Gemma tucked herself behind Meg as a guy from accounting almost stepped on her. "I mean, what are they waiting for?"

Gerald Dawson entered the room, and the hush went out in ripples.

"Right," Gemma said.

Gerald Dawson wasn't your typical zoo director. He was a short guy without the Napoleon complex who always wore pinstripe suits, loud ties, and bifocals, capped with a helmet of neatly trimmed, graying curls. He was a lot jollier than you'd expect from someone in his job or boxing class, though that was probably because he made middle management enforce all his budget cuts. Despite his usually pleasant demeanor, he knew how to command attention. Everyone in the boardroom fell absolutely silent as he calmly took the only vacant seat, at the head of the table.

"It seems we have a miracle on our hands."

All the shuffling stopped.

"Antonio Rodríguez tells me that parthenogenesis prevents Komodo dragons from giving birth to female offspring. This fact leads us to some logical conclusions." He ticked the possibilities off on slight, gnarled fingers. "The Komodo did not reproduce parthenogenically." One finger. "The hatchlings are not female." Two fingers. He paused on the third fingertip, as if inspecting the nail for cracks. "What we know as scientific fact is not true. The science is wrong."

Gerald looked from face to face around the room. "Ladies and gentlemen, we are the Zoo of America, and we are committed to discovering the truth. We will not rest until the mystery has been explained. It is our privilege and duty to let the world know what has happened within our walls."

A murmur tunneled through the bodies.

"Well, I should say," Gerald acknowledged with a tiny smile, "that it is our duty to more fully explain what Ms. Yancy announced on Friday night. Is she here, by chance?"

Meg pushed a hand into the air. "Yeah."

Leaning forward, Gerald followed the hand and voice to pick Meg out of the crowd. "I can barely see you."

"That's fine," Meg said, and the entire room laughed.

"Ms. Yancy, come to the front, please."

If she was getting fired, it better not be in front of this suit-and-tie crowd. She pushed her way to the front with whispers of "Ow" and "Hey!" following her.

Out in the open now, she lifted an eyebrow at Gerald in silent invitation.

"You haven't done much public speaking before, I take it?"

She shook her head. Her nails bit into the flesh of her biceps.

"Let's keep it that way." He didn't laugh with the rest of the crowd but looked her over with a quiet amusement that wasn't quite condescending, wasn't quite hostile. It was the same look that crossed the older faces in front of the howler monkey exhibit. Hey, look at that one. Isn't that one funny?

She sighed and tried to relax in the shadow of apparent safety, but who knew when the spotlight would return? Channel 12 hadn't aired anything about the reception yet, but the longer they waited, the more nervous she got.

"Now, let's briefly outline the parameters of our three possibilities." Gerald steepled his fingertips together and nodded at Antonio, who stood up and cleared his throat.

"Right. Well, my team and I have been researching all weekend, but nothing has broken loose yet. As for the first possibility—that the adult Komodo did not reproduce parthenogenically—we have to consider the idea of long-term sperm storage."

"Can that happen?" someone asked.

Antonio nodded. "It's been recorded in other reptile species during periods of drought or lack of available mates."

"Jata hasn't been exposed to a male Komodo since she was brought here five years ago." Meg didn't realize she'd spoken out loud until all the heads in the room cranked in her direction.

Antonio glanced at her and then at his notes. "Yes, but she would have been exposed to males in the community environment where she spent the first year of her life—the Wildlife Refuge in Jakarta."

Meg dropped her eyes to the table, not quite ready to look at him yet, but she couldn't let it go either. "She was sexually immature then. As a juvenile, she wouldn't have been selected for mating."

"You can't assume that."

"But it's ridiculous. Any interest a male would have shown in her at that stage in her life would have been as an afternoon snack."

"Ms. Yancy," Gerald interrupted. "We can't assume anything at this point in our research. We need to pool our collective expertise and examine all possibilities—no matter how preposterous they seem."

"Okay. Yes." Meg rolled her shoulders and repositioned herself closer to the table. "If she was capable of mating with a male five years ago, then we need to prove that Komodo sperm can survive for five years without fertilizing anything. Do you have a test set up for that, Dr. Rodríguez?"

"Of course not." He smiled at her as the room laughed again, but when he spoke, he spoke to Gerald. "There are other, equally as likely possibilities that we should examine first. My team is interested in scenarios such as amphibian DNA recombination or the possibility that the adult is a hermaphrodite."

"Don't forget about Mr. Dawson's second point," Meg interrupted. "The hatchlings might not be female."

Antonio nodded, and it was as if there were diagrams running through his head, strategies for dividing and conquering this phenomenon. It was the doctor in him. He discovered a condition and eliminated possibilities one by one until he could diagnose the problem. This was just another disease. "We're running a third set of blood tests on all three hatchling dragons and have also started blood tests on the mother."

Meg blinked. "When did you get Jata's blood sample?"

Where the hell had she been when this happened? She realized she was holding her breath and let it out slowly, deliberately, narrowing her eyes on Antonio.

"Yesterday."

"As her primary keeper, I should have been consulted."

"I e-mailed you on Saturday." His tone was professional, but there was a slight gleam growing around the edges of his eyes now. He knew damn well she never checked her e-mail.

"Let's back up for a second," Gerald interjected in a mild tone.

"For the benefit of everyone in the room, including myself, let's review the basics here. Antonio, these tests are looking for certain alleles in the DNA?"

"That's correct. Unlike humans, Komodo dragon males have identical ZZ chromosomes, and the females have ZW. So when the female clones her DNA in parthenogenesis, the only possible results are ZZ and WW."

The faces around the boardroom, with the exception of the vet interns, looked blank. Meg shook her head. "Here. I'll draw it out." She retracted the overhead projector screen behind Gerald Dawson's chair, and it hit the ceiling with a metallic crash, revealing a clean whiteboard. With a marker, she sketched the basic equations that were now scrawled over most of the surfaces in her apartment—from magazine covers to toilet paper, all staring back at her from nooks and crannies like crib notes from the edge of sanity.

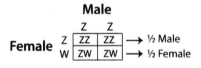

"What does the third scenario represent?" Gerald asked, shifting his chair toward the whiteboard.

"This is the possibility of DNA recombination, as I suggested earlier." Antonio walked around Gerald's chair and tapped the third equation. His knuckles sounded hollow on the board as he tagged her with an inviting look, letting her know it was her turn to say something, but her throat constricted, choking off anything she really wanted to say to him. Why hadn't he talked to her before containing Jata and drawing a blood sample? Who the hell was on this team he kept mentioning, and how could they know a fraction of what she did about Komodo dragons? Torn between the need to know and the shame of asking, she just shook her head. When she remained silent, Antonio took up the lecture again, addressing the room at large.

"We know that frogs are capable of gene switching in order to reproduce asexually during times of environmental stress. There's a species of whiptail lizard that is completely female, reproducing by cloning themselves. Given that our knowledge of Komodo dragons is so limited, it's possible that they may be capable of these same techniques."

"How can you say that our knowledge is limited?" Meg found her voice again. "I've read every study ever published. I regularly communicate with the Jakarta refuge."

"Collectively, Ms. Yancy." The name, from Antonio, was like cold water in her face. He didn't even turn away from the boardroom at large as he said it, squaring up beneath his lab coat in an easy, dismissive move.

"We have only known of the species' existence for less than one hundred years. They survived for millions of years in complete isolation from humans, thriving in their niche environment largely unchanged from the varanoids that appeared in the late Cretaceous period. They are living fossils, and if this aberration—for lack of a better word—can teach us anything, it is how little we truly understand about the Komodo dragon."

He sounded like a freaking textbook. Meg tried to find Gemma in the crowd, but taller people stood between her and the bay window where she'd left her.

"What do you recommend as our path forward, Antonio?" Gerald asked.

"Our best resource opportunity is Dr. Joyce Reading, the evolutionary biologist who I'm sure needs no introduction in this room. I've briefed her on the situation, and she has agreed to fly in tonight to lead our research efforts. There will be no cost to the zoo. She will work with us in exchange for non-exclusive publishing rights on the Komodo aberration."

"And what about our statement to the press?" the PR director, a suit sitting on Gerald's right side, asked Antonio. "Despite Ms. Yancy's unfortunate outburst the other night, we need to make a more cohesive and uniform statement."

"I would like to make a very short statement today and wait until Dr. Reading arrives for a full press conference." He had an answer for everything.

Bringing out a stack of glossy folders, Antonio passed them around the room. He held one out to Meg, and she hesitated, as if taking it would accept something about him that everything inside of her wanted to spit on. She understood in that second what had put that horrible pain on Ben's face last night, and it wasn't the unfaithfulness—it was the deception. Despite all their differences, she and Ben had always been honest people—honest about who they were and what they expected from each other. But she'd let him think that she was a better person, someone who wouldn't cheat on him, and now, after destroying every good thing he'd seen in her, here she was on public display with the man she'd cheated with, watching him turn into someone else, too.

Antonio must have seen her hesitation in accepting the folder because for the first time during the meeting, a shadow passed over his features, just the briefest flicker of the distraught Antonio she'd found at the reception, and that tiny glimpse moved her hand toward him to take the folder. Before she could say anything, though, he turned away, slipping back into the corporate persona that fit him so flawlessly.

As she flipped through the folder, it became obvious why he hadn't returned her calls or asked her in person about Jata's blood sample. The thing was full of easily digestible sound bites, bright charts, and pictures. He'd been too busy keeping the print shop running, and all of this was just step one—a bullet point even—in his plan to diagnose the disease.

The PR director, as well as most of the other people in the room, pored over the folders and discussed the best marketing techniques, ways to stretch the Komodo aberration—Antonio's term had immediately caught on in the meeting that they should also have renamed The Launch of the Miracle—into the highest possible return. It was impossible to follow their conversation; they were thinking out loud in that corporate, predatory language that swept over the entire room like a feeding frenzy.

"I'll allow today's statement then, as long as Ms. Yancy is not the speaker," Gerald Dawson was saying with a small nod, and again laughter rippled through the room.

Meg ignored it, ignored all of them, and squeezed the folder tightly against her torso as if she could strangle the threat out of it, when she knew the opposite was true. She couldn't even touch the whirlwind that was forming. She was the useless jerk who could only watch as their collective minds grouped up like a hunting pack, circling closer and closer to Jata.

Ben was gone when she got home that night. She'd sped through rush hour and run a stoplight to make sure she arrived in time for the six o'clock news, but now that she was here, she couldn't turn the TV on. Flipping a lamp on in the living room, she sat on the couch and stared at the dark and dusty screen. An open bag of potato chips faced Antonio's press release folder on the coffee table, and she didn't have the heart to touch either one. It was 5:52 p.m. Cold—funny how dread made you cold. She hugged herself and bent over her knees. Ben's news notebooks were piled on the floor by the opposite side of the couch, unopened. She picked up the one on top and turned to the first page.

This notebook covered the warring political factions in one of the Baltic states, threatening to split the country in two. She flipped through pages all marked by date and source. Some stations concentrated on the top players in the struggle. Others, she read, focused on the common people and what it would mean to them if their country were torn in half. On the bottom corner of each page, Ben had written in which party that news source was siding with. All of them, it seemed, came down on one side or another. That was the classic thing he always looked for—how the reporter skewed the story by taking sides or selectively editing facts. Maybe it was impossible for them not to, she thought as she sifted through the pages. Would there even be a story if it didn't lean to one side or the other? Humans saw good guys and bad guys no matter what they were looking at, unless they just didn't care. And that was the rub; it was impossible not to care about Jata, and that made the hatchlings prime news.

It was now 5:58 p.m. She swallowed hard, turned on the TV, and switched it to Channel 12. The room felt wrong without Ben there— hollow. How many hundreds of nights had they sat there together, comfortable to the point of lazy in their routine? Ben watched the news while she read *National Geographic,* and they ate dinner and talked about the zoo or whatever story was making headlines.

Sometimes on frigid January nights, she tucked her feet into his lap, and he would call her cold-blooded and laugh, but her legs warmed up in no time—he was like a great big electric blanket. She shouldn't even be watching the news without him. It felt more like cheating now than it ever had when she was sleeping with Antonio. Carefully, she placed the notebook back on top of the pile, brushed a piece of hair off the cover, and slid to the far side of the couch, as far as possible from the empty cushion where Ben should have been sitting.

"Good evening, and welcome to the six o'clock news. Tonight we'll talk to the police officer who arrested the man suspected of committing Saturday's South Side shootings and hear about the latest research in the fight against cancer, but first, Nicole Roberts brings us our top story tonight—a bizarre birth at Bloomington's Zoo of America."

The screen cut from the anchor to Nicole Roberts, who stood in front of the zoo's main entrance. The huge Zoo of America sign, a Godzilla-sized version of the logo on the back of Meg's uniform, glowed in spotlights behind Nicole's head, even though the sun was still well above the horizon. The last visitors streamed out of the gates and waved to the camera as they disappeared on their way to the parking lot or light rail station.

"Thank you, Don." Snug in her camel-colored coat, Nicole nodded. "The Zoo of America hosted a party last Friday night to celebrate the birth of three Komodo dragons, but the festivities abruptly ended with news that was confusing to some and outright shocking to others."

A clip from the reception jumped on-screen, and Meg sucked in a breath when the camera zoomed in to her own face, pale as paper, behind the stage podium. "They're girls. The dragons are female."

Nicole continued, confirming the birth as impossible and reading the published blurb that the zoo sent out earlier today. One of Antonio's charts flashed up on the screen, then photo stills of other Komodos.

"There have been a few other cases of parthenogenesis in the Komodo dragon population of the world's zoos, but as the Zoo of America explained, these were all male dragons born to an unfertilized female. Parthenogenesis is a mouthful, but it comes from the Greek words *parthenos*, which means chaste or virgin, and *genesis*, which of course means origin or creation. And that is exactly what the Zoo of America believed this to be eight months ago—a virgin birth. I interviewed the woman on stage about this very idea when the zoo originally announced the discovery of the Komodo eggs last August."

Meg appeared back on-screen, this time standing in front of Jata's exhibit, arms crossed, looking hostile and defending Jata all over again. "We have no documentation on Mary's sexual status, and Jata has done a lot more work to reproduce."

The sound bite was even worse than she remembered. It went on and on, the disaster replaying itself, reborn with twice the strength.

"Unfortunately, this zookeeper, Meg Yancy, was less willing to talk to us since the announcement last Friday."

The screen jumped to Meg at the reception again, except this time she was waving a huge angry hand in front of the lens. "This is none of your business."

"We're invited guests here," the off-camera reporter claimed as Meg glared into the frame.

"I didn't invite you."

In the living room, Meg buried her face into the side of the couch, but she could still hear, through the couch cushions, Nicole's distorted voice wrapping up the segment.

"Now it seems that Ms. Yancy was a little quick to judge. We have to consider, for lack of any other explanation, whether there might be divine forces at work here after all. Back to you, Don."

After they transitioned to the next story, Meg leaned over and picked up the press release folder. The exact words that Nicole had read were right there in black and white, just as Antonio had written them down. He'd planned it all out, exactly the way the story should air, but there was nothing in the folder to prepare for this. Nicole had taken each carefully phrased blurb and chart and hacked them up—piecing them all back together with that damning footage into a story that made Meg look like the worst keeper in the world. Nicole hadn't aired a story about Jata or the hatchlings at all; she'd leveled a direct attack on Meg.

Meg had no idea how to fight back, how to defend her comments or her name. She could count the number of people who would listen to her on one hand, while Nicole Roberts had the entire Twin Cities as her ready audience. Meg didn't know anything about dealing with the media. The person she needed right now, she realized with a sinking hopelessness, was Ben.

She should've gotten up to eat something, but the thought of food made her nauseous. Gemma called, having seen the story, too, but there was nothing to say after the initial confirmations. Meg sat on the couch for an hour, staring at the wall while the TV droned through programs, before dragging herself to the bedroom and passing out, exhausted.

～૭

Jata walked to her, hunger flexing in each lumbering step. Meg looked down, around the dirt floor, on top of the rocks, but the feed bucket was missing. Jata drew closer, breathing heavily. Hissing coated the underside of her tongue as she licked the air, and Meg felt it, as if she were the air circling Jata's jaws, being hit with stabs of forked, demanding flesh.

Food. Jata must eat.

Ben and Antonio stood behind her, and she picked up the feeding hook and pierced Ben's palm, ripping through his skin. His hand tore apart into bones and blood, and she knelt down to collect the pieces to feed them to Jata. They disappeared as fast as she could offer them: fingers, wrist, tendons, hairy skin. She moved to Antonio, stabbed the hook into his armpit, and tore his whole arm from his body. The blood pooled at her feet, rushing over her toes and swallowing her ankles, but when she looked down it was blue, a wide river that grew and grew. Jata nudged her, still hungry, and Meg snapped off her own fingers like happy firecrackers—relieved when each one popped and broke free—and fed them to her as the water rushed over them, sweeping them both downstream and out into the ocean. Jata submerged and was gone, her feet tucking into her sides and tail pumping steadily down into the depths of the water. Meg tried to follow, but she couldn't move and, looking behind her, she saw the stump of a tail growing out of her own back—severed and useless.

She woke up in a twist of wet sheets and blinked at the black, pre-dawn ceiling. Slowly, the white noise of the ocean receded until she could hear her heartbeat again, thumping out of her ears into the sweat drying cold on her pillow. Today was Tuesday, the day she fed Jata.

24 Days *after* Hatching

When Meg punched in for her shift the next morning, a crowd of keepers and cleaning staff huddled around the last computer terminal in the cage. Desmond, driving the show, peeked out from between hips and badges and called her over to check out an Internet site.

"Isn't anyone working today?" Meg muttered as she shouldered her way to the front of the group through thumps on her back and lots of comments: "Good job." "Nice work out there, ace." "Have you applied for PR yet?"

The site was hosted by the Cooperative for Christian Consumer Rights, or CCCR to their friends and pamphlet makers, a consumer watchdog group that had banned the Zoo of America at six o'clock that morning in protest of the virgin birth. An e-mail titled "Boycott the Serpent Abomination" had been sent to more than a million subscribers across the country.

Cyber thumpers, Desmond called them. They weren't part of any church, and they didn't have a leader or even a PO box. They were self-appointed keepers, making sure that their people didn't give a single American dollar to any business they felt, for whatever reason, didn't honor their beliefs. General Motors alone had lost 5 percent of its annual revenue when CCCR had decided a few years back that the Saturn was too gay-friendly in its ad campaigns. Apparently gay people were only allowed to walk or bicycle their way straight to hell. Somehow the CCCR caught wind of the Nicole Roberts broadcast with her hint at divine intervention, and their messengers tripped all over themselves to deliver it personally.

"The serpent abomination?" Meg asked.

Abominations, according to Desmond's elementary Catholic-school glossary, were like the anti-miracle, signaling the apocalypse and "all that jazz."

"It's like, to them, Jata is the serpent, the devil's messenger, you know, and you're the serpent's master." Desmond was straddling his computer chair backward and clearly loving the attention. All those starting their shifts had read the article already and were slowly donning boots, checking SAMs, all quieted down for the free show.

Meg took a big gulp of coffee, even though there wasn't enough caffeine in the entire cafeteria for this day, and wiped her mouth with a sleeve. "So I'm the devil?"

Gemma snickered from the next computer terminal.

"No, you're probably like a messenger, too. There're a lot of people in the apocalypse. Four horsemen and all sorts of angels and demons." He grinned. "It's like now you're a bitch with a higher purpose."

The laughter and remarks followed her all morning, so she switched off her radio and stayed off the main walking paths. Her coworkers weren't the real problem, though. It was the alpha males she worried about. Management should have been too preoccupied with how Jata had given birth to girls to worry about a little angst from the CCCR, but she doubted it. What good was a miracle if it hurt their revenues?

Standing outside of Jata's new exhibit door, the pungent smell of meat wafted up and made her stomach roll. She breathed through her mouth and waited for the nausea to pass, forcing herself to concentrate on the few things that mattered right now. She wasn't like Ben. She wasn't. She didn't get so overwhelmed by the sheer number of messed-up things in this world that she stopped trying. She didn't sit on her ass and do nothing just because she couldn't fix everything. She just had to focus. In a couple of minutes it would be time to feed Jata, and everything would break down to the bucket of pork sitting next to her in the hallway, the feeding hook propped against the door, and Jata's mouth. These things were all she needed to know. They had substance and texture, coming together in a basic dance for survival. Everything else had to disappear.

Gemma, who was slated to assist today, appeared at the end of the hallway and moseyed toward her. "Quite the little sideshow we've stirred up. Desmond printed the website out and posted it on the cage bulletin board with a sign that says 'Homo sapiens in constipated state.'"

"Desmond did that?"

"Well, I might have asked him to. The general sends her troops into battle so she can live to fight another day."

Gemma's mere presence made things better, chiller, and reproportioned. Meg wiped the clammy sweat from her forehead and slapped Gemma affectionately on the arm. It was time to feed.

They suited up and entered the brand-new exhibit. Glass surrounded them on all sides and above, making the space feel like the outdoors when the environment was actually completely controlled.

Meg had let Jata out here for the first time yesterday, holding her breath from the anxiety. New exhibits didn't always open smoothly around here. When the Amazon fish tank had opened, half the species died in the first two weeks because of pH problems in the water. Last winter, when they'd introduced a new lion to the pride, the poor thing had been chased and beaten to a pulp for ages, and of course everyone remembered the birds. Luckily Jata seemed completely at home so far. She was sprawling on a basking rock when Meg and Gemma entered the enclosure, and there were already dig marks in the back patch of dirt where she must have thought about burrowing.

Jata's head swiveled around, and she stood up swiftly, delighting the visitors that stood shoulder to shoulder on the walkway. The crowd was massive today, sparked by either the announcement of the hatchlings' gender or the protestors or both. Camera flashes exploded on the glass as Meg walked quickly to the feeding platform and speared a piece of pork to place on the top of the rock slope. This was the first feeding in the new exhibit, and she wanted to get Jata in position as quickly and smoothly as possible.

Jata swaggered toward her. She looked younger in the natural light; her thick torso seemed greener and more agile out here in the freshly planted grasses. Scales glistening in the sun's rays, Jata reached the base of the rock with one foot up and her claws digging into its surface. Her tongue flickered at the meat, and her head bobbed once, twice—but then, without warning, she stopped.

Meg's breath caught in her throat as Jata lowered her head and arched her neck, the skin beneath her lower jaw puffing out until all the folds of muscle and cartilage were distended.

It was a threat display. Jata was threatening her.

Meg swallowed and held her ground, watching the yellow fork of Jata's tongue work madly in and out of her mouth. There were twenty long feet of exhibit space between her back and Gemma, who stood guard by the door.

"Jata, chow time. Jata, Jata." Meg called the name low and steady, letting her voice wash over Jata's stiff spine and down the curving brunt of her tail. The unfamiliar exhibit was throwing her off—that was all—or it could have been Antonio and his veterinary lackeys who had taken her blood on Sunday and made her defensive. Meg heard Gemma rustling behind her and held her off with a slight shake of her head. They just had to work through this together, she and Jata, give themselves enough time and space to relax and forget about all the craziness.

"Come on, girl. That's it, Jata." The folds in Jata's neck reappeared as her skin slowly, painstakingly deflated. Her head bobbed again as she started to climb the rock, and her throat relaxed into the upward bend of an appeasement display.

"Chow time."

Jata reached the top, scooped up the hunk of pork, and threw her head back, letting a stream of drool fall out of the corner of her jaws. Vaguely, Meg sensed the rumbling of the crowd amid the bursts of light from cameras and fluctuating bodies as she speared another piece of meat and prepared to offer it to Jata. They thought this was the dangerous part. They didn't see that the danger had passed, how it had broken down and died right before their eyes.

~೨

"You have to log it." Gemma unsuited in the hallway and hung her body shield up in the closet next to the emergency box that housed the gun.

Meg stared at the case, shaking her head. "There's nothing to report."

"That was high stress and aggression. I saw it, Meg. Maybe I haven't studied every last piece of Komodo behavior ever published, but give me some credit here."

They walked down the hallway to the back side of the iguana exhibit, where Gemma dug out a feed bag from the cupboard and mixed the pellets into a bowl of fresh vegetables.

"She was just nervous in the new environment. It passed as

quickly as it came."

"Okay, hang on while I feed Ralph and Alicia, and then you can play animal psychologist some more for me." Gemma ducked into the iguana exhibit, and Meg kicked the door shut behind her.

She paced the hall until Gemma reappeared with some dead palm leaves in tow and threw them in the trash. Crossing her arms, Meg looked away. "Is there more debris out there? You want a hand?"

"No, I want you to go log the behavior. That's what we do. We don't rationalize or humanize. We do our job and log the behavior."

They walked to the next exhibit, and Meg glanced through the window to check the python's position. The ten-foot snake was named Bertha, and she was coiled up along the public side of the tank. The gloss of scale and muscle lay still, and it took a minute for Meg to follow the coils up to Bertha's head before she could give Gemma the all-clear to drop the rat carrion into the tank. When the rat hit the floor, Bertha didn't move.

What was it that made serpents the messengers of the devil? A whale could do God's bidding, but somehow pythons and Komodos were destined to be evil. The few Sunday school lessons Meg had endured were fuzzy at best. There was the snake in the garden with Adam and Eve, but she'd never understood that part. Snakes kept the vermin out.

"Meg, you're going to log the aggression, aren't you?"

She turned away from Gemma. "Of course I will."

∽

There was no way to trust written records because they could betray Jata so easily. Look at Ben's reporters or even Nicole Roberts, how they twisted words into anything they wanted. It was her job to log the aggression at the feeding, sure, but Jata had just become the hottest thing since SAMs around here. She might have to dodge the bullets, but hell if she was going to start passing out free ammo.

The only other person who went into the exhibit without her was Antonio, so he was the only one who really needed to be informed to mitigate the danger. And with today's SAM report hot in her hand, she was on her way to personally report the behavior, or something like it, to the head veterinarian himself. She just had to do it quickly—all business—then get out.

There was no answer to her knock on Antonio's office door, but she could hear his muffled voice, so, taking a deep breath, she pushed her way inside.

He wasn't talking on the phone; he was standing over his computer, and in his chair sat a thin, long-faced woman with a gnarled gray bun and heavy-lidded hawk eyes. A visitor badge was snapped to her tiger-print tunic, but Meg didn't need to read it to know who she was. As one, the two of them looked from the computer screen to Meg.

"Meg, I'm glad you stopped by. This is Dr. Joyce Reading, my professor and mentor." Antonio waved a hand between the two women. "Joyce, this is Meg Yancy, the primary keeper for the Komodo."

She avoided his eyes. "I thought you were a vet, Rodríguez, not an evolutionary biologist."

"I was lucky enough to study with Dr. Reading during an undergrad internship. A small group of us tracked the mating patterns of wildebeests across the West African savannah that year."

"Those were the worst horses I've ever ridden," Dr. Reading interjected, making Antonio laugh. She turned to Meg. "Halfway through the trip our jeep broke down, and I had the brilliant idea of renting horses from a local ranch."

"Horses would have helped us get closer to the wildebeests without all the disruptive jeep noise." Antonio was quick to defend her.

"Yes, that was the working theory, but the horses were barely broke. One of them threw that poor girl from Texas into the water, remember, and we had to distract a crocodile until she could climb out? The rest of us were all fighting with the reins and getting brushed off on scrub trees. Antonio was the only one who actually looked in control of his mount."

"What year was that again?" he asked.

"Don't remind me." Dr. Reading laughed, a trim ruffle of sound that was more like a punctuation mark than actual humor, and she held out a small, calloused hand to Meg. "Please excuse the reminiscing. I haven't seen Antonio in years, although we've kept in touch. I've discovered all sorts of fascinating stories about you, Ms. Yancy. Both spoken and in print."

"Hi." Meg shook the hand lightly, taking stock of the legend.

Dr. Reading could have been fifty or seventy. She had that skin-turning-to-hide look of someone who spent more of her life outdoors than in, and yet she couldn't have seemed more comfortable taking over Antonio's office than if she'd propped her feet up on the desk. Of course Meg had read her work. Everyone in freshman zoology studied the field papers of Dr. Joyce Reading; she was one of those iconic researchers that people tripped over themselves trying to describe with enough superlatives.

"I assume you're here for Antonio, Ms. Yancy?" Dr. Reading returned her attention to the computer. There was something about the way she said *Antonio*, a familiarity sliding through the vowels, that made the hair stand up on the back of Meg's neck.

"I wanted to inform him that—" She glanced down at the report. "I just wanted to say that I did the weekly feeding for Jata today, and she seemed to show some signs of elevated stress."

She shoved the SAM report across the desk to Antonio and

tucked her forearms into her rib cage. He seemed oblivious to everything in the room except Dr. Reading.

"I'm sure it's a result of the new exhibit environment or maybe the veterinary team"—Meg paused on the words, trying to glare at him and hide it at the same time—"that contained her on Sunday without my supervision."

"Look at that adrenaline spike." Antonio set the paper in front of Dr. Reading and launched into a huge explanation about the different SAM charts and how, for each animal, they deciphered the target ranges for serotonin and adrenaline. Meg gritted her teeth when he got to the SAMs' statistical analysis capabilities and then something she'd never heard him talk about before: an Automated Behavior Indicator.

After the mini-lecture, he looked back up at her, completely ignoring her tight, angry posture. "This spike couldn't be due to an unchanging environment. This is an adrenal event. Was this when you were in the exhibit?"

She nodded and refocused. "I entered the exhibit at one o'clock, so yes, I was in there. The event, I think, happened because someone hit the glass."

The lie slid so easily off her tongue, coated in a delicious reasonability.

"There was a huge crowd today, bigger than I've ever seen, even bigger than when the parth was announced, and right as I came outside someone hit the glass. A real loud crack. The noise made her stop right before climbing the feeding rock, but I talked her through it, and she climbed up and ate just like normal. All in all, I think it was a good feeding for our first time in the new exhibit space."

"Excuse me, Ms. Yancy, did you say you talked a Komodo dragon out of a stress reaction?" Dr. Reading pierced her with those hawk eyes, and her sandpaper voice bounced off the diplomas and framed articles on the walls.

Meg faltered under her speculative gaze. They were the same eyes that had first noticed how bonobo feeding patterns anticipated drought seasons and had observed the territorial dance displays among snowy owls. It actually took a minute for Meg to shrug and swallow. "Yeah. I've been the primary keeper for this Komodo since she was one year old, and we've established a relationship."

"A relationship?" A thin eyebrow arched.

"A recognition pattern." The old college jargon snapped back into place. "The Komodo has responded well to the environment I've designed and has shown a huge aptitude for non-aggressive interaction with familiar humans, specifically me."

"Until today." Dr. Reading dropped her gaze to the SAM report.

"This was extremely rare, and brought on by the foreign noise. She recovered very quickly, which was why I wanted to report the behavior to Antonio—I mean Dr. Rodríguez—to discuss how well she was doing in the new exhibit." Meg groped backward for the door, trying to escape those eyes. The temperature of the office had gone up at least five degrees since she got here. A ten-by-ten box just wasn't big enough for three people.

"There you are." Chuck stepped into the doorway and practically bowed toward Antonio and Dr. Reading. "I hope your accommodations here are satisfactory, Dr. Reading."

"Excellent. Thank you, Mr. Farrelly," Dr. Reading said, in the same tone people used to dismiss waiters.

"Megan, a word." Chuck nodded, backed out of the office, and stalked down the hallway toward the cage. If there was any other way out of the vet area she would have run for it, but this Wonderland only came with one rabbit hole. Muttering good-bye to no one in particular, she caught up with Chuck at the double doors, where he shoved a piece of paper into her hand. His usual albino complexion was steaming toward red, and a vein pulsed through his fleshy forehead.

"What's this?"

"The official notice of your partial suspension."

"What did I do?" She threw her hands into the air, crunching the notice.

"Do you really need to ask that? After the CCCR boycott?"

"Chuck, that's not my fault. They're boycotting us because Jata's babies are female. Tell me how I could have possibly caused that."

He moved in closer than she thought his comfort zone would allow, leaning over her, squashing all the denials and arguments dead in her throat. His eyes were wide and surrounded by dark, bloated sockets—the cement-weighted stare of a sleepless night. "I saw the Channel 12 story. In fact, everyone on the management team watched it together in the boardroom again this morning. As of today"—his voice went flat—"you are no longer to talk to any media, PR, or public liaisons of any kind. You are done leading tour groups. You will not answer any e-mails that are sent from outside this institution. You will work with the animals and no one else. Do you understand the parameters of your suspension?"

It should have made her gleeful. He'd revoked almost everything she hated about this job in one giant sweep, but instead of celebrating she felt cold, icy cold, and when he spoke again, his voice was coated with an angry frustration that turned her chest inside out.

"Management is overwhelmed by this ... aberration. They don't know what step to take next, but it's their step to take, not yours. Do you understand that? They own the animal. This suspension is coming from the board, Megan, not me. If you make another wrong move, or jeopardize the Zoo of America's reputation in any way, my hands will be tied. They'll terminate you."

27 Days *after* Hatching

It was barely a week after the reception, and everyone had cut Meg out. She was like the asshole at the party who chased everyone away from the punch bowl. Antonio buried himself in the vet lab with Dr. Reading, and all the other staff seemed too intimidated by the doctor to question anything either one of them demanded. When Meg asked an intern why he was ordering 2,000 cc's of frog plasma, all she got in reply was, "It's for Dr. Reading." Dr. Reading had become the great Because, the new SAMs, the only thing anyone needed to say on their purchase order. Chuck shut Meg up every time she asked him anything, Gerald Dawson lived inside closed-door boardrooms, and even Gemma had acted icy around her since the other day when she'd asked Meg about Jata's log again and Meg hadn't given Gemma a straight answer.

The only person in the world who did want to talk to her was Nicole Roberts. She'd been waiting at the entrance with her camera guy today, both of them ready to swarm as soon as Meg punched out.

"Ms. Yancy, do you have a minute?" The two of them chased her heels.

She wanted to rip the microphone out of Nicole's hand and stuff it in her mouth, but Chuck's warning pounded in her head. Checking behind her, she saw the cashiers staring and pointing at them.

"Ms. Yancy, over one million Americans belong to the CCCR. Can you confirm if there's been a drop in attendance over the last few days because of their boycott of the zoo?"

Meg ducked under the gate into the employee parking lot, but Nicole followed her all the way to her car, firing questions at her back. As Meg turned to open the car door, Nicole took the opportunity to shove the microphone in her face as the cameraman stood right behind her. Meg didn't even know what Nicole's last question had been.

"No comment." She smiled sweetly and stepped down hard on one of Nicole's high heels before getting into her car, but the whole way home she was torn between satisfaction and the dread that somehow management would find out what she'd just done.

As she pulled into the driveway after work, she saw Ben's pickup backed up to the kitchen door and piled high with boxes and garbage bags—Ben's signature luggage set. She hadn't seen him since their fight five days ago. As she walked through the house, it became obvious that all his things were gone. His bedroom dresser drawers were open and empty. The hallway closet was cleaned out of everything except her stacks of *National Geographic*s, and a break in the dust on the back of the toilet was the only trace of his shaving kit. He always left. That wasn't news. Every winter he drifted in and out of the house, but she could still follow the trail of his life: an empty cereal bowl in the kitchen sink, a half-smoked cigarette in the ashtray on the porch, a picture sent to her cell phone of a snowman holding a beer in its tangled branch hands. His territory wandered around the perimeter of hers in a comfortable, piss-marking familiarity, until the spring when he packed up and disappeared as if their relationship were just something he hibernated inside. She always knew he would leave, but then she always knew he would come back, too. And now ... now there would be no coming back.

Circling into the living room, she found him on the couch chucking his news notebooks one by one into a garbage bag.

"You're leaving." It wasn't a question.

He didn't glance up but nodded tightly.

A few minutes passed, and there was nothing to do but watch him pack, each notebook hitting the last with an angry plastic hiss of the bag. The silence stretched out. Ben was the one who filled the silences, not her, whether he was explaining the latest in-depth coverage of a breaking story or finding out what she wanted for dinner or telling her who Paco had pissed off lately. Even when she was only half-listening, he still talked. But that was before, when he thought she was someone worth talking to.

"I have some crates you could put those in. They'll get all mixed up like that."

He kept tossing notebooks.

"I'll go get them."

"Don't." He spit out the word. "These aren't coming. They're trash."

"What?"

He finally looked up at her, and the echo of their last conversation haunted the air between them, the crashes of his boot against the couch, his voice bellowing, *Why are you fucking him?* They both froze, as though the last five days apart had never happened. When he finally spoke, his voice was harsh and low.

"The notebooks are pointless. I never did anything with them. Isn't that what you always said?"

"Yes, but—" Watching him destroy all his research, all the carefully constructed files on which he'd spent so much time and passion, broke her heart. Ten months or even ten minutes ago, she'd have said they were a waste of space with no hope for anything to come of them, but suddenly she desperately wanted him to keep them going. "I was wrong. Your thesis. You need them for your manifesto."

"Don't patronize me."

"I'm not. I mean it." She came around the couch and scooped up the folders he hadn't gotten to yet. "Don't throw them all away now, after everything you've written."

"So let me get this straight." He stood up, glaring. "You're the one who wanted these notebooks in the garbage for years. Whether you said it or not, I knew, okay? And now that I'm finally agreeing and doing exactly what you wanted in the first place, I'm the asshole?"

"No—"

He grabbed the last of the notebooks out of her hands, shoved them into the bag, and walked out of the living room. "Even when I'm on the road, they always remind me of your place—sitting around the TV together while we both did our research. I can't stand the sight of them anymore."

"Don't do this because of me." She ran after him as he left the house and crossed to the garbage cans on the far side of the garage. The recent rain had turned the ground around the cans into a muddy mess, and she slipped, unsteady, pulling on his arm. "Ben, please. You'll regret this. Someday you'll wish you'd kept them. I know you will."

"Forget it, Meg. You're going to get exactly what you want, and you're not going to make me the bad guy for it this time, all right?" He pulled the cover off the garbage, rearing back and jerking out of her grip at the same time. It wasn't a punch, but the effect was the same. She flew backward and lost her balance, hitting the mud with a bruising splat. He didn't even look over.

"I always did everything you wanted, you know? You never wanted people over here, so I never had parties. You were obsessed with those animals, so I started collecting all those stories for you." Ben shoved the bag of notebooks into the can and crashed the cover back down. "You needed someone to blame, someone to be your designated whipping boy. Well, guess who that was."

The weight of his words pressed her further and further down. Everything sank into the wet ground—her shoes, her hands, her hips—as if the mud had no bottom, as if she could keep sinking forever. He was right, everything he was saying. She'd blamed him completely for the reception, refusing to accept any responsibility for what happened. She'd thought that he was the one who didn't care enough about her. She'd hated him because he supported her most terrible decisions.

After a long silence, she hitched in a breath and choked on it. He sighed and offered her a hand up, but she shook her head. Here, where everything had turned to cold mud and shadows, there were things that had to be said.

"You were easy to blame."

The words were choppy, but she forced them out.

"It was so much simpler to be angry with you than admit … everything. That I could never make things right, not between us, or for Jata, or … the baby. That guy—he was just so excited about the hatchlings. I never thought anyone could want them as much as I did and … it was terrible what I did to you. I'm sorry."

He mumbled something that sounded like *yeah*, and then there was silence, the kind where nothing comes afterward, as when she'd stood at her mother's grave or raked into the sick crunch of a hidden egg—the moments that shatter a person into something else.

After a minute, he sighed and shuffled back into the house, coming back out with the last of his bags. Before climbing into the pickup, he stared at her across the yard. She hadn't moved from the ground next to the garbage. She lifted a hand—cold and invisible in the black silhouette of the building—and watched Ben leave.

30 Days *after* Hatching

L adies and gentlemen of the press, thank you for coming on such short notice. I sincerely apologize for the weather."

The woman had been here less than a week and was closeted away with Antonio in that laboratory love nest most of the time, but Meg had still managed to learn a few things about Dr. Reading. Fact one: She liked to remind people how old she was. Like at this press conference, standing behind the podium in her Asian tunic with her stone-gray hair scooped into that perma-bun, she said shit like *ladies and gentlemen of the press*. Who said that? No one had said that since Cary Grant, and Dr. Reading probably wanted to remind everyone that she'd known him and given him pointers on filming *Bringing Up Baby*.

The dozen reporters who'd turned out for the conference—probably the largest press group they'd ever had for a single zoo announcement—all laughed when she mentioned the weather. Yeah, it was mid-May in Minnesota, which meant cool with a chance of soaked, freezing upholstery if you left your car windows down. So what? Dr. Reading had only mentioned the weather because it let her bring up fact two: She constantly reminded people how important she was.

"Everyone tells me this isn't bad weather for this time of

year"—Dr. Reading gestured to the people flanking her, including Gerald Dawson and Antonio—"but I flew in from Costa Rica a week ago, where it's just a few degrees below boiling."

Apparently because she'd been studying the predatory habits and population density of jaguars, everyone at the zoo was supposed to kiss her ass for dropping the project to come help them. And that was another thing: going from jaguars to Komodo dragons? Most zoologists and biologists found an ecosystem or particular fauna that called to them and dedicated their lives to becoming experts in their chosen area, but Dr. Joyce Reading eco-hopped her way around the globe looking for the next high-profile assignment, writing books comparing the great white shark to the T. Rex that rocketed up the best-seller lists, narrating Omni theater documentaries, and speaking at black-tie fundraisers in her spare time.

Meg would have been anywhere else on the property, shoveling shit, wrestling the alligator—hell, even reading her in-box—rather than lurking behind the Channel 12 van in the front parking lot, but they were talking about Jata. It wasn't just some random animal on the poster this week; it was *her* animal, and they hadn't told her anything outside the standard lines. We're working on it. We're just hypothesizing right now. There's nothing concrete to say. We can't assume anything at this point.

She wouldn't have even known about the press conference this morning if she hadn't started waiting for Chuck outside his office every day after she punched in. He was a douche, but he was a well-informed douche. Details just dripped off that handy clipboard.

"You aren't going, Megan," he'd warned. "Even appearing there would lead to questions that you know you are prohibited from answering. It's just a formality, to address the influx of calls and e-mails."

"Yeah, like I want to be anywhere near that circus." A quick sneer was all it really took to shrug off his suspicious stare, and twenty minutes before the conference began she snuck out through the shipping and receiving dock to wait in her car. As long as no one on staff spotted her, she was fine. Maybe Chuck was being honest and this whole thing was just a formality, but she wasn't going to take his word for it, not after she'd been shut out of all the meetings and research.

As Dr. Reading ran through the usual explanation of partheno-genesis, Meg paced back and forth, watching the cameramen film the podium with the huge Zoo of America sign blazing behind it in all its red, white, and bald-eagle glory. Standing next to Dr. Reading, chest out, shoulders squared, looking as if he'd waited his whole life to get there, was Antonio.

He wore a suit, probably the same suit he'd worn at the recep-tion, but that was so long ago now, another life even, when she'd been too distracted trying to soothe and listen to him than to pay attention to what the hell he was wearing. Here, though, it was the only thing to see. His lab coat was gone, and he wasn't holding any papers or folders or stethoscopes. The suit just swallowed him up in shades of tar and ash, and from way back here he almost looked like a pallbearer. That was fine. She didn't want to get any closer, to see how the designer lines were probably tailored to his body or how he basked in the attention of the media.

Dr. Reading opened the podium for questions, and the protestors were the first topic thrown up from the crowd.

"We deeply regret the CCCR's decision to boycott the zoo." Gerald Dawson stepped in to comment. "There is simply no way we can address their concerns. Jata is a beloved animal at this institution, and she has no more invited the apocalypse than any other mother on this planet. That is all we have to say on the matter."

"Has the boycott affected the zoo's plans for the young dragons?"

"Not in the least. We've received an unprecedented number of bids on these extraordinary hatchlings coming in from all parts of the globe, most of them after the CCCR's announcement." Gerald gestured around them as if the world fit into the parking lot.

"Is it mostly other American zoos?" a reporter asked.

"The majority are, yes, but we've had offers from Europe—Amsterdam and Dublin, I believe—and even as far away as Indonesia."

Meg kept pacing. Chuck had filled her in on most of the bidders, the ones he knew of anyway, and she'd started surfing their websites on breaks, measuring each of them up and taking notes on their climate, facilities, staff, the usual. The hatchlings weren't going to be shipped off to some half-assed menagerie that happened to wave the biggest check.

"How has this happened? You just said it was impossible for Komodos to have female offspring by parthenogenesis." Another reporter, with the ten-billion-dollar question.

"We have put forth a number of hypotheses at this point but can propose no conclusions without extensive scientific research." Antonio leaned over Gerald and took control of the microphone. "Dr. Reading and I will be heading a cross-functional research team here at the Zoo of America in collaboration with the National Wildlife Foundation and the University of Minnesota. A number of prominent biologists, geneticists, and ecologists will work together to test and research the various hypotheses that have been brought forward."

As Dr. Reading outlined the various theories for the female hatchlings, her gaze panned to Meg, and she cocked her head and squinted. Meg ducked behind the van, heart pounding. The cold metal numbed her back, and she slid down until her butt hit the rear bumper. Dr. Reading couldn't have ID'd her, not fifty feet away in under a second. Shivering, Meg stayed out of sight as she continued listening.

"But how would you test any of those theories?" Meg recognized the voice of Nicole Roberts.

"Blood tests, DNA experimentation, computer modeling. Technology affords our team a number of options that would have been impossible twenty years ago. Believe me, I would have loved to have had some of these resources when I was proposing new migratory patterns for released golden eagles in the 1970s." After an obvious pause for the required laughter, Dr. Reading continued. "But I believe that the most compelling evidence is always gathered at the source. To fully understand the reproductive system of this Komodo, we will need to perform some medical procedures on the animal. X-rays and echoes, of course, as well as some more invasive but completely safe procedures that will enlighten our path to … "

Meg didn't hear anything after that. The blood roared in her ears, the same hissing that chased her awake from the ocean of her dreams. Invasive procedures.

They wanted to take Jata apart.

31 Days *after* Hatching

What she couldn't get over was how Jata's new exhibit had a false veneer of summer. When she'd supervised the concrete basin of the pool being poured less than two months ago, or the parade of dump trucks hauling dirt, trees, and thick slabs of glass, it had been hard to sit back and soak up the façade. Even though the freshly planted grasses and shrubs around the enclosure were as real as the oak trees flanking the giant, metal wing of the Bird Kingdom across the pond, they looked like AstroTurf against the oaks' barely budding May branches.

Standing outside the glass looking in, no one would notice the disparity. All they would see was a tropical savannah housing a giant dragon, a brushstroke of the place where they imagined this animal actually lived and hunted and played and died. They stopped. Said, *Oh, look at that*, then moved to the next brushstroke.

The world was entirely different on the other side of the glass, where the ventilated, plucked, pruned, and crafted environment was eclipsed by the stark and messy reality of things. From here, Meg saw the shadow box for what it was.

She gazed through the window of the newly installed keeper's door, squinting painfully into the sun. Jata lay behind the far basking rock, head down and legs spread, as if she were hiding from the constant crowds. She had become more antisocial—Meg had recorded that in the logs—choosing to spend most of her indoor exhibit days in her cave, away from the cacophony of visitors. There was no cave out here, though. The outdoor space exposed her completely, except for a line of long grasses Meg had planted to simulate the Komodo's natural hunting terrain. Today Jata's tail curled around the edge of the basking rock and disappeared into those grasses. The stalks waved only a foot and a half off the ground, but in the wild it was all the height Jata would've needed to hide from approaching prey. Did she know that instinctually, despite her lifelong captivity? Meg half-smiled. Maybe a stray bird would somehow flutter through the ventilation system someday, so she could observe Jata's predatory skills.

"Meg, we need to talk."

Her sun-baked cheeks went stiff; it was amazing how quickly skin could go cold. Antonio walked down the hallway, his footsteps making hollow and urgent pings on the concrete floor. The lab coat was back today, but she wasn't fooled by it anymore.

"No, forget it. We needed to talk a week ago. You needed to tell me what you and Dr. Reading were plotting."

Dropping the bucket of chicken on the floor, she slammed open the keeper closet, grabbed a pair of leather gloves, and yanked them on.

"You're right. I should have—"

"But you didn't. Not even a word in the hallway. I had to find out about your plans for medical experiments at a goddamn press conference."

He stopped short, as if he'd seen the wall coming and smacked into it anyway. Shaking his head, he watched her slam around the closet. "Honestly? I didn't tell you because I knew you would act like this."

"Like what? Like I wouldn't let you touch her with a ten-foot pole after this?" She gave up the pretense of looking for something and squared up, leveling him with a glare.

"Yeah, like an overreacting bitch."

"I get a little cranky when someone wants to cut apart my animals." She propped her fists on her hips, and he mirrored her, taking a step closer.

"It's highly unlikely that surgery will be our first method of study."

"First?" She spit it out. "As in, you'll get around to it eventually, whenever you and your precious Dr. Reading get too bored with frog plasma and giving speeches?"

"We're talking about a fucking miracle, Meg! Sexual animals can't spontaneously reproduce. Not like this. You knew we were going to have to look at Jata's physiology, so don't act stupid. I know you better than that."

"Sure you do. You've got everything and everyone figured out, don't you?"

He plowed ahead, not listening. "This is a once-in-a-lifetime opportunity. No scientist could ask for better circumstances to study this phenomenon. She's contained. Her history is completely documented. We have a five-year record of her blood pressure, for God's sake. She's on my watch now. You're going to have to trust me with her, and you should know by now that I'm not going to let anything bad happen to her on my operating table."

"You don't have control over that!" she shouted, inches from his face. "Get it through your head. You can't control her or what happens to her any more than I can. How can you stand there and call something a miracle and then claim to be able to dissect it? What do you think that makes you?"

She whirled around and grabbed the feeding bucket. Gemma, who must have come from the opposite end of the hallway, stood a few feet away with her mouth open and features frozen in shock.

"Are you ready?" Meg demanded.

"Not quite." Gemma crept between them and pulled on the safety boots and gloves. Antonio leaned across Gemma's hunched back.

"If you don't trust me, then fine, but Joyce is a legendary biologist. She understands the circumstances and has the pull that it takes to get the resources we need for this research. She was my mentor. For Christ's sake, she studied under Jane Goodall."

Gemma, up to speed now, winked at Meg through her honey-colored bangs and muttered, "I bet Jane Goodall hated that bitch."

"Stay out of it, Gemma," he said.

"Actually, she can't stay out of it. She's assisting me with the feeding today." Meg shook the bucket at his face. "Remember the animal that you're taking such great fucking care of? Yeah, she needs to eat."

"Fine. No problem." He stripped off his lab coat. "I'll assist you."

"Piss off, Antonio. We're done here."

"We're nowhere near done." His eyes were bright, like coal right before the flame catches, and they focused in on her with brutal intensity. And that's when she realized it was still there. The pull, riding his tight, angry shoulders, drawing him into her. The excitement, twisting her gut and responding, God, jumping to return the anger, the heat. Despite everything that had happened in the last week and a half, despite the fact that the sane part of her wanted to kill him right now and feed him to the shark exhibit, that gut-sucking, heart-pounding attraction was still alive, tugging at her, humiliating her.

No. Not this, Antonio. Not now. She unlocked the exhibit door and stumbled through it just to get away and breathe.

Sunlight blinded her. Shouts and happy chatter filtered through the edges of the glare. People. Right. There were people waiting to watch her feed Jata. She blinked and shielded her eyes with a shaking leather glove. Antonio appeared beside her, pulling on work gloves.

"This isn't about Jata, and you know it. It's about us."

"There is no us."

He grabbed her elbow and steered her back toward the feeding rock. She tried to twist away without the crowd noticing, but he sensed it and held her tighter. On the far side of the exhibit, Jata circled around the sunning boulder. She swaggered eagerly, almost aggressively, around the rock bed. The direct sunlight washed out her scales; the greens and grays looked like sea foam being swallowed by a dirty ocean. Licking the air in greeting, Jata bowed her head with each step, and her eyes locked on Meg.

"Jata." Her voice shook. "Feeding time, Jata." And underneath, only to him: "Let me freaking go and get out of here."

Children were pressed up to the glass, their faces squished into pancakes of fascination. Tourists angled their cameras over others' heads, trying to get a good shot of the dragon. There were so many of them. Meg had the fleeting impression of bodies shuffling around one another in a mosaic of color and sound before she pushed them all out of her mind and tried to focus her attention on Jata. Only Jata.

"Smile for the people, Meg. They're here to see our baby."

As they reached the feeding rock, Antonio's teeth flashed in a flirting, crowd-pleasing grin, and before she registered anything beyond that flare of white—too white; how could any feeling person's teeth be that shockingly white?—she jabbed her elbow into his ribs.

Grunting, he crumpled a little and let go of her arm. In that split second, Jata stopped at the base of the feeding rock—the same place she became aggressive last week—and peered through the long stalks of grass from the bucket to the man.

"Take it easy, Meg," he was saying behind her. "I'm just assisting ... "

His words trailed around her, the syllables breaking apart into abstract, meaningless sounds as her gaze sharpened on her Komodo, less than five feet away.

Jata's tongue whipped the air. Antonio had accompanied Meg into the exhibit before. Jata knew him. She did. She wasn't like other dragons, who had to be handled through bars and barriers. She—

Meg's heart tripped and a breath trapped itself in her throat as she saw Jata's legs stiffen through the waving grasses, her head bent low, and a strange hiss eclipsed the growing rumble of the crowd. It was the hiss from her nightmares.

"Get out of here," Meg repeated, choking out the words this time, but there was too much noise. The hissing grew louder, like a snake ready to strike, and filled her head with a dreamlike panic, the kind that paralyzes as it obliterates everything else. For a moment that was all there was in the world, a drowning hiss that severed time into only before and now.

Then Jata lunged.

Meg dropped the bucket, shoved Antonio back, and together they stumbled toward the exhibit door, twenty feet away. There was nothing between them and the door—no trees to climb, no fences to jump. The emergency supplies were in the keeper's closet. Years of training videos and exercises echoed through her mind in seconds. Gemma, who must have already hit the panic button, was holding the door open, shouting and braced behind a body shield. They raced for the opening, chased by the sudden screams of the crowd.

Out of the corner of her eye, Meg saw a flash of black as Antonio went down, and then a weight struck her behind the knees, knocking her legs out from under her. She hit the ground and rolled. The sky tumbled over itself, and she inhaled dirt and bruised grass.

Someone was screaming. She pushed herself up and saw Antonio crawling toward her, shock and pain crunching his face.

Jata stood over him, her jaws digging into the back of his thigh.

She arched her neck and shook her head back and forth, the folds of muscles undulating with a savage power, slicing her teeth deeper into his leg. Meg heard the sick, wet tear of flesh that her brain associated with feeding and saw Antonio kick Jata in the side with his free foot.

God, no. She didn't know if she was thinking or screaming. No. No. Suddenly Gemma was there, pulling Antonio by the shoulders, trying to extract him from Jata's jaws. Gemma yanked backward on him, but she was even smaller than Meg, and Jata was 180 pounds of scale and muscle.

No. Meg ran into the darkness of the exhibit door and felt blindly through the supply closet until her fingers closed over the cool, etched metal. In the hollows of the reptile building came a distant pounding of feet on concrete. She wiped her eyes furiously and ran back into the sun.

Jata had released Antonio's leg and was standing near the bucket Meg had dropped. Blood stained her snout, and the sweet stink of copper filled the air. Gemma dragged Antonio across the grass toward the door, and Jata slowly followed them, stiff-legged and hissing, pink saliva hanging in strings from her open mouth.

Meg lifted her arm to point at Jata and braced her legs the way she had been trained. The gun wavered in her hand, shaking violently.

No, this isn't happening. It isn't real. Voices shouted in every direction, and a siren pierced the air. Acid clawed up her throat as she aimed the gun at the animal she loved. A heartbeat passed, then two. Gemma lifted Antonio through the door.

With a sudden burst of speed, Jata charged again.

Meg pulled the trigger.

31 ½ Days *after* Hatching

It was a cage within a cage—two rows of bars, roughly welded at the corners with thick balls of misshapen iron, and its sheer size made it impossible to imagine movement or liberation of any kind. It wasn't transported here. The bars were brought in, beam by heavy beam, dragged down the stairs and through the long vet hallway into this windowless room, then welded and hammered, erected into immobile place. A quarantine. A prison within a prison. And inside of it all, at the very heart of captivity, was Jata.

Meg watched Jata's body, the unnatural stillness of her drugged sleep. Her SAMs read like surgery. Heartbeat: 38 bpm. Blood pressure: 80 over 65. Adrenaline: 12 ppm. A robot dragon. Meg hugged her still grass-stained knees tighter into her chest, rubbing one hand over the ripening welt across her forearm. It was turning from shocky to numb, and the reds and purples had started to bloom in a diagonal column between her wristbone and inner elbow.

The desk she sat on looked completely abandoned in the corner of the room, the cracking wood veneer covered in dust and random sheets of paper. Resting her back against the cold concrete wall, she tucked into herself like a switchblade, rocking slightly. She'd come into the quarantine room how long ago? She'd wanted to be here when Jata woke up; she remembered that much. That was her intention.

She dropped her head into her knees. Intentions. What a useless word. You either did something or you didn't. You controlled something or couldn't. That was it. End of show. Intentions were worth as much as all those other bullshit words, like *wishes* or *hopes*. They were used by powerless people who couldn't control what was happening two feet in front of their tiny, blindside d faces.

She had control over nothing. Her relationship with Ben was over. She couldn't protect Jata from Dr. Reading now, and Antonio might be dead. Meg couldn't tell if Jata had severed one of his major arteries, because there had been so much blood covering his legs from not one attack—but two.

~~9~~

The Telazol dart Meg had shot sank directly into Jata's neck, blooming a little red flower out of her throat as she lunged for Antonio's injured leg. The dose was high but not instant. Only a bullet could have brought her down immediately. This time she bit below his knee, tearing through pants that were already dark and sticky, but she didn't hold her grip as she had during the first attack. It was a taste, a warning this time. Her tail dropped slightly, and she seemed to be losing momentum. Meg grabbed the body shield Gemma had dropped and used it to push Jata back in shoves and halting steps. *Stop it, Jata*, she'd screamed. *Get back*. She got Jata to turn around by throwing the emptied gun at her; the sick, dull thud on her side broke the buzz of hissing. Meg kept walking and yelling, watching the animal she had trusted retreat unsteadily to the back wall of the exhibit. By the time Jata collapsed, the medical team had already arrived.

They didn't tell her where they had taken Antonio. She might have gotten him killed, and she didn't even know where he was. They wheeled him away in a cloud of frantic people with Gemma jogging alongside the stretcher, her braid bouncing and uniform splattered with blood, holding on to one of Antonio's hands. She'd thrown a last, desperate look back at Meg before disappearing around the staff corridor.

Meg stayed behind to help load Jata onto the cart, taping her lax, bloody jaws shut and binding her feet. Numb, she walked alongside as the security staff and keepers silently wheeled Jata's body out of the reptile building, across the zoo amid stares and frantic pointing, down the freight elevator to the veterinary wing, and into the quarantine room. One by one they all left, leaving Meg pacing next to the cage and thinking—insanely—that Jata would be all right as long as she was there with her when she woke up. Tranquilizers worked unevenly at the end of the dose, and most animals came out of the drug in fits and slow starts. But Jata was different. Meg paced the room, turning back and forth, back and forth, until suddenly she stopped in mid-stride.

Jata stood at the cage door, staring at Meg. Her tail hung in a downward docile position. Her legs bowed out slightly farther than normal, but that was natural enough, considering the dose of anesthetic. Jata's head tilted forward, eyes unclouded and focused on Meg, as if waiting to be told how and why she had come to be in this strange place.

"Jata!" Unconsciously, Meg rushed toward the cage and the cool metal of the outer layer of bars. "It's too cold in here, isn't it? I'll have the heat turned up so you don't get sick."

She leaned into the metal, meeting Jata's quaking stare.

"It's okay. It's okay." Her voice rose in pitch, as if unsure of who she was trying to comfort. Then it happened.

She snaked her hand through the outer layer of bars toward Jata, reaching half-heartedly in a pathetic attempt to reassure her. Without warning, Jata lunged at her.

She jerked forward, throwing her entire weight at the cage. As her jaws cracked into the metal inner bars, Meg's hand flew back and slammed into the outer bar. The pain shrieked through her arm, but she didn't scream; she didn't make a sound. Uncurling her throbbing forearm from the bars, she shuffled backward until her legs touched the desk, lifted herself onto its surface, and grasped her knees to her chest.

∽

What time was it now? It was hard to tell down here where there was no sound from the zoo, no bustle of tourists or animals or hassled staff. The only other presence was the damp, mossy smell of the river soaking through the walls. They said the river used to be hazardous in the spring before the dams were built, that it ruined basements and moved whole houses off their foundations. The planners had done a study before they built the zoo to be sure that all the buildings were sufficiently elevated and the bluffs couldn't be flooded anymore, but the smell still permeated the lower levels. That smell filled Meg's nose, and she wished the river still had the power to rise up over its banks, pour into the zoo, and break the quarantine room apart, sweeping them both away, freeing them.

Meg sat rocking for an hour, two hours, and beyond, while the world passed above them. No one came to tell her what happened to Antonio, and she was too terrified of the answer to go ask.

"I'm sorry," Meg whispered to the massive back that was shadowed in stripes. Her voice sounded tiny and whimpering. She couldn't force anything else out. There were no other words, and no river could save them.

5 Years *before* Hatching

She'd called her mother the week after Jata arrived at the zoo. It was Christmas or something, one of those obligatory phone-call holidays.

"A dragon?"

"Komodo dragon."

"I never understood why you liked those slimy creatures. Remember when you brought that snake into the house and scared poor Daphne to death?" Her mother laughed over the phone. "Her coat stunk of fear for weeks after that."

"If you'd ever let that dog outside the yard she might have seen a garter snake a time or two in her life." Or a prairie, or a swamp, or another dog that wasn't inbred and reeking of Aveda.

"Here we go again." The weight of a ten-year argument groaned through her mother's voice.

"You never let her be a dog, Mother. This Komodo dragon is just that—a dragon. Not some trophy or a twisted, surrogate child. They put me in charge of her care, and I'm going to do everything I can to give her a good life at the zoo."

"I know this is what you wanted and you think you're making a difference, but these lizards … they don't have the slightest capacity to understand what you're doing for them. Say whatever you want about Daphne's life, but she loved being a show dog, remember? She would absolutely prance around that ring, and she loved us for putting her in it."

"Keep telling yourself that, Mom."

"I know you, Meg. You act so tough and above it all, but you crave that same recognition. You need to feel loved and needed by those animals. You call Daphne my surrogate child? That's rich."

Trust her mother to make the issue about rewards. What was the point of doing anything, according to Theresa Whittaker, if you didn't get something in return? Her whole life she'd hungered for those ribbons and trophies, and now she was trying to group Meg in with her, as if there were any similarity between shoveling shit at the zoo and parading a purebred whippet in front of hundreds of adoring eyes.

~9

One day Meg hauled a bucket of dead rats to the exhibit and peeked through the window. Jata lay on a large boulder, a behavior she'd recently developed in the afternoons that was a natural mirror—Meg had read—to the thermoregulation activities of island Komodos. They stayed inactive so their bodies didn't overheat.

When Chuck made her the primary keeper of the new Komodo exhibit, Meg had been shocked. She'd been working at the zoo for six months, busting her ass while more senior keepers put their gossip and smoke breaks before their animals, but the whole time Chuck acted as if Meg didn't know a fish from a damn monkey. Then, out of the blue, he called her into his office and handed her the file for a *Varanus komodoensis*, an eight-month-old female wild capture, already crossing the ocean in a freight ship from Indonesia.

"I know your background is more domestic lizards and alligators, but we don't have anyone experienced with Komodos on staff. I'll expect you to liaison with the refuge and get the habitat set up prior to the specimen's arrival. There will be a lot of research expected of you, Megan, above and beyond your position. Are you ready to handle the responsibility?"

"Yes. Yes, I'm ready." There had to be something more professional to say—maybe ask about the budget or space she would have to work with—but only one question surfaced. "What's her name?"

Chuck sighed, but she was starting to see how the tic that crunched his overworked eyes had more to do with him than anything he thought about her.

"Jata. It says the name is Jata."

Jata was fascinating. When she arrived at the zoo, every behavior seemed new and mysterious to Meg. Why did she cock her head toward the viewing platform but not actually look around before she took a swim? How did her claws grip the rock when she climbed to the top? Why did her tail look long and stiff when she first arrived, then limp and dragging after she'd been at the zoo for a few weeks? Was she getting comfortable or depressed? Did she need stimulus or solitude? After exhausting all the zoological studies on record, Meg started calling other Komodo keepers around the U.S. and even Gus, Jata's transfer contact from Indonesia. She watched the delicate mosaic of sage- and slate-colored scales until they blurred into a curious splotch that darted around the exhibit with the agility of a dog. Ben started to think she was obsessed and, considering the stack of books and absently scrawled notes littering her studio, it wasn't hard to see his point.

The exhibit door had a built-in chute to send the food inside, but that was for later, when Jata tripled in size. At a little under three feet long and with jaws no bigger than the palm of Meg's hand, there was no real danger. Meg unlocked the door and stepped into the exhibit.

Jata looked toward the door and zeroed in on her. That was the first thing Meg had noticed after Jata arrived, the intelligence that lingered behind those black eyes. They didn't reflect light, Komodo eyes, and maybe that was part of it. Jata just took everything in with that piercing gaze and locked it inside.

This was usually Jata's cue to run. She played the old duck-and-cover game every time she got her water changed or her exhibit cleaned, hightailing it for her little makeshift cave like they were going to shoot her—which they'd only done once for that stupid microchip—and then she waited until the door was shut and locked tight before reappearing. Today, though, she didn't run. She stood up on the rock and darted her tongue in and out, maybe getting a whiff of the carrion in the air.

"Chow time, little one." Meg dumped the rats in a pile on the dirt while Jata just stood there, staring. Instead of leaving like she normally did, Meg took a couple steps back, leaned deliberately against the back wall of the exhibit, and held her breath. Just to see. Jata looked down at the food and then up at Meg—a big, slow-motion yes—and then she climbed down the rock and walked over. Before digging into her meal, she glanced sideways at Meg one last time with her head cocked and humble near the ground, and flicked her tongue in one brief loop. Hello.

~⸲

"Just say anything. It doesn't matter. I'm looking for intonation and clarity of sound, not specific words."

Meg pointed the microphone at Gemma Perkins, the new part-timer who was still working on her zoology degree at the U, who shrugged and took the mic with a smile creeping up one sunny-apple cheek.

"Hello. Perkins here, reporting for KP or Cage P, as it were. I do not create the assignments. Not this newbie. You say speak, and I speak. The newbie must be torn apart before she can be made whole. One must destroy in order to create."

"Mmm-hmm," Meg muttered, playing with the volume level on the computer.

"I have been in love with Meg Yancy since my first day, and I jump at the chance to help her science project, no matter what nefarious scheme it might be."

"I think that's good. We can break it up from there." Meg nodded, noting the length of the sound bite. Laughter shredded her focus, and she looked up to see Antonio Rodríguez holding his side and leaning on her computer station.

"Do you want something?"

"You might want to check that last part," he advised, winking at Gemma.

Meg tucked the pen behind her ear and glanced between the two of them. "Why, was there some feedback?"

Playing back the recording, she heard Gemma's words this time—*I have been in love with Meg Yancy since my first day*—and her face started burning as Antonio busted out again, thumping the back of the monitor.

"Nothing gets past you, Yancy."

"Go screw an intern, Rodríguez." She slashed the file into pieces and started renaming them.

"Well, I would"—he leaned over the top of the screen, dangling muscular forearms into her line of sight—"but all my interns are on winter break. Isn't that a shame?"

He was talking to Gemma now.

"You want me to tell you what I think about you, or are you just going to shove a microchip up my ass?" Gemma asked, with a voice like honey.

He stood up and retreated to the vet wing, still chuckling loudly, as Gemma nudged Meg with an elbow.

"Sorry about that. I just like to play, you know?"

"Well, you found the player." Meg cocked her head toward Antonio and proceeded to splice files and move them around.

"Yeah, no." She drew both words out like caramel, stretching her arms above her head. "I don't mean like that. I have a toddler, and sometimes I forget to leave the teasing mommy at home, you know?"

"Okay, sure. Thanks for the recording."

Meg inserted a CD and burned the files over, glancing at the keyboard, the monitor, anywhere that wasn't near Gemma. She didn't have anything against kids, really, as long as they didn't throw their toys into the exhibits or whine about how boring the reptiles were.

Gemma kept stretching in her chair, contorting her body into strange letters. "Are you going to tell me what this is for, or am I going to hear myself dubbed over a kung fu movie one day?"

She shrugged. "Come see if you want."

～ᦞ

The trails thinned out as the last visitors made their way back to the parking lots and the light rail station. Meg motioned for Gemma to be quiet as they approached the viewing platform for Jata's exhibit. She set a small boom box on the railing and hit play before tugging Gemma back behind a nearby shrub.

The CD sounded tinny and hollow, with plenty of clicks and bleeps between her spliced recordings. It played three voices:

Gemma, Michael—the veteran mammal keeper—and Meg. A voice spoke for a minute or two, then the CD switched to someone else.

From behind the shrub, Meg touched Gemma's arm and mouthed, "Look."

Inside the exhibit, Jata rested halfway into her lagoon, submerging her back legs and tail in the water that rippled with reflected exhibit lights. Eyes closed, she paid no attention to the recording when Michael's deep voice rumbled out of the speakers or when it switched over to Gemma's casual declaration of love.

When Meg's voice started, though, Jata's head swiveled 120 degrees above and behind her body toward the viewing platform.

She searched the empty space until the voice switched back to Gemma, then she turned back around, disinterested again. The CD bounced from Gemma to Michael and back a few times. Nothing. No reaction. Meg hadn't noticed she was still touching Gemma's arm until Gemma covered her hand with her own and squeezed.

The next time Meg's recorded voice played back, Jata immediately stood up and walked out of the water toward the platform with her head cocked to one side. Her eyes swept from side to side, searching for the body that went with the voice, and she licked the air to locate the matching scent. Jata recognized her voice. A bubble of excitement swelled in Meg's chest as Jata came too close and disappeared from view under the platform ledge.

Jata knew her. Jata wanted her. Meg wasn't imagining the hello in the dragon's eyes, or the familiarity between them during her feedings.

The knowledge filled up every part of her body with a bright, basking glow. She squeezed Gemma's hand with fingers that had become warm and slick, but just as Gemma mirrored her wide-eyed grin, she stuttered and sank down on the floor.

"What is it?" Gemma whispered.

Meg shook her head and shrugged, but she felt as if she'd been slapped in the face: Out of nowhere, her mother's words had flashed into her head—*you crave recognition, you need to be loved*—like an insistent, clashing overlay as Meg's voice looped around and around on the CD.

This is Meg Yancy. Does the Komodo dragon know me? This is Meg Yancy. Does the Komodo dragon know me?

32 Days *after* Hatching

Meg slammed through the double doors separating the vet wing from the keeper's cage a half hour before her shift was supposed to start. The cage was empty except for Chuck, who sat quietly on the bench directly in front of her locker. He wasn't fidgeting or poring over lists. His clipboard lay ignored in his lap. Rather than acknowledge her, he dropped his gaze from her locker when she came in and looked to the floor as if for support. The incredibly un-Chuck-like picture sucked all the rage out of Meg's limbs and filled them back up with a cold, knowing dread. She walked to her locker, keeping her back to him.

"Why the hell doesn't my badge work on the quarantine room?" The words came out jerky and strange. "I got here early so I could see her, and I can't even get in the door."

"Clearance is determined by the veterinary department."

"What department? Antonio's gone." She kicked her street shoes into the back of the locker and pulled out her work boots, trying to swallow the rush of fear at putting those two words together. He wasn't *gone*. He couldn't be gone. Chuck had to be there for some other reason. Maybe if she didn't look at him he would go away. If she could just put on her work boots and get to work …

"Sandra Mienkewicz is taking over as head veterinarian for the time being. She's proven very capable over the last few months."

Sandra was the part-time vet, but Meg rarely worked with her; Sandra mainly handled mammals. "Tell her to get me some freaking clearance. I'm Jata's keeper."

"That's why I'm here." His voice was flat under the weight of things she couldn't bear to turn around and face. "We have to go upstairs."

∽

He took her to the same boardroom that had been crammed full of excited and mystified people a week ago. Now it was empty except for two people: Gerald Dawson and Dr. Joyce Reading.

"Come in, Ms. Yancy. Have a seat." Gerald sounded exactly like Chuck—quiet and dead sober.

She sat two chairs down from them, and Chuck awkwardly filled the gap, setting his clipboard down on the table. Stacks of papers and dog-eared books lay in front of Dr. Reading, but the space in front of Gerald was empty except for a glossy black pen, and its very alone-ness held ten times the weight as anything else that could be sitting on that table. It drew the eye.

Gerald took a deep breath and began. "Yesterday's incident was a terrible and tragic event, made worse by the number of guests who witnessed and, in some cases, recorded the attack. We are extremely lucky that Antonio Rodríguez was not killed. The surgeons tell us that he may still lose his leg; it's touch and go at this point."

Antonio would live. The sudden relief overwhelmed her, and she tried to reach past the sound-bite crap and cling to that piece of information. Her carelessness hadn't gotten him killed. He was going to live.

Gerald looked straight at Meg, his eyes kind yet implacable. "He owes his life to you, Ms. Yancy, and to Ms. Perkins, too. I have not received a satisfactory explanation as to why he was in the exhibit in the first place, but if it had not been for your quick and well-trained responses, he might not be here to worry about a leg."

"Perhaps Ms. Yancy can give us an explanation." Dr. Reading's fingers were calmly laced together on the edge of the table, but her eyes flashed at Meg. "I agree that we were extremely fortunate that Antonio was only injured, but one of my brightest, most accomplished students could have died yesterday. I think you and this institution deserve some answers."

Meg crossed her arms. "I was already in the exhibit preparing for the feeding when he entered."

Dr. Reading leaned past Chuck to address her directly. "He spoke to you when he grabbed your arm."

How did she know that? Meg blinked, trying to remember if Dr. Reading could have been in the crowd.

"It's all over the news and the Internet," Dr. Reading said. "At least three tourists took videos of the attack. The publicity is raging."

"We were arguing about the research options for Jata." She met the doctor's gaze with a tight glare. "I don't remember exactly what he said."

Chuck jumped in, eager to put his conflict resolution skills to work. "This isn't an investigation, Megan. Not yet."

"Not ever," Gerald interjected. He made a steeple out of his fingers and nodded over the fingertip peak at both of them. "The board has studied the footage and found no deliberate misconduct by any involved party. There will be no disciplinary action toward any staff member."

So she still had her job, but they didn't bring her up here for that—Chuck yelled at her and let her keep her job every day. They were right. It wasn't an investigation; it was what came after that, after everyone with heavy, black pens made up their minds. She swallowed, hesitated, and forced the next question up her raw throat.

"What about Jata?"

A long silence filled the room, engulfing everything inside. Meg looked from Chuck to Gerald to Dr. Reading. No one seemed to want to speak.

Finally, Gerald sighed and met Meg's question full in the face.

"We have decided to euthanize the Komodo."

"No."

Meg shot up. The verdict had been there all along, building underneath everything Chuck and Gerald were saying and choking her with dread. Now that it was out, its gut-wrenching terror unleashed, the fight broke loose inside her. She dashed to the head of the table. "No, you can't. I won't let you."

"The decision has already been made. The procedure is scheduled for ten o'clock today."

Today. They wanted to kill Jata today. Hysteria swelled in her throat, and she clamped down on it.

"Mr. Dawson, she's not dangerous. I swear. She has no history of violence. Look at the entire archive of her logs. Look at her SAMs. She could eat out of my hand."

She leaned over the table, speaking only to Gerald. "This was an isolated incident, brought on by the unfamiliar environment and excessive crowds. I promise you it will never happen again."

"I'm afraid that's not true, Ms. Yancy," Dr. Reading said.

"What do you know?" She whirled toward the doctor. "You've been here a week. You don't know anything about Jata. I've been by her side every day for the past five years."

"You reported the animal's previous aggressive behavior to Antonio in my presence and lied about the reason for it. I don't feel this can be considered an isolated incident, and neither does"—Dr. Reading glanced at her notes—"a Ms. Gemma Perkins."

"What?"

Chuck cleared his throat. "Gemma, ah, stepped forward to speak to me last week and reported the aggression that both of you witnessed at the animal's last feeding before the incident. Her version was different than yours, and she voiced concerns over the level of human interaction with Jata. In view of her testimony, and the fact that you didn't log the behavior, well, it seems that there is a pattern of instability in the animal and probably more than what has been recorded."

Gemma. The floor had been stolen from underneath her feet. She was in free fall. The words floated in the stale boardroom air. Gemma came forward. Gemma voiced concerns.

"In other words, Ms. Yancy, how many other times did you manipulate the logs for this specimen?" Dr. Reading asked.

"None. That was the only time, and I reported—"

"What I want to know is why, in light of this pattern, you chose to stock a tranquilizer gun in the exhibit with no lethal measures available? Antonio could have been killed in the time it took for the dose to have an effect. Komodo dragons are alpha predators. They will attack humans without provocation, and yet you neglected to stock the appropriate contingencies?"

"I don't have to prove my procedures to you," Meg retorted. "You don't have any authority here."

Gerald cut in. "I would like an answer, too, Ms. Yancy, for the record. I know the reporters are going to be asking that question, and we want to be able to respond with confidence."

"Jata trusts me. I knew if I could get between her and Antonio, I could regain control of the situation. And that's exactly what happened. If it's all over the Internet, you must have seen that part, too."

"Yes, we've seen a lot of footage this morning." Gerald Dawson nodded to Dr. Reading, who pressed a button on a remote control.

A video popped up on the projection screen at the far end of the room. It was a fly-on-the-wall view of a dark room filled only with a giant cage and a small, wiry woman with a brown ponytail pacing the outside of the bars. Meg stared at the grainy picture of herself from yesterday in the quarantine room. When was it? She was pacing, so that must have been right after they brought Jata there, just before...

Oh, God.

She closed her eyes so she didn't have to see it twice, but the picture was still there, playing over and over on the back of her eyelids.

"Jata!" The tinny recording distorted the name. Meg pinched her eyes shut tighter, shaking her head at the floor, willing the past not to happen. Not here in this soulless boardroom. Her voice sounded hollow and small, and it was followed by the crash of Jata's body against the cage—the horrible, bone-crunching lunge—and finally a rustling before a heavy silence.

"You were saying something about the animal trusting you?"

Meg spun around to Dr. Reading. "She was drugged and scared. I shouldn't have approached her so soon and especially not while she was in quarantine. That was my fault. And Antonio shouldn't have been in the exhibit at all. You don't call that deliberate misconduct?"

Gerald replied, "He has already been punished enough, Ms. Yancy."

"Punish me! Don't take this out on Jata! Please. Please, I beg you. Suspend me. Fire me. You can't kill her for something that's my fault." She leaned toward Gerald, pleading with the black pen.

"It's obvious from the public feedings that you had Jata's trust for a long time, Ms. Yancy, but the bonds between a keeper and a young animal change during maturity." Dr. Reading turned off the projection screen and continued. "How many times have we heard of a person who was mauled to death by an adult tiger that they bottle-fed as a kitten? Remember the keeper in Bruges who was decapitated by the orphan polar bear that imprinted on him? The list goes on and on. The fact is that Jata is now a liability to this institution and has become too dangerous to maintain."

"Maintain." Meg whispered the word.

"Your judgment is clouded by loyalty, Ms. Yancy," Gerald said, standing up and nodding solemnly at her. "It's an admirable trait. I'm very sorry to have to make this decision."

"What can I do to change your mind? What do you want? If you want me to quit, I'll quit. I'll feed myself to the CCCR if that will make you happy. We'll ... we'll stop the feedings." She swallowed once, hard. "I'll keep Jata behind bars and glass for the rest of her life, if that's what you want. She'll never come into contact with a single living thing."

"The decision has already been made," Gerald said.

"You're just doing this because you want to take her apart." Meg's voice shook. "This is just an excuse."

"That's not at all true," Gerald said.

Dr. Reading stood up and paced over to the bay windows, her back to the rest of them, as Gerald continued. "The public will abandon the zoo if we don't respond appropriately to the attack. No one wants to take their kids to a place that they feel is dangerous in any way. We could lose a significant amount of private funding and public revenue, and we can't neglect the safety of our staff."

"The bottom fucking line? You're killing her to save the bottom line?"

"Watch yourself, Ms. Yancy." Gerald's voice sharpened; he was getting angry in his own right. He squared off, face to face with her. "This zoo provides shelter and safety to hundreds of species, twelve of which are endangered. We educate the public about ecological concerns as well as introduce new generations to the importance of animal diversity. We need money to do all that. I know this decision grieves you, so I understand your reaction, but we don't tolerate that kind of attitude here."

With that, he walked her to the door, and Chuck followed silently behind. Dr. Reading didn't even bother turning around. She just stood at the window looking down, as if she owned every last godforsaken animal on the grounds beneath her.

"You may be present during the injection if you wish. It's against policy, but I've cleared you for the procedure. I know what this specimen means to you."

Did she nod? The door shut behind her, then she and Chuck stood alone in the executive hallway. Neither of them moved.

"She gave us a miracle," Meg whispered.

His face blurred and she looked away, letting the burn of tears overflow.

Chuck cleared his throat. "I know."

"I have to see Jata. Before they take her."

"I've got clearance. Let's go." Chuck took her elbow and gingerly led her down the hallway. His clipboard was missing; he must have forgotten it in the boardroom. Dumb with grief—that was the only thought she could form as his clammy fingers helped her into the glass and chrome elevator. His clipboard was gone.

~Ꝍ

Chuck stood quietly by the door as Meg knelt in front of the quarantine cage. Tears ran dully out of the corners of her eyes and streaked down the metal bar that held her head up. When they'd entered the room, the smell of feces permeated the air, and Jata had been curled up awkwardly in the far corner of the cage. She'd risen when she saw Meg and stood expectantly for a minute, hopefully. Her tongue grazed the air in greeting—the old Jata saying hello. It was too much.

The raw chicken Chuck watched her steal from the cafeteria was balled up in a plastic bag in her fist.

"It's almost time," Chuck said.

She nodded and carefully unwrapped the chicken, digging her fingers into the soft meat and pulling apart the chunks of flesh and fat.

Jata lumbered up to the front of the bars, her head bowing and claws scraping harshly on the metal floor. If she stayed in quarantine a few more days, the cage would eat her claws down to the marrow.

"Jata, chow time, Jata," Meg whispered, elongating the syllables, feeling her way around the familiar chant. She tossed the chicken pieces gently through the bars, one by one. They sailed in like ticks of a clock, each one closer to the last.

"Jata, Jata."

Jata ate the chunks in eager bites, scooping them from the floor. Her scales looked dull in the half-lit room, and her tail rapped awkwardly against the confines of the cage. Meg had a flash of her basking spread-eagle on a boulder, feet sprawled, full and sleepy after her weekly feeding. There were so many other moments—the late nights she'd spent swimming after minnows in her pool, how she'd burrowed that cave out for herself so many years ago, the time she tore apart a Frisbee and dumped the chunks of it so proudly at Meg's feet—but this one ripped at her heart. Just Jata, content and basking on her favorite rock.

"Will they do it in here?"

"Yes. They'll inject her here and then take her to the morgue."

"They'll do an autopsy."

It wasn't a question, but Chuck answered anyway. "Yes."

Jata settled uncomfortably back down on the hard floor of the cage, watching Meg. "Did you know this was how they used to exhibit Komodo dragons, in cages just like this?"

"Really?" He played along.

"They died pretty quickly, just couldn't handle it. I studied everything I could find about Komodos when you made me her keeper. I researched for hours at night and made calls to Indonesia. Do you know how much it costs to call Indonesia? I read about this one specimen in Germany named Bubchen. She was the tamest Komodo I ever found on record. She took walks with her keeper through the public zoo grounds, posed with children for pictures— children, Chuck, tasty little meals—and never once took a bite out of them. They said she was afraid of planes when they first got her, that she'd hide whenever a plane flew by. Do you know how she died?"

He didn't answer.

"The zoo was bombed to the ground by the Allied forces in World War II. Frankfurt burned. The keepers had to shoot all the injured and escaping animals, and the rest died of hypothermia or starvation. Planes killed her. Isn't that funny? What you're scared of really does kill you in the end."

She swept her hand back and forth over the bars, absently petting them, scratching the metal with fingernails that were broken and still crusted over with dried blood from yesterday.

"When I first read about Bubchen, I felt like I was waking up. I thought I knew what I had to do. I had to make sure that Jata was never scared of anything, that she accepted us and enjoyed her life, because just the least little thing could kill her. As soon as she spooked, as soon as the environment couldn't soothe her anymore, I knew it was all over. Every captive life is a deprived life, I know that, but I wanted to give her the best captive state she could have. And now she's given us the most precious, impossible gift"—her throat closed and she fought against it, shoving the words into the room— "and we're still killing her. So maybe it doesn't matter anyway. Scared or not, the planes still kill you in the end."

Chuck's head was lowered. The building creaked above them as people walked; they were circling closer, preparing the injection. Time was running out.

He cleared his throat, a low, wet noise. "I've always believed in progress, you know. That we can build on the past, learn from our mistakes, and reach higher. Do better. That's why I made you her keeper, Megan. I knew you would do better for her, better for all your animals, than some of the people we had working here when you started. You could teach your coworkers how to care for their exhibits, and they could teach you how to relate to people without getting the zoo in a lawsuit."

She smiled, her face heavy against the bars.

"But Jata"—he shook his head—"she's just gone beyond anything I understand as progress. She's part of a—a larger order now ... and I just don't think we were equipped to handle it. I don't think we were able to evolve with her."

He paused, shoulders stooped and his face in shadows. "You can't blame the men inside the planes, Megan. You have to blame the war."

The noise above them grew louder, the feet on the floor pounding harder. The cafeteria must be opening. That meant it was ten o'clock. It was time.

"Give me the dosed gun. I want to do it."

"That's not what Gerald—"

She stood up and laid a hand on his arm, silencing him. She had to do this.

"I want to be the last thing she sees. I don't want her to be scared.

Please, Chuck. It's the only thing I'll ever ask you."

It didn't take him long, but she'd dried her face on her uniform by the time he got back. This time when she raised the gun, there was no panic or overwhelming fear. Her hand was steady, and a horrible calm stole over her body.

"Jata." At her name, Jata looked up, and her eyes were black trusting pools, focused on her keeper. Meg fired, and the dart with the euthanizing dose sank into her right shoulder. She watched her dragon—the only thing in the world she had truly loved—until Jata's head lowered slowly and gracefully to the ground, and only when her jaw was resting on the floor did her eyes close for the last time.

34 Days *after* Hatching

Meg sat at the last computer terminal of the keeper's cage, in the far corner of the room. Her coworkers kept their voices low and moved in wide circles around her, keeping a quarantine distance, a mourning distance. Everyone knew that today was the autopsy.

She'd been here for the last three hours, even though Chuck told her to take the rest of the week off. *Take a vacation, and don't talk to any reporters*, he'd said after she'd shot Jata. *Relax. Spend some time with your family.* She'd even tried to follow his advice, which showed how far gone she really was. She went to the cemetery and stood by her mother's grave, but Jata stared up at her from under the budding grass. When she called her father, he tried to convince her to come see him again, but all she heard was Jata's hiss snaking through the static on the line. When she went to the hospital to visit Antonio in the intensive care ward, the nurse stopped her and asked if she was family. *Sister-in-law*, she'd almost said—the words were on the tip of her tongue—but she shook her head instead, too cowardly to go in to face him. The nurse filled her in on the surgery schedule, saying he was still dangerously close to losing his leg. The infection wasn't under control yet. Meg nodded and went home, threw up her breakfast, and cried for most of the day. She came to work this morning because it would have been torture to spend any more days "relaxing" like that, but when she found out that Dr. Reading had scheduled the autopsy for today, even bringing in some hotshot university veterinarians for assistance, it became pointless to try to work. She had to be nearby.

They rarely did autopsies at the zoo, unless one of the charismatic mega-vertebrates died mysteriously, and that had only happened once as far back as anyone could remember. This autopsy, though, had nothing to do with Jata's death; they were taking a corpse apart to dissect a life. To pretend to distract herself, Meg searched through the website of the Association of Zoos and Aquariums, looking at the zoos that had placed bids on the hatchlings. Chuck came in and out of the vet hallway periodically after they started the procedure, and each time he passed through he nodded to her corner of the room, as if to say, *Yes, they're still working. I'll keep checking back.*

Gemma walked into the cage. The last time Meg had seen her had been the day of the attack, running down the corridor alongside Antonio's stretcher, her uniform covered in blood. She walked straight to the computer opposite from Meg and sat down. Clicking and typing, Meg concentrated on ignoring her. It was almost comforting to have something else to focus on.

An e-mail popped up in her in-box from Channel 12; they wanted her to comment on the death of Jata. She deleted it.

After a while, Gemma remarked offhandedly to her computer screen, "Didn't expect you to be here in the thick of things."

"I'm looking for something. Ben took his computer with him when he left."

Gemma let that pass, typing for another quiet stretch of time. "Funny how they keep logs on our logs, tabs on everything we do in these computers. Really is a cage, isn't it?"

"Are you trying to be on my side now?"

"I've always been on your side." Gemma gave up the pretense of typing and leaned across the station toward Meg. There was something like guilt creeping around the edges of her eyes. "They were wrong to kill Jata, but she was dangerous, Meg. She couldn't be controlled anymore."

"And you made damn sure that they knew that."

"That's our job. I did what the policies tell us to do. There was no way I could have known Jata would attack Antonio."

As she leaned in to meet Gemma's pleading stare, the shreds of grief curled in Meg's stomach, clawing to get out. "Well, you still have your job. Congratulations. Now you can go home and tell Allison that you helped kill her."

Gemma's expression shriveled into hurt, giving Meg a sour kind of satisfaction to see Gemma wearing the same thing that was tearing her up inside. Gemma Perkins, who was never bothered by anything—and what a horrible reach *anything* turned out to have—was finally touched, finally shit-splattered by this mess. Gemma leaned even farther over the computer and worked her mouth over the pain, tasting it, spitting it back.

"It's so easy for you, isn't it? You can be a bitch, shut everyone out, ignore the rules, screw your coworkers, and what does it matter? If they fire you, it's just you. You'll just pack up and move on to the next zoo. I can't do that. I have a daughter. She wants to go to summer camp at the science museum this year. Did I tell you that? Four hundred and fifty dollars without meals. And then there's college. Do you know how much I've saved for Allison's college? Two thousand dollars. Two grand in eight years. I have to keep this job. I can't afford to lose my paycheck or my benefits. And if Chuck has a heart attack or retires, you'd better believe I'm going to get in line for his job. So if they say jump, I'm going to jump. If they say shoot the animals, I'm going to shoot the animals. And if they say log the aggression, log every behavior you observe, guess what else I'm going to do."

It was as if the autopsy was happening right here in front of her, as if the Gemma she'd known was ripping into pieces, breaking irreversibly apart.

"How can you be so spineless? Don't you believe in anything?"

Gemma nodded, then laughed once, a humorless, empty laugh. "I believe in the way things are. Here we are sitting in the cage, and if everything goes well, we'll get to come back tomorrow. But you—you're just better than everyone, aren't you? Meg Yancy, the perfect fucking keeper, right?"

Meg dropped her face into a hand, trying to hold it together, but the words followed her. It all closed in on her—the other keepers pretending not to eavesdrop, Gemma's hurt and disgust, the pretty and sterile images of the AZA on the computer screen—they all crowded in like the autopsy vets, cutting deep into her bones, severing her into little pieces, and every slice was flawed. Nicole Roberts, the reception, lying to Ben, sleeping with Antonio, Antonio in the exhibit, Antonio screaming, failing Jata, shooting Jata, killing Jata.

She jerked to her feet.

"Meg—"

"No." She left the cage, stumbled down the veterinary hallway to the operating room window, and leaned into the glass. Three masked people in blue gowns stood around the table holding Jata's body. She lay awkwardly on her side with her head tilted back, throat gaping open as if she were ready to feed. Meg couldn't see her eyes. Hands fisted, salt choking her throat, she was paralyzed as they hacked into Jata, taking out pieces of stomach, heart, and bowels like glistening trophies. The perfect fucking keeper. She held back a sob as one of the doctors glanced at her, indecision clouding the unmasked part of his face. After a minute he bent back down, and she watched him flay the base of Jata's tail, dissecting her genitals. They were looking for a penis or some other deformity, something that could explain Jata's daughters in neat, black-and-white diagrams and win them all grants and fellowships. They sliced and sectioned tissues and put them into containers. An intern stood in one corner of the operating room, labeling everything.

As Meg stood there, the water buffalo from her nightmares appeared behind the glass, staring at her with glassy, dead eyes, except this time it was Jata, shaking and helpless in the mud pit as the humans burrowed their way into her in a wet dance of blood, knives, and intertwining hands. Jata was the water buffalo and she—the perfect fucking keeper—she was the dragon.

36 Days *after* Hatching

Someone from the Mammal Kingdom stole her hose again.

"Leprechauns," Michael said as he returned it, piling it around her shoulders. "They love moving stuff around and playing tricks on you. Must've been the leprechauns."

Meg pointed to the howling freeway that cut through the river. "Next time it happens, I'm going to throw you off that bridge so you can go meet the troll."

He didn't point out the fact that he had a good ten inches and nearly two hundred pounds on her, but then he didn't ask about her red-rimmed eyes either, or hound her for the results of the autopsy, which she still didn't know. He just clapped her on the shoulder, let out his big, rumbling laugh, and sent her down the south walkway toward the Reptile Kingdom.

It was warm today, already in the sixties and not even lunchtime. Spring was here. The river valley hit her in an unreal, distant way with its transformation. The trees on the far bank created a horizon of lush, rippling green, and the only bare branches in sight were the driftwood bones rising from the runoff ponds that swelled along the base of the bluffs. Everything on the water breathed life, from the waving marsh grasses and darting songbirds, all the way up to the raptors circling overhead and the perfume of the first purple wildflowers drifting past her as she walked. She'd missed it completely. The budding plants, the long, rainy days—she couldn't remember a single moment of it.

She started to veer left on the fork in the path that separated the main grounds from the Bird Kingdom but stopped when she glanced over and saw Dr. Reading sitting alone on one of the benches halfway down the path to the towering, golden wing. Her back was to Meg, but the neatly coiled gray bun and the slight, stooped shoulders were hers—no question. Without knowing exactly why, Meg veered toward the doctor, trying to fold her arms over the coils of hose and make use of her suddenly useless hands.

Dr. Reading's gaze hovered over the river, her hands folded in her lap as if they were squeezing something tightly against her abdomen. She looked older when she wasn't moving. Maybe it was because they were here on death row, the path to the ill-fated birds, but Dr. Reading had that unfocused twitch in her eyes—that knowledge that haunts the elderly when someone dies and they know there is nothing left to be done. There were a thousand things Meg wanted to say to the doctor, but that blank look stopped them all. She shuffled up to the railing and kicked it, scuffing one boot and then the other, wondering how to begin.

"I've always had a hard time with places like this," Dr. Reading commented, as detached as if she were talking to the empty bench. "Tight spaces and imposed environments. When I was a girl, I hated classrooms—all those walls and the teachers standing in front of them with their rules, trying to keep us contained. I spent most of those years staring out windows, wishing for the day to end so I could escape to the creek and my woods. I wasn't made for classrooms or zoos; I belong out there, with the animals in our natural habitat."

Meg didn't know what to say. Maybe this wasn't such a good idea.

"It's lovely out there, isn't it?" Dr. Reading's voice might as well have been coming from that far bank of blooming trees, it sounded so far away.

Meg shrugged and turned to leave, but then Dr. Reading looked over and asked, "Has the river always been this shallow?" and Meg saw her eyes. They were hollow and dark, completely unconnected to her mouth. As soon as Meg registered them, dread clenched her chest. This wasn't about a river.

"Antonio ... did something happen?"

Dr. Reading shook her head, and Meg started breathing again. She turned to the river, hugging the coil of hose tightly to her chest, and played along. "There's a lot of sediment runoff from the north. It clogs the water, chokes it off into sandbars and pools."

"Where does it lead?"

"It links up with the Mississippi a couple of miles down, and then they head south for the gulf."

"And the ocean beyond," Dr. Reading added, then was quiet for a moment. When she spoke again, her voice still had that disconnected quality, as if she wasn't here at all.

"My creek led to a small lake in the New England woods. It was a tiny thing, but I was just a little girl then. It was a fine place to tramp around and explore. I catalogued all the native fauna in my notebook."

"Oh." It was hard to tell what kind of a conversation they were having.

"What about you?"

"What about me?" Meg turned around on the off chance Dr. Reading was talking to someone else, but there was no other staff in sight.

"How did you get started? Forgive me, but you don't really seem like you fit in around here, Ms. Yancy."

Meg huffed out a laugh and shrugged. "I don't know. I didn't have a creek, if that's what you're asking. I grew up in the burbs."

"People don't just end up in our profession, Ms. Yancy. You must have had a calling."

No one had ever asked her that before. Granted, she didn't exactly invite idle chitchat with her coworkers, but it wasn't anything anyone talked about anyway. It was just who they were, something imprinted into each of them in their own way.

Eyes unfocused, she let herself remember when it had been imprinted into her. How old was she then? Twelve or thirteen at the most.

"My mother was into dogs, and we traveled a lot," she said. "Once a year, we'd go to Florida for a show and stay with one of her friends who bred border collies. I liked it there; she had a pool. Anyway, one morning we woke up to a lot of barking, and then my mom's friend started screaming. We ran out and saw an alligator swimming in circles in her pool, with one of her dogs locked in its jaws. The other dogs were going crazy in their kennels, and my mom ran to call the police. Her friend kept shaking and screaming next to me on the patio, but I couldn't do anything. I just stared at it. There were streams of blood trailing out along the alligator's back, turning the water red. I guess any other girl my age would've been freaking out, but I just couldn't believe I was so close to this huge, powerful predator. I knew better than to walk forward, but I couldn't walk backwards either.

"The dog was long gone by the time this guy showed up in an unmarked truck. He said he was a trapper. He noosed the alligator and wrangled it out of the pool all by himself. I remember noticing he wasn't a very big guy, just wiry and tough. I watched him the whole time and handed him rope and tape when he asked. I wanted to help. I thought he'd take it to some alligator farm or a marsh somewhere, but after he loaded it in the back of his truck he said he was happy it was so big, that he'd make a lot of money off of it.

"Later I asked my mom's friend what he meant, and she said the trappers got to kill all the nuisance alligators and sell their meat and hides. She said she wished she could have killed it herself. My mom and I argued the entire drive home, all the way from Florida to Minnesota. She kept sticking up for her friend, saying how horrible it was that her dog was dead, that the alligator deserved to die. I argued back, saying there had to be someone somewhere who could've looked after it, made sure it had enough to eat so it didn't have to attack pets.

"After that I became kind of obsessed. My mom hated it." Meg smiled, remembering. "I knew I wanted to take care of animals—the outcast, unfriendly ones always appealed to me the most, go figure— but I was naive and idealistic then; I thought I could change people's minds about them, too, and it seemed like the best place to do that was at a zoo. Look at all the people that come to zoos."

A noisy group passed behind them, the mothers' warnings and kids' shrieks echoing down the path.

"And now you don't want to change people's minds?" Dr. Reading asked, watching them go.

"Look at them." Meg faced the receding group. "They're way too preoccupied raising their offspring and managing their own crazy lives to think about the ethical treatment and care of animals."

"Maybe you're looking at the wrong people."

"They're the only people here most days."

Dr. Reading shook her head. "No, not the parents. Look to the children."

They tracked the group's progress down the path, listening to the kids' shouts and laughter. One of them pointed at a hawk circling the river, and then they disappeared inside the Bird Kingdom. A minute of silence passed, punctuated only by the breeze and the traffic on the bridge. Meg was thinking she should probably get back to her exhibits when Dr. Reading took a deep breath and braced her hand on the arm of the bench, leaning forward.

"There were no deformities."

Meg's jaw dropped.

"Her reproductive system was textbook female. The blood and tissue samples are all coming back normal. We haven't been able to substantiate the DNA recombination theory at all. We discussed the possibility of cloning to try to duplicate the scenario—"

"Oh my God." Meg's back hit the fence with a dull clunk of the hose.

"—but even if we recreated the same genetic dragon, there's no guarantee that she'll reproduce by parthenogenesis again. I think that idea is on its way out already. At this point, we're setting up some long-term tests on the sexual argument, but after that—we're just hoping that it will happen again and give us a chance to gather more data."

Dr. Reading met Meg's shock and relief with a microscopic shake of her head. Meg could see an emotion swelling at the edges of her eyes and cheeks, but it was locked underneath the grid of meshed lines and tendons tightening her face. "I have no explanation."

Never in a million years did she think those four words could come out of Dr. Joyce Reading's mouth. The impact of it sank through the shock of the results and gave Meg a hollow, bitter satisfaction. "So despite everything, with all your fancy tests and Jata's dead body laid at your feet, you can't explain this any more than I can."

"We've eliminated many possibilities and are working to seg-regate more. When and if the aberration appears again, we'll have a solid foundation of research to draw from."

"Why can't you just admit it?" Meg took a step closer.

"Admit what?"

"That you can't force evolution into a cage. That these animals who are stuck in the tight spaces you hate so much are free in ways you'll never understand." She knew how she sounded, could hear the snottiness in her own voice, but she couldn't seem to help it.

Dr. Reading's eyebrows and voice both shot up. "I'm not trying to cage evolution, Ms. Yancy, but we should be able to explain it like any other scientific principle."

Meg shrugged. "Komodos are running out of mates, both here and in the wild. It's only logical that if they couldn't reproduce sexually, they had to find another way to do it."

"What, you think your Jata looked around, saw there was no available male, and switched on some parthenogenic code in her body?"

"No. Obviously it had to be inherited, but the species has been threatened for some time now."

Dr. Reading leaned farther forward, in full professor voice now. The lost old woman on the bench had completely disappeared. "Define 'some time.'"

It had begun with the Western explorers or maybe even before, when the locals started settling on Komodo Island. "At least a hundred years."

"A hundred years isn't enough time to evolve an extra toenail, let alone an entirely new reproductive method."

"The environment forced it to happen."

"Now you sound like Lamarck."

Meg barely remembered the name—he was one of those European guys putting out evolutionary theories before Darwin came along and made everyone look like idiots. Dr. Reading stood up and started pacing up and down the railing next to Meg.

"Lamarck's adaptive force stated that acquired characteristics would transfer genetically to the next generation. A giraffe, stretching her neck to the higher leaves, would give birth to giraffes with longer necks."

Pausing at the far end of her pacing circuit, Dr. Reading nudged a wildflower with her foot and watched a moth flutter to the next patch of flowers down the bluff. When she finally looked up, her expression was condescending.

"What you're proposing, Ms. Yancy, is even more ridiculous. If every species that sensed it was threatened could spontaneously reproduce, there would be no such thing as extinction." She swept a hand across the river. "There would be a brontosaurus over there, chewing on those trees."

"Fine," Meg practically yelled. "You explain it then."

"I can't, and I won't presume to."

Toe to toe, they stared each other down, the anger congealing on both their faces as the seconds ticked by and neither threw back another retort. Eventually Dr. Reading sighed and turned back to the river.

"Jata's daughters are a biological mystery—like unearthing a bone that has no match in the fossil record. You can barely begin to speculate about what it is without the rest of the skeleton."

Meg looked at the ground. "Maybe they were right. Maybe it really was a miracle."

"It's unexplained." Dr. Reading's tone said the discussion was closed. She smoothed a loose strand of hair back into her bun and looked toward the Reptile Kingdom building across the pond. "It's still a shame she had to be locked up in here, that any of you have to. I'd go crazy here."

"We'd put you in a really nice exhibit."

A smile cracked over Dr. Reading's face, and she patted the hose on Meg's shoulder before heading back toward the main grounds. "I'm sure you would."

Meg watched her for a minute and then, on an impulse, ran to catch up with her. Dr. Reading cocked an eyebrow at her but kept walking. Apparently the time for sitting still was over.

Meg swallowed. "I need a favor."

～◊

A few hours later, in the boardroom, management called a meeting to review the bids on the hatchlings. Gerald Dawson, Dr. Reading, Chuck, and a bunch of admins all sat around the table going through a list of the bidding zoos and the highlights of their offers. Borrowing one of Chuck's pens, Meg crossed out every zoo on the list except one.

"The Tallahassee Zoo wants to take just one hatchling in exchange for—"

"No," Meg said, making Chuck pause.

"It's one of the top five bids we've received, Megan. They're offering an albino alligator in exchange, which is an exceedingly rare specimen, in addition to a generous sum."

"All they have there is the old alligator exhibit space, and when I say 'old' I'm talking about both the alligator and the space. We're not a nursing home, and their exhibit is a ten-by-twenty-foot box with a concrete floor and an unfiltered pool. We can't give those people one of Jata's hatchlings."

"I would concur," Dr. Reading added.

"Well, there's also an offer from Anchorage that—"

"No."

Chuck turned in his seat, the vein in his forehead starting to pop. "You haven't even heard what they're offering."

"They get less than six hours of daylight in the winter. It's incredibly difficult for a tropical animal to regulate in those conditions."

"So we'll have them buy a UV light." One of the finance guys chimed in, throwing a disgusted look toward the head of the table.

"Ms. Yancy." Gerald steepled his fingers and gazed down the table at her. "We're going to move two of these hatchlings out of the Zoo of America. That's a non-negotiable fact. I think we can all appreciate your concerns, but no zoo is going to be perfect."

"No, but we can get closer than this." She waved the list in the air and dropped it, facedown, on the table. Too keyed up to sit any longer, she pushed out from her chair and stood up to pace the room.

"All the zoos that you've listed in your top slots are U.S. zoos. They're all registered members of the AZA. I have, uh, every respect for the AZA, but everyone in this room knows that there's no way they'll allow all three of these hatchlings to breed. The Komodo population in the U.S. zoos is so limited that the three of them would completely unbalance the gene pool."

She walked over to a world map at the end of the room and stood in front of it, pointing at all the hulking countries that floated on top of the blue graphs. "We have to send both hatchlings outside the U.S., where the AZA won't have jurisdiction."

She turned around and faced the silent rows of faces. "There are maybe less than four thousand Komodo dragons in the world. Isn't it more important to make sure they can breed than to get some old white alligator in return? After everything we've been through, after Jata somehow managed to give these dragons to us, don't we owe them the chance to flourish? They need space. They need mates. They need care. And we can give them all of these things."

She looked toward Dr. Reading, who gave her a tiny, tight nod and broke in. "Speaking of jurisdiction, I know that I don't have any here in this room, but throughout my extensive research and travel, I've worked with many zoos, and I have a recommendation, Gerald—a place that I'm confident will fit all of the needs addressed in this discussion." Dr. Reading glanced back at Meg. "And there may be some bonuses with it as well."

40 Days *after* Hatching

Aweek after Jata's death, Meg paced the public trails of the Reptile Kingdom. When anyone asked what she was doing, she said she was looking for Gemma, and so far that had been enough to get people to stop talking, drop eye contact, and back away. The one time Meg bumped into her in the staff hallway outside the iguana exhibit, Gemma had acted as if nothing had happened. She'd actually stopped to ask if Meg needed a hand, leaning on the wall and flipping her radio from hand to hand, all nonchalant. Hip Gemma. Casual Gemma. Paycheck-dangling-out-of-her-back-pocket, let's-let-bygones-be-bygones Gemma. Meg had walked into the iguana exhibit and shut the door in her face.

Nobody said anything. Nobody asked her for her assistance. They all kept their distance, but the strange thing was that she kind of was looking for Gemma. She missed the joking, the stories, the easy, quiet work between them when they overhauled exhibit after exhibit—but most of all she missed the not knowing. She missed not knowing what Gemma would do to save herself.

At least she could move around freely today. The media had mobbed the zoo all weekend, looking for interviews to follow up Jata's attack, death, and autopsy—the bizarre chain of events had captured national attention—but today there were new stories, more shootings on the North Side and tankers tipping in the middle of rush hour on the cross-town. The city was blooming with disasters, and the reporters, good honeybees that they were, had all buzzed on to the next flower.

Since she'd formally signed the deal in Gerald Dawson's office, Meg spent more and more time on the public side of the zoo, the formerly dreaded area now an anonymous refuge. She didn't have the energy to explain to the other keepers what she'd done for the hatchlings, why it seemed like the right thing. Instead, she stopped to answer every question from visitors along the path, happy to show a group of tourists how to tell the geckos apart, and even give a little girl a quick lesson about the birds and the bees.

"So that opening right up there"—Meg pointed to a diamond-shaped skylight—"is how the stork can fly in and drop off the babies. There's a special latch on the window that only storks know how to open."

She waved off the mother's grateful beam and watched the two of them walk over to the last exhibit before the exit—Jata's exhibit. Meg crossed to the railing nearby and leaned over it, tracing the lines of Jata's space without even really looking at it, just feeling the sink of the sandy beach under her boots, smelling the hints of algae that lingered in the empty, drained pool, and sliding her arm along the bumpy stone façade of the back wall. They'd transferred one of the big tortoises into the new outdoor exhibit to distract people, make them look for something other than bloodstains dyeing the grass, but the indoor space wouldn't be filled until the hatchling left the baby building. The place was empty and yet so full of everything she remembered—all the years of feedings, cleanings, and play—and the contrast between the empty and the full just kept rubbing her raw every time.

"Momma, what does it say?" The girl pointed at the sign.

"It says, 'Komodo dragons live on a few islands in Indonesia. They can grow up to ten feet long and are the world's largest lizard. Jah-tah ... is a six-year-old female dragon, named for a serpent goddess. The Dayak people of Borneo believed that Jata the goddess ruled the underworld and rose up from the ocean to create everything between the sea and the sky.' Pretty neat, huh?"

"Where is it? I don't see it." Head pressed up against the bars, the girl strained to see directly below the viewing platform, as if by sheer force she could will the animal into sight.

"The dragon's not here anymore," Meg said flatly.

"Where'd it go?"

"She died."

Without any warning the kid's eyes watered up, and she buried her head in her mother's legs. The mother rolled her eyes and whispered, "We just watched *Bambi*."

Kneeling down, she rubbed her kid's back and made soothing little noises. She glanced up at Meg, a supplication in her eyes. "It's okay, sweetie. The zookeeper was just kidding. She's not dead; she just went away, right?"

"Uh, right," Meg lied. Her first instinct was to run away, but there was something compelling in the kid's naked sadness, how a child could be shaken by the death of an animal she'd never heard or seen. She remembered what Dr. Reading had said about children's minds, about children being the ones who were reachable.

"She's not dead," Meg reiterated, trying to sound confident.

"How do you know?" The kid looked up, all tears and disbelieving red cheeks. She was going to be a hard sell.

"Honey," the mother said, "she's the zookeeper. It's her job to know things like that."

"But she said—"

"What I meant was that she's gone. I watched her go."

The tears had stopped falling, but the kid's face was still wet. Meg dug a clean but wrinkled tissue out of her pocket, handed it to the mother, and watched her carefully wipe the girl's face dry. She was no good at guessing ages, but it was a weekday, so the kid was definitely too young for school. Four years old, maybe? How did a four-year-old wonder so many things? It was mind-blowing, to think of what it would be like to be responsible for a life like that, to field the infinite questions of a growing mind and somehow try to teach them everything you ever learned. The kids that churned through the zoo every day were like some massive, chaotic ecosystem unto themselves. As a whole they inspired irritation and frustration, and on bad days you could kind of see where that guy got the idea for *Lord of the Flies*. Individually, though, there was something undeniably amazing about them. A kind of pull, like the first time Meg picked up a hatchling and saw its perfection.

She didn't realize she was staring until the kid cocked her head back at Meg, returning her gaze.

"Where did the dragon go?" she asked.

Shaking her head, Meg looked away toward the exit doors, glimpsing the river valley and its far, sun-washed banks. The water moved sluggishly downstream, on its way to meet the Mississippi and the ocean beyond.

"She went swimming," Meg murmured. "She decided to swim home."

2 Months *after* Hatching

The regular hospital wing was noisy and crowded. A hassled-looking nurse thumbed the way to Antonio's room after Meg leaned over the top of her station and asked three times. The rudeness was fantastic after all the polite whispers and creepy pats on the hand in the ICU. She wandered in the direction the nurse had pointed, glancing into rooms as she passed. Every door was open, the TVs all pumping out tinny distraction, family members walking in and out, and attendants wheeling gurneys, wheelchairs, and dollies up and down the hallway.

She stopped outside Room 248 and kicked the tile floor for a minute. After visiting the hospital every week, this was the first time she'd actually come to his room. There'd been no point before. The nurses gave her a quick update each time on the progress of his leg. Surgeries went well, infections were controlled, skin grafts, physical therapy, and on and on. Why stand around a hospital bed telling someone he was going to be fine and trying to think of stupid conversation?

But this was the last visit, and she couldn't avoid going inside anymore. There were things that had to be said.

The Twins game was on inside the room; she could hear the announcer whooping over a double play. Smoothing her T-shirt over her hips, she heaved a sigh and walked in.

Antonio was sitting up in the first hospital bed; a curtain bisected the room, concealing the window and anyone who might have been on the other side. When Meg appeared, he looked over, and his face lit up. His usually oak-colored skin was as pale as maple after spending the last month indoors, but the same gleam colored his eyes. They came alive, eager and hesitant at the same time, locking into her face as if he'd been expecting this moment since he'd woken up in the hospital four weeks ago.

They didn't say *hi*. They didn't say *how are you* because *how-are-you*s were for people who didn't give a shit how you were and only needed to fill the empty air, and *how are you* between her and Antonio—if they meant it, if they each really wanted to know—could take hours, or days, and she doubted he could handle what she would say.

He propped himself up higher against the pillows, stretching his hospital gown over a sling that dangled his left leg above the bed. "I was wondering if you'd show up before they released me. You're cutting it close, Yancy."

A line of staples closed the skin together over his calf. It looked like a Frankenstein zipper running up his leg. One of the ICU doctors said it was so the air could get to the wound and bring the infection to the surface.

"Yeah, well, I've been busy." She stood in front of the olive-green chair that flanked his bed and crossed her arms.

"Too busy to see if I'm dead or alive?"

She shrugged. "I'm sure I would've gotten a memo if you kicked it."

"Wow, that was beautiful. You should freelance for Hallmark."

"They keep lowballing me."

He grinned, but it didn't last, couldn't survive on his face as other emotions started flooding over it. She turned away, pacing the length of the wall as he turned the TV off and left them in silence. Now that she was here, the words were gone, squeezed out of the room by the weight of that day. It wasn't just a memory; it was everywhere, staring at her from the fat, black staples in his leg and the dark hollows riding under his eyes. Jata's carnage was still twisted up inside him, living in this hospital bed, leveling him. Meg kept pacing the edges of the room, blindly, unable to look at him and face the blame that she knew was there.

"Meg."

She stopped and dropped her head. His voice was low, almost buried by the hallway noise. She didn't say anything.

"Will you look at me?"

She turned around and looked at him from across the room. He nodded, his eyes burning into hers, and repeated her name.

Shaking her head, she started to speak, but he held up a hand to stop her. He dropped his head back against the pillows, stared up at the ceiling, and swallowed. His Adam's apple bobbed up and down, exposed.

"Have you ever had a dream, something you wanted so badly and worked so long to get that it seemed like everything in your life was either building toward it or getting in your way?" He swallowed again and paused.

"My father told me not to come to the U.S. The American dream is dead, he said. Everything you could want is right here. My family was happy, and they had their little place carved out in the world, but I wanted more. I wanted to make a difference, to change the world around me. The fish were disappearing from the ocean, but did my father get depressed? No, he just stopped being a fisherman and started working for the tourists. He adapted, but I couldn't. I thought, why accept this when there's got to be a way to make it better? We can fly around the world or into space; we can split an atom into pieces. Why can't we save the animals, too? We can do anything, can't we?"

As he talked, she skirted the foot of the bed, not even realizing she was moving until she'd drawn up near his side, where his hand lay limp and pale on the sheets. He stared straight up, past the water-stained ceiling tiles, through the roof, looking at things that were miles away from this stale room.

"Jata—when we found out about the parth, and you and I started ... you made me see things differently. It was the first time in years I started to think that maybe we couldn't control animal populations, couldn't put things back on track the way I had dreamed, and I kind of hated you for it."

She exhaled in a laugh, and he smiled, too, just a ghost of a smile at the sky, and then he turned his head and looked at her.

"I was interested, too. Obviously. But then you just kept shutting me out."

"I shut you out?"

"Yeah, you did. And then I got the test results back, and everything changed. It was an entirely new game, a game with no rules, and I thought that this was my chance. This was the opportunity I had worked so hard to prepare for, to prove that the technology could help us understand the phenomenon. I thought I could show everyone, that somehow I could capture that miracle and reproduce it. The cure for Komodo extinction, right? It was the first step to saving other threatened species, every endangered animal on the planet."

The whole speech was too perfect, the words chosen as if he had pulled every one off the hospital shelf and examined it, making sure it was exactly what he meant. He had been waiting for her, she realized. He thought she blamed him for Jata's death.

Now he shook his head in disgust. "When I followed you into the exhibit, I didn't even see Jata. I looked right through her."

"I should have made you leave the second you walked in." She twisted her arms around her stomach, searching for the words that came so easily to him and tripped her up every time. "It was my fault. She was under so much stress, and then I pushed you. It was like waving a red flag."

"It wasn't your fault."

She nodded, the same way she nodded at everyone at the zoo who said that. As if they thought that as a collective, speaking the words would actually displace the blame, would exempt the keeper from keeping her animal from harm.

He reached out and touched her, sliding his fingers into the hand that she'd locked into her ribs, and squeezed.

"I'm so sorry about Jata."

It was his touch that broke her. She pressed her lips together and nodded, nodded, fighting the salt that glazed her vision. He muttered something in Spanish, pulled her down around the gurney, and tucked her into the space between his chest and chin. Dropping her head on his shoulder, she felt the paper-thin gown turn hot and wet under her cheek as his arm circled her back, rubbing comfort into her bones. He held her, rocking for long, silent minutes while she cried, letting all the hurt unravel and pour out.

"We killed her, I know," he said, but she felt the words more than heard them as the scratchy vibration of his throat pulsed through her forehead. She closed her eyes. "Not you or me, but all of us. We all did."

After a while the tears slowed and then stopped, crystallizing into tight, raw tracks on her face. The quiet strung out, and she stared at the wall as the bustle of the hallway filtered into the room. They didn't speak. It was a mourning silence, a space wide enough for Jata to swagger into, claim her place, and bask.

After a few minutes, she sat up, wiped at the dark splotches on his shoulder, steadied her breathing, and then spoke quietly. "I'm sorry, too."

"I keep thinking what if, you know, what if I had done something differently that—"

She laid a finger on his lips and smiled, cracking the dried tears open on her cheeks. "There you go again."

His eyes locked on hers. He took her wrist and moved her hand from his mouth, pulled her down, and kissed her. It was a smooth, lingering kiss, sweet and salty, a first kiss—because for the first time they weren't fighting—and it tasted like the last. Eventually, she pulled back but didn't know what to say. What was left? As the silence turned from comforting to awkward, she got up out of the bed.

Antonio cleared his throat. "The doctors say I'll make a full recovery. Two legs and all. I would have been out of here a lot quicker if I let them amputate, but I had this weird thing about having two feet."

She didn't say anything, so he kept talking. "They're discharging me in another few days, ready and certified to take care of some hatchlings."

"Only one hatchling." She glanced up, relieved that she remembered. This was why she'd come in the first place.

He shifted in the bed, trying to sit up higher. "What? Did something happen? Chuck didn't say anything about it when he was here last."

"Nothing bad." She kicked the floor with her sandal. "The Wildlife Refuge in Jakarta is taking two of them. We signed the final agreement last week."

"They're too young to travel now."

"Conventionally, yes. You're right. But there's been some special arrangements."

He waited, but she didn't continue. As the silence drew out, a kid in scrubs knocked on the door. He wore a pink Mohawk and a cheesy grin.

"Supper time." He carried a tray over to the bed and set it down in front of Antonio. "How's it going, man?"

"Fine, thanks."

"We got some tasty soylent green tonight. Goulash and a killer veggie medley." He whipped the cover off the tray and sent waves of greasy meat sauce wafting across the room. Meg's stomach clenched. She tried to breathe through her mouth, but the pools of saliva were already forming at the back of her throat. Shit.

"Is this the bathroom?" She didn't wait for an answer before running through a side door by the TV and slamming it closed. Flushing the toilet to cover the noise, she gagged into the basin. So much for the whole-wheat sandwich and apple.

She started to rinse her mouth out but spit the metallic, lukewarm water back into the sink. No wonder it took so long to get healthy around here, when it tasted as if they were pulling tap water straight from the Mississippi.

Antonio was watching the door when she came out. He'd put the cover back on the tray, thank God, and the Mohawk guy was gone.

"You okay?"

She nodded. "Yeah, I guess. The autopsy was hard."

"That's not what I meant. You look pale. You're shivering."

She sidestepped the look of concern and brushed the covers around the end of the bed. "There's a virus going around." She tossed him a smirk as she reached the top of the blanket. "I probably should have told you that before you kissed me."

"Well, I guess I can't say you didn't bring me anything." He flashed her a smile, the old cat grin, the one she used to want to slap off his face, and reached out for her hand.

"I should get going so you can eat." She glanced at the leg in the swing. "I'm glad that you're going to be okay."

"I always land on my feet." He squeezed her hand.

"Yeah, I know you will." She looked at the floor. It was time.

Reaching into her back pocket, she pulled out the faded picture of Bubchen and her keeper and pressed its curled edges into his palm. "See you around."

2 ½ Months *after* Hatching

The ship's horn blasted—a low, bleating siren—as the bow pulled away from the berth. Meg stood on the balcony outside her room, five stories above the churning froth of the Pacific Ocean, and watched the land recede into gray, choppy water. Industrial warehouses and shipyards faded behind a huge suspension bridge that spanned the width of the port of Los Angeles.

"See you later, suckers!" someone shouted from a deck above her. A woman laughed and added an ecstatic, "Good-bye!"

Meg didn't say anything; she just watched as the United States disappeared, with no idea when she'd ever see it again.

As of last week, she was no longer Keeper Level 1 at the Zoo of America. She, Meg Yancy, the zookeeper who could barely keep her own job, had accepted the position of Behavioral Studies Head Researcher at the Wildlife Refuge in Jakarta, and they expected her to arrive with the hatchlings in two weeks. They were launching a new research department and—after Dr. Reading highly recommended her—asked Meg to head up the project. Her goal, the one they had given to her in neat, black letters on the contract, was to find ways that humans and Komodo dragons could coexist. They wanted her to find hope for Komodo survival. It was a base-jumping job, pure professional suicide to go halfway around the world in search of a holy grail with a tiny budget, coworkers who spoke Malay, and virtually no legal way of preventing the invasion of people into the dragons' territory. How could she say no?

Hope. They wanted her to bring hope to the dragons. The word intimidated her; she had no idea what it even looked like—was probably the last person in the world qualified to find it—and all she'd brought with her was a newspaper. It was the closest thing she had.

Last week they ran the headline she'd been waiting to see: MIRACLE BIRTH ENDURES! LEGENDARY SCIENTIST STUMPED BY VIRGIN BIRTH. She'd barely crossed the Minnesota state line when the story hit the AP wire, and it kept popping up in local papers the whole way to California, like some giant middle finger unearthing itself from the Rocky Mountains and stretching its shadow all the way back to the Zoo of America. The zoo wasn't giving any further press releases about it, but Dr. Reading—who was back in Costa Rica by now—co-published the breaking story in a trade journal with Antonio. The two of them were planning on writing a book together, but Meg didn't need to read it to know what it would conclude: Jata's miracle lived on.

Despite all the new press, she'd managed to make the cross-country trip without drawing any attention. She'd convinced Chuck and Gerald not to use airfreight to transport the hatchlings. People went back and forth on which was better—air or ground—but she'd seen too many arriving specimens come off the plane sick or traumatized. It was far less stressful, if a bit longer, to transport animals by ground with a familiar keeper. Driving the hatchlings herself, she'd checked the rearview mirror obsessively, watching the dark pools of their eyes for any signs of tension. During the whole drive she'd never turned the car off or left them for longer than the time it took to get a coffee, pee, and pay the gas station attendant. She talked to them all the way across the country, telling them a little about the refuge and Jakarta, but mostly stories about Jata—like when she'd stolen one of Meg's gloves and wouldn't give it back, and the time she'd ripped apart the shrub that used to grow in front of her cave, meeting Meg at the exhibit door with a mouthful of branches. She'd been so pleased with herself. Though neither generation would have had any interest in the other, Meg felt as if she were bridging a gap, if only to mend the jagged pieces in her own mind.

The sea transport didn't even cost that much more than a plane ticket because, as luck would have it, two round-trip tickets from New York to Dublin easily converted into a single one-way suite from LA to Jakarta, with a few stops in between. She'd called her father from the motel last night and told him the news. He was shocked and a little hurt that she'd cashed out his present, but he didn't say much after asking the usual questions—where would she live, how was she moving her stuff. The stuff part was easy enough. She'd sold most of it to Neil so he could rent the place out as a furnished apartment, and her entire wardrobe and *National Geographic* collection fit into the trunk of her car. As for living arrangements, Gus—who was over the moon about welcoming Meg to his team—had found her a little house right next to the refuge and even arranged for a woman to cook and clean. Her father asked if the house had a spare bedroom, somewhere the old man could crash if he flew down to see her for Christmas. She said it did and was surprised at how good the idea sounded. He congratulated her one more time, and when they hung up, neither one of them said good-bye. The Yancys didn't say things like good-bye.

The call she hadn't expected came right after that. Ben had heard the news about the hatchlings, of course, but he hadn't known she was poised to leave the country for good. She'd left him a message to call but never really thought he would. After filling him in, there was an uncomfortable silence before Ben sighed.

"I'm glad for you, Meg. I really am."

"Thanks, Ben. I feel like … like this is what I never knew I always wanted."

He laughed. "Yeah, well, neither of us were too good at thinking about the future. I'm glad yours found you, anyway."

"What about yours? Did you get my package? I didn't know where to send it besides Paco's place."

"Yeah, I got it. We stopped back there between Tulsa and Montana."

She'd pulled his garbage bag full of notebooks out of the trash can after he'd left that last night but didn't know what to do with them. They'd sat in the corner of the living room, next to the TV, until she was cleaning out the rest of her personal items from the apartment and came across them again. Ben had recorded years' upon years' worth of news analysis in those pages, and it wasn't just idle note taking, she'd seen as she flipped through them. He really did have a gift for seeing the true stories, understanding the psychology of what was said and the cost of what went unspoken. He simply had to keep them; it was impossible to throw them away.

"I don't know what I'm going to do with them," Ben said after another long silence.

"You're going to keep writing in them. I bought you some fresh ones and something else, too."

"Yeah, I saw that." There was some rustling in the background and then he cleared his throat, reading. "*Mother Jones.*"

"I read through a whole rack at the bookstore before I found it. That's where you'll publish your paper."

"So now that you have a fancy new job, you're just going to tell everyone their future? Psychic dragon lady. You could work a good hustle at the fairs."

She laughed. "That would require contact with people, right?"

"Yeah, maybe not your thing."

"Well, I read a little about Mother Jones, too, the actual one. She spoke out against mining bosses, I guess, but the union organizers didn't like her either because she was an agitator. She just got people worked up."

"Yeah, I know."

"I figured you would." Meg paused, enjoying the unexpected easiness between them, knowing it was more than she deserved. "Anyway, she reminded me of someone, a fellow agitator. I bought myself a subscription, so you've got twelve months to get it published."

"Look at you, bossing everyone around, acting like you know best. Soon they'll put you in charge of the whole damn island."

They talked for a while longer about what her job was going to be like, the daily grind of the fair circuit, where Ben was going to live in the fall. Maybe because they hadn't really talked to each other in so long, or because they'd had more than a month apart, or because there was a thousand miles between them—whatever the reason, something had changed. They weren't lovers and they weren't friends, but on her last night in America, Ben wished her well, and it seemed as if he meant it. And when she told him to lay off the pot and take care of himself, she meant it, too.

She hadn't felt any nerves or nostalgia driving through Los Angeles this morning. She'd already left her home far behind; this was just the last U.S. stop on the way to a new, unknown home. At the port she got through customs fine with the whole freaking book of required permits and visas, but the coast guard had been a little more difficult.

"The permits allow you to take the lizards, ma'am, not these other undocumented animals." The officer shook the container and tried to peer through the opaque lid.

"What am I supposed to feed them? I can't exactly take them to the dining room with me and give them table scraps."

"I don't know. My cousin had an iguana, and it would eat just about anything. Loved mashed potatoes."

She leveled him with a glare. "Well, I'll just call the government of Indonesia and tell them their *Varanus komodoensis* specimens died at sea because the American coast guard is afraid of crickets."

After a few more threats and a telephone call to his supervisor, he eventually let her board the ship, crickets and all, but the hatchlings' tank had to be stored in a quarantine hold. They absolutely refused to let her keep them in her cabin and only granted her the clearance to visit them twice a day to check the heater, humidifier, and ventilation system.

"What am I supposed to do with the rest of my time?"

The ship officer shrugged and locked the quarantine door. "Go say *bon voyage*."

Now, as the United States and everything she knew disappeared into the horizon, the edges of something started to unfurl in her chest. It was a foreign, wild feeling, but she let it grow anyway, trying not to kill it the way she'd killed everything else. Let it breathe. Let it go. The last stripe of land vanished into the ocean. She waved goodbye to no one and leaned over the deck railing to look in the other direction.

Ahead, the water moved, choppy and blue on the horizon. It was the water she'd read about all of Jata's life, where the great Komodo kings destroyed their bindings and cages and smashed their way into the ocean, escaping into the waves that called them back to the rocky shores of Padar and the forests of Rinca. Without knowing anything else, they chose freedom over life. Staring at the water, Meg heard what they'd heard as the waves broke against the ship. She felt their desperation and their hope, even if it was the hope of the damned, for the first time in her life.

As if it sensed the feeling, the baby fluttered deep inside her abdomen. The doctor had said it was too early to feel anything, that such fluttering was just indigestion or a cramp, but when the hell did a cramp flutter? Besides, this was the same doctor who told her the birth control patch was foolproof. She wasn't exactly buying stock in that guy. Automatically her hands cupped her belly, rubbing the skin through her shirt.

"I'm glad, too," she said to the ocean.

All those weeks of nausea and bizarre dreams, and she'd only figured it out a few weeks ago, after her breasts had started to throb every morning. A child.

She hadn't told anyone about the baby before she left because, for one thing, she didn't know who to tell—according to the date the doctor had given her, the father could have been either Antonio or Ben—but also because it didn't matter. Even though she'd enjoyed talking to Ben on the phone last night, it was obvious their relationship was spent, and she hadn't spoken to Antonio since that day at the hospital. She'd already packed up and left town by the time he returned to work, although just after she'd crossed the Minnesota border she'd gotten his one-line e-mail on her phone: *Learn how to write, Yancy.* It made her smile, but she didn't write back. If and when she did, she wasn't planning on mentioning the baby. Neither Antonio nor Ben were daddy material, and especially not to her child, not after everything that happened. Telling them and then moving to the other side of the world was just cruel. And maybe she was harsh and cynical, but she had never been intentionally cruel. This baby was hers and hers alone. After all the chaos and grief of the last two months, this was the one thing that finally made sense to her—starting a new life with all of her fatherless children.

She leaned farther over the railing and looked ahead to the open water and overcast sky. A plane climbed through the clouds and roared ahead of the ship toward the place where West became

East, where her baby would be born. The kid would have so many questions someday. How much time would she have to fit the pieces together and try to make sense out of events that rebelled against logic? That defied all human knowledge of nature? Somehow she had to stand in the place where humans met animals, where the planet's conquering species struck the reptiles' unyielding will to survive, and explain a miracle that she could never fully understand.

Rubbing her stomach gently, she watched the waves crash against the hull and whispered into the wind something that felt like a beginning. "Once there was a woman who didn't like people very much, and her best friend was a dragon, a very special dragon ... "

Acknowledgments

The Dragon Keeper owes its life to some very special people. Midge Raymond and John Yunker of Ashland Creek Press, for their faith, hard work, and enthusiasm. My mom and dad and all my family (that means you, too, Liz) who have always given me their unconditional support. Philip, who puts up with me no matter what. Sheila O'Connor, who was water and sun when this book was just a tiny seed of a story. Mary Logue, for her invaluable critique and encouragement. Dr. Steve Reichling and Michelle and Mike Wines of the extraordinary Memphis Zoo, who gave me a glimpse into their dragons' lives. The Komodo research and scholarship of Walter Auffenberg in *The Behavioral Ecology of the Komodo Monitor*; Dick Lutz and J. Marie Lutz in *Komodo, The Living Dragon*; and editors James B. Murphy, Claudio Ciofi, Colomba de La Panouse, and Trooper Walsh as well as all the contributors to the comprehensive *Komodo Dragons: Biology and Conservation*. Phillip Watts, et al., whose "Parthenogenesis in Komodo dragons" in *Nature* inspired the fictional diagrams in the book. George David, who began the ESP program that allowed me to learn the tools every writer needs. And, of course, Flora and Bubchen, who inspired it all. Thank you.

About the Author

Mindy Mejia was born and raised in a small-town-turned-suburb in the Twin Cities area. She received a BA from the University of Minnesota and an MFA from Hamline University. Other than brief interludes in Iowa City and Galway, she's lived and worked in Minnesota her entire life.

Mindy generally focuses her fiction writing on the novel, though she also writes short stories, which have appeared in *rock, paper, scissors*; *Things Japanese: An Anthology of Short Stories*; and *THIS Literary Magazine*.

The Dragon Keeper is Mindy's debut novel. She's currently working on a murder mystery set in rural southern Minnesota.